ALEXANDER PUSHKIN

Eugene Onegin

A Novel in Verse

Translated with an Introduction and Notes by
STANLEY MITCHELL

PENGUIN BOOKS

PENGUIN CLASSICS

Published by the Penguin Group
Penguin Books Ltd, 80 Strand, London WC2R ORL, England
Penguin Group (USA) Inc., 375 Hudson Street, New York, New York 10014, USA
Penguin Group (Canada), 90 Eglinton Avenue East, Suite 700, Toronto, Ontario, Canada M4P 2Y3
(a division of Pearson Penguin Canada Inc.)
Penguin Ireland, 25 St Stephen's Green, Dublin 2, Ireland (a division of Penguin Books Ltd)
Penguin Group (Australia), 250 Camberwell Road, Camberwell, Victoria 3124, Australia
(a division of Pearson Australia Group Pty Ltd)
Penguin Books India Pvt Ltd, 11 Community Centre, Panchsheel Park, New Delhi – 110 017, India
Penguin Group (NZ), 67 Apollo Drive, Rosedale, North Shore 0632, New Zealand
(a division of Pearson New Zealand Ltd)
Penguin Books (South Africa) (Pty) Ltd, 24 Sturdee Avenue, Rosebank, Johannesburg 2196, South Africa

Penguin Books Ltd, Registered Offices: 80 Strand, London WC2R ORL, England

www.penguin.com

First published 1833
This translation first published in Penguin Classics 2008
4

Translation and editorial material copyright © Stanley Mitchell, 2008
All rights reserved

The moral right of the translator and editor has been asserted

Set in 10.25/12.25 pt PostScript Adobe Sabon
Typeset by Rowland Phototypesetting Ltd, Bury St Edmunds, Suffolk
Printed in England by Clays Ltd, St Ives plc

ISBN: 978-0-140-44810-8

www.greenpenguin.co.uk

Contents

Acknowledgements

I should like to thank the following for their help: Peter Carson, my editor for his constant scrutiny; Nina Zhutovsky (St. Petersburg) who cleared up every mistake; Robert Chandler for his devotion and counsel; Angela Livingstone for her careful reading and improvements; Ruth Pavey for her pertinent comments; Carla and Dan Mitchell for their common sense; the late Hannah Mitchell for her enthusiasm and encouragement; Leonid Arinshtein (Moscow) for his suggestions; Yu D. Levin (Moscow) for his criticism; Sergei Bocharov (Moscow) for his advice about the map; Martin Thom for his clarification of the role of the Carbonari in my Introduction; PKS Architects and the Art History Department of University College, London for the use of their photocopy facilities; Tom Dale Keever for sending me an audiotape of Innokentii Smoktunovsky reading *Eugene Onegin*. In retrospect, I am grateful to the late Isaiah Berlin and John Bayley for having blessed my very first stanza.

I thank the following for their warm support throughout my work on *Onegin*: Antony Wood, Natalia Mikhailova (Deputy Director of the Pushkin Museum, Moscow), Nicholas Jacobs, Dmitry Gutov (Moscow) and Gina Barker. Above all, I am indebted more than I can say to Barbara Rosenbaum for her love of the poem and her unstinting efforts to ensure that my translation was poetic. Whether it is or not is my responsibility not hers.

Stanley Mitchell

Chronology

1799 26 May   Born in Moscow. Father of ancient Muscovite aristocratic lineage; mother a granddaughter of Abyssinian General Abram Gannibal (hero of Pushkin's unfinished novel *The Negro of Peter the Great*).

1811–17 Educated at newly opened Imperial Lycée at Tsarskoe Selo. First poetry (earliest publication 1814).

1817–20 Nominal government appointment in Foreign Office, St Petersburg. Life of dissipation. 'Free-thinking' acquaintances (future Decembrists).

1820 Completed first major narrative poem, *Ruslan and Lyudmila*. Exiled to south for a handful of 'liberal' verses on freedom, serfdom and autocracy.

1820–24 'Southern exile' (via Caucasus and Crimea to Kishinev and, from July 1823, Odessa). 'Byronic' narrative poems, including *The Captive of the Caucasus* and *The Fountain at Bakhchisaray*. Began *Eugene Onegin* (1823). Recognition as leading poet of his generation.

1824–6 After misdemeanours in Odessa, exile continued in greater isolation of parental estate of Mikhailovskoye. *The Gipsies* (1824); *Count Nulin*; *Boris Godunov* (1825). Misses Decembrist Revolt of 1825, ruthlessly suppressed by new emperor, Nicholas I.

1826 September   Summoned to Moscow by Nicholas I. Freed from exile, with tsar as personal censor; subject thereafter to the surveillance of Count Benkendorf, Head of the Third Section (Secret Police). Resumed life in Moscow and St Petersburg; restlessness, search for stability.

1828 *Poltava* (narrative poem on Peter the Great and Mazeppa).

1829 Four-month visit to Transcaucasia. Witnessed Russian army in action against the Turks.

1830 Proposed to Natalya Goncharova (1812–63). In September–November stranded by cholera epidemic at new estate of Boldino: first and most productive 'Boldino autumn' (*Onegin*; lyrics; *Little Tragedies*; *Tales of Belkin*; *The Little House in Kolomna*).

1831 Married in February. Settled in St Petersburg. Completed *Onegin*.

1833 Historical research. Travelled to Urals. Second Boldino autumn (*The Bronze Horseman*; work on *The Queen of Spades*).

1833–6 Unhappy period in St Petersburg: humiliations at court (with requests for retirement from government service refused), mounting debts and marital insecurity. Relatively little creative work: *The Captain's Daughter* (completed 1836) and some outstanding lyrics.

1837 27 January Provoked into duel with Baron D'Anthès, adopted son of Dutch ambassador, and shot in stomach. Died two days later. 'Secret' burial decreed to avoid expressions of public sympathy.

Introduction

Alexander Pushkin (1799–1837) is by the common consent of his compatriots Russia's greatest writer. He is to Russia what Shakespeare is to England, Goethe to Germany and Dante to Italy. He lived at the springtime of Russian literature, which had gained its independent language only some fifty years before his birth. There was no unified language before Mikhail Lomonosov formulated it in his famous grammar of 1755. Before that, Church Slavonic coexisted with the disparate dialects of the civil service and the business community. With the growth of a centralized state a national language appeared.

In this new period Russian writers leaned heavily on Western models, and the nobility, to which Pushkin belonged, spoke French before it did Russian. French phraseology, often in its more flowery form, left its stamp on dramatists, novelists and poets during the reign of the German Empress Catherine the Great (1762–96), who loved all things French, corresponded with Voltaire and invited Diderot to St Petersburg. She freed the nobility from the service imposed on them by Peter the Great (1672–1725) and encouraged them to use their leisure in the pursuit of literature and the arts, as long as they didn't question the fundamentals of the Russian state, in particular serfdom. Enlightenment figures at home were imprisoned or sent to Siberia.

While it would be wrong to say that Pushkin was the first authentically Russian writer, since predecessors like the fabulist Ivan Krylov and the playwright Denis Fonvizin were already

incorporating the vernacular in their work, nevertheless he was
the first to treat the major events of Russian history and society
in an accessible way. He borrowed themes and styles from
Western literature only to give them new twists from a Russian
perspective. Although he tried his hand at most genres, he was
essentially a poet. The new literary language had blossomed
into a poetic culture in the generation preceding him, dominated
by the Romantic Vasily Zhukovsky and the more classical
Konstantin Batyushkov. Zhukovsky gave the language a new
expressiveness and musicality, Batyushkov a fresh clarity and
precision. Pushkin learned from them both. In his own genera-
tion a cluster of poets appeared – Yazykov, Delvig, Baratynsky
– who became known as the Pushkin pleiad and appear as
minor characters in *Eugene Onegin*. As elsewhere in contem-
porary Europe this poetic heyday was short-lived, superseded
by the prose novel – Gogol, Turgenev – with which Western
readers are more familiar. Pushkin himself went on to produce
an historical novel, *The Captain's Daughter* (1836), and other
works of prose. His poetry reflected a time of hope among the
younger members of the nobility, epitomized by two dates –
1812 and 1825.

In 1812, Russia's armies defeated Napoleon. Yet on reaching
Paris their younger officers were drawn to the ideals of the
Enlightenment and the Revolution. Back in Russia, they were
keen to introduce reforms – abolition of serfdom, a consti-
tutional monarchy, even a republic. Having no influence on the
increasingly reactionary Tsar Alexander I (1777–1825), who
headed the Holy Alliance, they began forming secret societies
on the model of the Western Carbonari[1] movements, aimed
at overturning the government. Pushkin, then aged thirteen,
befriended some of these officers when they were quartered in
the grounds of his *lycée*. Several of his close schoolfriends would
later join the secret societies. For the liberal nobility 1812
was a wake-up call. Officers were impressed by the courage of
their serf soldiers. Soon, on leaving the *lycée*, Pushkin was
writing poems deploring serfdom. Circulating all over Russia,
they earned him the honour of becoming the Tsar's first political
victim, exiled in 1820. The years of hope came to an end

when the young revolutionaries attempted an ill-organized *coup d'état* on the death of Alexander, which was mercilessly crushed by the new Tsar, Nicholas I (1825–55). The date of the revolt, 14 December 1825, gave the participants the name 'Decembrists'.

Pushkin was still in exile at the time. During the previous years he had met the conspirators, but was not admitted to their ranks because of his volatility and indiscretion. However, when the new Tsar called him to Moscow and asked him what he would have done had he been present at the attempted revolt, Pushkin replied that he would have stood with his friends on the Senate Square in St Petersburg, the chosen place of the insurrection. Nicholas played a cat-and-mouse game with him, revoking his exile and promising to be his personal protector and censor. In fact, the task fell to the chief of the secret police.

Pushkin married the beautiful Natalia Goncharova in 1831, who had no interest in his work and was happy only at court functions, which Pushkin hated, particularly after having been assigned a demeaning rank by the Tsar out of keeping with his age. Nor was he, either as a small landowner or a professional writer, able to pay for his wife's expensive tastes.

From this moment Pushkin was trapped by the court until his death in a duel with a French émigré officer, the Baron D'Anthès, who was paying attentions to his wife. Pushkin was thirty-seven. Later, the symbolist poet Alexander Blok remarked that it was not D'Anthès's bullet that killed Pushkin, but 'lack of air' in the court environment.

Although the Pushkin age was short-lived, and Pushkin himself died at thirty-seven, his work provided the seeds for the later Russian novel and several operas. *Eugene Onegin* inaugurated a lineage of superfluous men and self-sacrificing women in the novels of Mikhail Lermontov, Alexander Herzen and Ivan Turgenev, and in Tchaikovsky's opera version of Pushkin's novel-in-verse. Pushkin suggested the plots of *Dead Souls* and *The Inspector General* to Nikolai Gogol, appreciating the latter's gifts for the grotesque that were outside his more classical bent. Leo Tolstoy emulated Pushkin's storytelling manner, comparing it with Homer's, and his novel *Anna Karenina* describes what might have happened to Tatiana had she given in to Onegin. With Fyodor Dostoevsky, who condemned the Onegin type as a Western intrusion and glorified Tatiana as the exemplar of Russian womanhood, a nationalist cult of Pushkin began that has not ceased. Radicals and conservatives fought over Pushkin's characters as if they were real people. Opponents of Tsarism saw Onegin, Lensky and Tatiana as kindred victims of feudal Russia.

By birth Pushkin was deeply embedded in Russian history. On his father's side he could boast a 600-year lineage as a nobleman. On his mother's he was the great-grandson of an African princeling, stolen from the harem at Constantinople for Peter the Great, under whose tutelage he rose to the rank of general. The features of Gannibal, as he was called, still showed in his great-grandson, whose African roots gave him the romantic feeling of an outsider wanting to get back to his native land (Chapter I, stanza 50). But Pushkin was equally attached to Peter, who played a dominant part in his outlook and work (see *The Bronze Horseman* (1833) and *Poltava* (1828–9)). At the same time he was envious of the new aristocracy who owed their advancement to Peter (and then to Catherine), ousting the older nobility to which his family, on his father's side, belonged. Unloved as a child, he found a new family in his *lycée*, where he made lasting friendships. He was famed for his love poetry, but friendship nevertheless remained his chief value, as *Onegin* attests, where friends form an invisible audience or enter directly into the novel.

2

On 4 November 1823 Pushkin wrote to a friend, Prince Vyazemsky, from Odessa: 'I am writing now not a novel, but a novel in verse – the devil of a difference. Something like Don Juan – there's no point in thinking about publication; I'm writing whatever comes into my head.'[2] Odessa was Pushkin's second place of exile after Kishinev, in Bessarabia. In Odessa he was in the employ of the Governor Count Vorontsov, who

had little appreciation for his poetry, calling him 'a weak imita-
tor of a writer whose usefulness may be said to be very slight –
Lord Byron'.[3] The zest with which Pushkin wrote his new work
reflected a hectic life that included an affair with the Governor's
wife.

In 1825, he was removed from Odessa, at the request of
Vorontsov, to Mikhailovskoye, the Pushkin family estate in
north-west Russia, which was to be his third and final place
of exile, From there, in a letter to another friend, Alexander
Bestuzhev, Pushkin wrote, in a different vein, about *Onegin*
and *Don Juan*:

> No one respects Don Juan more than I do ... but it hasn't
> anything in common with Onegin. You compare the satire of the
> Englishman Byron with mine, and demand the same thing of me!
> No, my dear fellow, you are asking a lot. Where is my satire?
> There's not a hint of it in Eugene Onegin. The foundations of
> Petersburg would crack if I touched satire. – The very word
> 'satirical' should not have entered the preface. Wait for the other
> cantos ... Canto One is merely a rapid introduction.[4]

Bestuzhev, himself a writer, was also a Decembrist. Many
Decembrists were literary men, who, like Bestuzhev, saw their
craft as a means of political struggle against autocracy and serf-
dom and were puzzled by Pushkin's apparent departure from the
radical poems that had sent him into exile. Why was Russia's
foremost poet, they asked, wasting his talent on the trivial lives
of the gentry? In 1824, four years into exile, Pushkin declared in
response to the most significant of Decembrist works, Kondraty
Ryleyev's *Dumy* (*Reflections*), that the aim of poetry was
poetry. In a series of poems Ryleyev had evoked heroic figures
from the past as models to be followed in the present. Pushkin
questioned the accuracy of Ryleyev's work, claiming that he
was on the contrary projecting present ideals into the past.

Pushkin spent the first three years of his exile (1820–23)
in what he called the 'accursed town' of Kishinev, capital
of Bessarabia, serving in the office of General Inzov, Adminis-
trator for New Colonies in the South. By 1823, when the

Decembrist movement was gathering steam, Pushkin had disavowed his earlier idealism. In 'The Sower of Freedom in the Desert', a poem written in Odessa, he scorns himself for philanthropy and the people for passivity. Indirectly, the poem targets the Carbonari and their followers in Western Europe (1820–23), crushed by the Holy Alliance. Pushkin writes to a friend that he is parodying the parable from the Matthew and Luke gospels that tells of Christ going out to sow. In Pushkin's incarnation the saviour is 'a moderate democrat' who sows in vain. The Decembrists were, like the Carbonari, largely a military organization, operating through secret societies and equally disconnected from the people they wished to liberate. Pushkin's sympathies for the Greek insurgents, whom he met in Kishinev and Odessa, likewise vanished. Could these dregs, he asked, be the descendants of Themistocles and Pericles?

Exile brought Pushkin into closer contact with his own countrymen, learning of their folklore from his beloved serf nurse, Arina Rodionovna, who appears as Filipevna, Tatiana's nurse, in *Eugene Onegin*. Her songs about the seventeenth-century rebel Sten'ka Razin inspired Pushkin's own songs about him (1826). In a letter to his brother (1824) he called him 'the only poetic figure in Russian history'.[5] The magnetic Emelyan Pugachov (1740?–75), who led a massive peasant revolt against Catherine the Great, dominates *The Captain's Daughter*. These rebellions were popular, not directed by another class. Smaller peasant revolts were innumerable during the entire period of serfdom. Where the Decembrists wished to import Western constitutional models into Russia, Pushkin delved ever more deeply into Russian history to seek political answers for his own time. On the eve of the Decembrist revolt he completed his Shakespearean drama *Boris Godunov*, set in the so-called Time of Troubles (1604–13), the interregnum between the Riurik and the Romanov dynasties. Here, the people, who take centre stage, appear by turn passive, fickle, savage, murderous and finally mortified by the assassination of the deceased Boris's family, to which they have been party. Their horrified silence at the end, when asked by the Boyars to applaud yet another Pretender, passes judgement not only on their time, but on ruling-class manipulation in every age. The centrality of the people in *Boris Godunov* goes beyond any of Pushkin's Shakespearean models. But the play is Shakespearean in the sense that no one is the victor other than history. With this lesson in mind Pushkin writes to a friend, on hearing of the Decembrist defeat, that they should look upon it through Shakespearean eyes.

3

Eugene Onegin is certainly about the life of the nobility down to the niceties of Onegin's toiletry. But the popular element is very strong there and even decisive. Filipevna, based on Pushkin's nurse, is also storyteller to Tatiana, who is rooted in peasant superstition and the Russian countryside. Of course, she also reads French and English novels and writes Russian with extreme difficulty. Her declaration of love for Onegin has to be translated by Pushkin into Russian. Nevertheless, it is clear where her roots are when, as the Princess whom Onegin is courting in Chapter VIII, she repudiates the aristocratic flummery that surrounds her and expresses her longing for the countryside and her nurse, now dead.

The language of the novel, although largely the idiom of the nobility, extends into popular speech, for which Pushkin was often taken to task at the time by conservative critics. Surpassing previous writers in this respect, Pushkin took his Russian directly from the streets, the market-places and the country estates. In *Onegin* he honours his Decembrist friend Pavel Katenin for translating Corneille's *Le Cid* (Chapter I, stanza 18). French neo-classicism and its heroic language were a model for the revolutionary nobility. Pushkin's *Boris Godunov*, by contrast, abounds with ordinary speech, as does his historical novel *The Captain's Daughter*. 'Vulgar' expressions enter into the most intimate of Pushkin's lyrics. By and large, writers came from the gentry, that is the minor nobility, and shared on their estates a common culture with their serfs, as the Larin family does in Onegin, despite differences in status and education. The

Larin family is not wealthy. It does not employ foreign tutors or governesses. The Westernized Onegin, by contrast, grows up, handed from one to another. Only the serf nurse looks after the two sisters.

As early as Chapter III of *Onegin* Pushkin announces that he might give up poetry for prose. At this moment in the story he is responding to the harmful effect of Western novels and tales upon Tatiana. In the place of these he proposes to write an idyllic novel about innocent love and the ancient ways of Russia, but does no such thing, instantly returning to his heroine's romantic agony. Towards the end of Chapter VI, as he contemplates his passing youth, he considers again the abandonment of poetry:

> To Spartan prose the years are turning,
> Coquettish rhyme the years are spurning;
> And I – I with a sigh confess –
> I'm running after her much less.
>
> (Stanza 43)

The novel-in-verse, as Pushkin chose to call his poem, is a workshop out of which his later prose fiction emerges. His *Dedication* to his publisher, written after he had completed five chapters, pinpoints the character of his new work:

> Accept these chapters and their rhymes,
> Half-comic and half-melancholic,
> Ideal and down-to-earth bucolic . . .
> The intellect's cold observations,
> The heart's impressions marked in tears.

Pushkin prefaced his first chapter, which he published on its own in 1825, with 'A Conversation Between a Bookseller and a Poet', in which the poet argues the rights of poetry against the requirements of the market. After a flood of Romantic protestation the poet suddenly accepts the bookseller's case, abandons his verse and negotiates the sale of his manuscript in three short sentences of prose: 'You're perfectly right. Here's my manuscript. Let's come to terms.'

What Pushkin calls his 'descent' to prose is, however, more than a matter of using ordinary language. The death of the poet Lensky in Chapter VI not only sounds the knell of Pushkin's youth, too, but questions the future of his own poetry in a world that kills imagination:

> Let not a poet's soul be frozen,
> Made rough and hard, reduced to bone
> And finally be turned to stone
> In that benumbing world he goes in,
> In that intoxicating slough
> Where, friends, we bathe together now.
>
> (Stanza 46)

From now on the tone of the novel changes. Pushkin completed Chapter VI about four months after the five Decembrist leaders were hanged. Repeatedly, in his manuscripts he draws sketches of his friends on the gallows, in one case adding 'this might have been me'. In an omitted stanza he suggests that Lensky, too, had he lived, could have swung from the gallows like the Decembrist poet Ryleyev, who was also Pushkin's acquaintance. Pushkin's distancing from the Decembrists was part of his 'descent' to prose, yet the executions of his friends haunted him for the rest of his life, as they do the pages of *Onegin*.

Chapters VII and VIII present a post-Decembrist world full of nonentities with the exception of his poet friend Vyazemsky, who comforts an unhappy Tatiana on her entry into the *monde* – the same Vyazemsky from whom the epigraph to Chapter I is taken. Both Tatiana and Onegin are hopelessly isolated in this new milieu, despite the former's well-schooled endeavours to behave *comme il faut*, which, as she confesses to Onegin, are a pretence. The term 'prose' refers not only to language, but to the prosaic world of Russia at all its levels. In *Onegin* Pushkin turned this prose into a new kind of poetry.

Pushkin belongs to a European shift from poetry to prose

that Edmund Wilson characterizes in his excellent essay 'In Honour of Pushkin' (1937):

> It was as if in those generations where Byron, Shelley, Keats, Leopardi, and Poe were dead in their twenties or thirties or barely reached forty, where Coleridge and Wordsworth and Beddoes and Musset burned out while still alive, where Lermontov, like Pushkin, was killed in a duel, before he was twenty seven – it was as if in that great age of the bourgeois ascendancy – and even in still feudal Russia – it were impossible for a poet to survive.

He adds:

> There was for the man of imagination and moral passion a basic maladjustment to society in which only the student of society – the social philosopher, the historian, the novelist – could find himself and learn to function. And to deal with the affairs of society, he had to learn to speak its language, he had – as Goethe and Hugo did, as Pushkin did just before he died – to train himself to write in prose.[6]

A heroic age had come to an end that began with the French Revolution and of which the Decembrist revolt was Europe's last echo. In poems of 1821 and 1824 Pushkin mourned the death of the epoch's giants, Napoleon and Byron, despite his fluctuating attitudes to them. (Onegin's study is adorned with a portrait of Byron and a statuette of Napoleon.) Pushkin was already concerning himself with the role of prose in 1822, at the height of his Romantic period, a decade before he embarked on prose fiction, insisting on the need for 'precision and brevity', as well as 'thought and more thought'. While poetry, he acknowledged, was different, it, too, he declared, would benefit from 'a larger stock of ideas', adding: 'Our literature won't get very far on memories of vanished youth.'[7]

Pushkin is referring here to elegiac poetry, including his own, which prevailed in his day. *Onegin* is, of course, full of 'memories of vanished youth', largely in the digressions. An ironic seesaw turns between 'remembrance of things past' and the narrative demands of the present. Recidivist memories are quenched by a brisk couplet, allowing the story to continue, as in the 'little feet' digression from Chapter I:

> Their charming words and glances cheat
> As surely as . . . their little feet.
>
> (Stanza 34)

Or a digressive stanza tunes back into the narrative, as when Pushkin, having mourned the absence of ballerinas he has known in the past, whisks his hero into the theatre of today:

> My goddesses! Where now? Forsaken?
> Oh hearken to my call, I rue:
> Are you the same? Have others taken
> Your place without replacing you?
> When shall I listen to your chorus,
> Behold in soul-filled flight before us
> Russia's Terpsichore again? . . .
>
> The house is full; the boxes brilliant . . .
>
> (Chapter I, stanzas 19–20)

The digressions are slower in pace than the narrative, more insistent, impassioned, full of questions. The language is more archaic, more 'poetical'. Pushkin's narrative in general is precise, brief and straightforward. Rarely is a noun accompanied by more than one adjective. But Pushkin's recourse to the past is more than a question of 'vanished memories'. It is also an attachment to past values, traditions, institutions, sometimes ironically expressed, but not always. In a world dominated by Western fashions Pushkin likes to return to the 'good, old days'. He is constantly calling his generation 'light', that is, without depth, not rooted. The digressions refer either to the past or the future, to 'vanished memories' or future hopes. Tatiana and Onegin are likewise immersed in their past, while Lensky thinks only of a happy or heroic future. Nevertheless, the narrative takes place in the present, although told mostly in the past tense. Here is the real world which Pushkin describes with a mixture of realism and irony – from the benevolent evocations of country customs to the repugnant chatter of the *monde*. The most Romantic episode in the novel, Tatiana's dream, is firmly based in folklore. The digressions remain the locus of romanticism, but they are always tempered with irony, as in the examples given above, and they get fewer towards the end of the novel. Romanticism and realism contrast most starkly between Lensky's elegiac poem written on the eve of the duel and Pushkin's meticulous account of the duel itself. Where Lensky writes:

> Whether I'm piercèd by an arrow
> Or whether it should miss – all's well:
> A predetermined hour will tell
> If we're to wake or sleep tomorrow
> (Chapter VI, stanza 21)

Pushkin describes, as if from a manual, the loading of pistols:

> The pistols glistened; soon the mallets
> Resoundingly on ramrods flicked,
> Through cut-steel barrels went the bullets,
> The cock has for the first time clicked.
> (Chapter VI, stanza 29)

Irony bridges the several, often contradictory planes of the novel – linguistic, stylistic, cultural, social. There is scarcely anything in *Onegin*, from characters to environment, from convictions to sentiment, that is not touched by it. The one exception is Pushkin's description of nature. *Onegin* reflects a world in flux. Some commentators have compared his irony with that of the German Romantics. This is wrong. The latter conceived the world as an illusion to be ironically punctured, not in favour of the real world, but a primordial chaos. Postmodernists have interpreted Pushkin in a similar way. Like the Romantics, Pushkin uses irony to remove illusion, but this makes his fictional world more rather than less real, which is how it was taken to be by his contemporaries and the generations that followed them.

Of Lensky and Onegin, for example, Alexander Herzen, exiled revolutionary of the decade succeeding Pushkin, wrote:

> Between these two types – between the dedicated enthusiast and poet and, on the other hand, the weary, embittered and useless man, between Lensky's grave and Onegin's boredom – stretched the deep and muddy river of civilized Russia, with its aristocrats, bureaucrats, officers, gendarmes, grand-dukes and emperor – a dumb and formless mass of baseness, obsequiousness, bestiality and envy, a formless mass which draws in and engulfs everything.[8]

Or, as Pushkin puts it, that 'slough/Where, friends, we bathe together now' (Chapter VI, stanza 46). I have already referred to Dostoyevsky's praise for Tatiana as the epitome of Russian womanhood.

Nevertheless, the characters are not of the kind we find in a realist prose novel. They are silhouettes. The encounters between Onegin and Tatiana are few, and the decisive ones are the responses to letters. There is a simple symmetry about their relationship: Tatiana falls in love with Onegin and is rejected; Onegin falls in love with her and is rejected. It is the symmetry of a mathematical equation or a chemical formula of the kind that Goethe pursues in his novel *The Elective Affinities* (1809). It gives the relationship between hero and heroine a spare objectivity that is consolidated by the central preoccupations of the novel – the nature of passion, romantic love, romantic literature, libertinage, marriage, the position of women, morality. Neither Onegin nor Tatiana develops slowly; they jump from situation to situation like film cuts. Pushkin agreed with his friend Katenin that the result of omitting the former Chapter VIII (*Onegin's Journey*) was to make 'the transition from Tatiana the provincial miss to Tatiana the grande dame ... too unexpected and unexplained' (Foreword to *Fragments of Onegin's Journey*). But it is not just a question of excising a chapter. The characters are not the 'independent' actors of prose fiction. They are half-lyrical, half-novelistic. This is obvious in Chapter I, where Pushkin enters the story as Onegin's friend, sharing the same discontent. They cross one another's paths twice again in the novel, in *Onegin's Journey* (stanza 10), when Onegin traverses the same route in the Caucasus that Pushkin had taken at the beginning of his exile, and in a variant, when they meet face to face in Odessa. Yet Pushkin is quick to disclaim identification with him. What we see in Chapter I is a fusion of poet and hero, followed by their parting, when Onegin is invited to his uncle's deathbed, and resumes his separate status. But Pushkin's friendship and their travel plans give Onegin a deeper sensibility than was evident before. The theme of exile unites them both – self-imposed for Onegin, who flees his killing of Lensky. Even after this Pushkin continues to speak indulgently of his hero. At the end of the novel Pushkin bids farewell to his 'strange comrade' (the Russian word *sputnik* can mean 'travelling companion'). Onegin is part Pushkin's earlier self.

In Chapter VIII Pushkin's Muse embodies each of Pushkin's feminine ideals in turn until she becomes Tatiana. (In *Onegin's Journey* (stanza 9) he embraces the ideal of the housewife!) Pushkin's friend the poet Wilhelm Küchelbecker remarked that he saw Pushkin himself in the new Tatiana. It has also been suggested that Pushkin intended his heroine as a model for his future wife to follow. There has been an industry of attempts in Russia to identify Pushkin's characters with real people. But the direct source of his characters is his poetry. They are poetic creations. They proceed from his lyrical self. Pushkin constantly refers to them as 'my Eugene', 'my Tatiana', 'my Lensky'. Each is endowed with a specific vocabulary that accompanies him or her through the story. Onegin is 'strange', 'odd', 'eccentric', 'addicted to dreams', 'abrasive', his mind is 'sharp' and 'chilled', his humour 'bilious', his epigrams 'dark'. Nor is he just a Russian type. Pushkin noted in a draft that Onegin always took three novels with him: Charles Mathurin's *Melmoth the Wanderer*, François-René de Chateaubriand's *René* and Benjamin Constant's *Adolphe*:

> In which the epoch was displayed
> And modern man put on parade
> And fairly faithfully depicted:
> With his depraved, immoral soul,
> Dried up and egotistical,
> To dreaming endlessly addicted,
> With his embittered, seething mind
> To futile enterprise consigned.
>   (Chapter VII, stanza 22)

The epithets attending Tatiana belong, by contrast, to elegiac poetry. She is 'wayward', 'silent', 'sad', 'shy', 'dreamy', 'contemplative', 'languid', 'pale', 'strange' – 'strange' not in the manner of Onegin, but as an anomaly in her family, in rural society and later in the *monde* where she hides her true feelings. In the early chapters she is always to be found at a window, contemplating the moon. Tatiana is transformed when she becomes a princess, but when she tells Onegin that this is only outward show, she speaks as she used to when she first met him. Like Onegin she is characterized by the foreign novels she reads. These, however, are the pre-Romantic or sentimental novels of the eighteenth century rather than the early nineteenth-century Romantic fiction that Onegin enjoys. She identifies with the heroines of Samuel Richardson, Jean-Jacques Rousseau and Mme de Staël, whose novel *Delphine* appeared just at the beginning of the new century, in 1802. Although Tatiana is 'Russian to the core' (Chapter V, stanza 4), her letter to Onegin is not only a translation of a non-existent French original, but, as Nabokov has shown, French translators have found no difficulty in rendering it back into their own language more or less literally. It echoes not only phrases from Rousseau's *La Nouvelle Héloïse*, one of Tatiana's favourite novels, but other French sources beyond Tatiana's ken. The letter can be decoded as a palimpsest of borrowings, while it retains the spontaneous passion that has moved generations of readers in Russia.[9]

Lensky, the poet, is, like Onegin, part of Pushkin himself, writing the kind of elegiac poetry that his creator had written in an earlier phase and that recurs in the digressions. But there is also an exalted strain in him that belongs, on the one hand, to the civic Romanticism associated with the Decembrists and, on the other, to the libertarian ideals brought back from his studies in Göttingen. In the text Pushkin chooses a more prosaic future for Lensky, had he lived – that of the gouty, cuckolded landowner. It is unlikely that this Lensky could be added to Edmund Wilson's list of poets unable to survive in a world of 'prose', since he is not of their mould, and his alternative future – to become another Ryleyev, Nelson, Kutuzov – is left tongue-in-cheek in the omitted stanza. Among the epithets attaching to Lensky are: 'virginal', 'pure', 'sweet', 'tender', 'rapturous', 'exalted', 'enthusiastic', 'inspired', 'ardent', simple'. The words 'vague', 'obscure', 'limp', 'ideal', 'tearful' apply to his poetry. The subjects of his verse are 'love', 'despond', 'parting', 'graves', even 'Romantic roses'. The last image of him is his own grave. He and Tatiana share to some extent a similar sensibility. Not for nothing does she refer to Onegin as 'the slayer of her brother' (Chapter VII, stanza 14).

Olga, too, has her linguistic aura, more limited than those of the main characters. These vocabularies have their counterparts in European literature. Tatiana's and Onegin's reading are entirely European. The comic Russian debate on the merits of the ode and elegy contextualize Lensky's poetry in Chapter IV (stanzas 32–4). These ramifications extend the range of the characters, turning them from individuals into types. Nor is it just a linguistic matter. Pushkin is quite serious about the 'immorality' of contemporary Western literature and its baleful effect upon vulnerable young female readers in Russia. In testing the characters against these influences Pushkin creates a clearing-house for a new, as yet undefined literature. But this clearing-house was to become its greatest monument. In his novel-in-verse Pushkin takes the same path of 'lost illusions' as Balzac was to do. Lensky is pointlessly killed without becoming either a hero or a cuckold; Onegin is left stranded at the end of the novel. Tatiana alone adapts herself sorrowfully to the high society she loathes, unlike the heroines of her favourite novels who die in order to save their integrity.

4

The Romantic narratives that Pushkin wrote in the first four years of his exile throw more light on the place that the novel-in-verse occupies in Pushkin's life and work. Written under the influence of Byron's early 'Southern' poems (*Childe Harold's Pilgrimage*, *The Corsair*, *The Giaour* – all referred to in *Onegin*), each bears the imprint of exile. A fortuitous holiday took Pushkin away from Kishinev at the beginning of his exile to the Caucasus and the Crimea in the company of a friendly family, the Rayevskys. From them he discovered Byron and was helped by the English governess and the sons and daughters of the family to read him in English, of which he had no previous knowledge. However, he never developed sufficient mastery of English to read Byron satisfactorily in the original and depended on French prose translations. Two of his Romantic poems, *The Captive of the Caucasus* (1820–21) and *The Fountain at Bakhchisaray* (1821–3), germinated in this exotic environment. The first directly anticipates *Onegin* in its aim 'to depict that indifference to life and its pleasures, that premature ageing of the soul, which are the distinctive features of the youth of the nineteenth century'.[10] A nameless nobleman, fleeing into nature from the constraints of civilization, falls captive to a Caucasian tribe among whom he languishes amid the splendours of the mountain scenery. Emotionally dead, he cannot respond to the local girl who helps him to escape across a river and drowns herself while he looks on without response. He is an early Onegin, lethal to himself and others, yet elegiac rather than demonic in disposition. Just as he bears no name, so he is hardly a character, which Pushkin was the first to admit. The poem is more a series of lyrical and descriptive fragments. One of these is an invocation to freedom by the Prisoner that appealed to the young Decembrists:

> Ah freedom! It was you alone
> He sought still in the desert world;
> With feeling driven out by passions,

> Grown cool to dreams and to the lyre,
> He listened with excitement to
> The songs inspired by you, and full
> Of faith, of fiery supplication,
> Your august idol he embraced.[11]

If Onegin did join the Decembrists in the fragmentary Chapter X, as some scholars suppose, then this passage anticipates how he might have felt on the rebound of his disappointed love for Tatiana.

A more demonic figure, this time with a name, Aleko, a perhaps conscious variant of Pushkin's first name, appears in *The Gipsies* (1824), written concurrently with the first chapters of *Onegin*. When living in Kishinev, Pushkin had apparently spent several weeks with a roving gipsy tribe. In this poem a disaffected Russian nobleman once more seeks refuge in a more natural way of life, this time in a gipsy encampment, where he returns the attentions of a fiery young woman, Zemphira, who, through Prosper Mérimée's translation, was to become the prototype for Bizet's Carmen. When, after two years, Zemphira tires of him and takes a younger gipsy lover, Aleko, in a fit of jealousy, kills them both. Zemphira's father, the Elder of the tribe, dismisses him with the sentence: 'You want freedom for yourself alone',[12] a phrase repeated by Dostoyevsky to condemn what he diagnosed as the corrosive individualism infecting Russia from the West. Pushkin's Tatiana, he pointed out, refused the freedom Onegin offered so as not to build her happiness on the unhappiness of her husband. Both the indifference of the captive and the possessiveness of Aleko enter into Onegin's character – from his dismissal of Tatiana's early love for him to his overwhelming passion for her when she is married and distinguished. Already in her dream, when he silences the monsters crying 'mine' to her with his own grim uptake of the word, Tatiana recognizes this egotism. As in *The Gipsies* possessiveness and murder go hand in hand. Tatiana sees the destroyer in Onegin. The killing of Lensky in the dream foretells the duel. Was he an angel or a tempter, she had asked Onegin in her letter. In the dream he is truly demonic. In both the Elder's judgement on Aleko and Tatiana's rejection of Onegin, Dostoyevsky discovered a Russian ethos, and perhaps he was right. Certainly, Pushkin's work, from *The Gipsies* and *Onegin* onwards, may be summed up as a debate with the West and a search for Russian values. The concept of the nation, first raised by the French Revolution, was being discussed throughout Europe at this time, and not least in Russia.

The earlier poem, *The Fountain at Bakhchisaray*, has no relevance to the novel apart from its elegiac epigraph and a recollection of the fountain in *Onegin's Journey*. The epigraph reads: 'Many, like myself used to visit this fountain; but some are no more and the others are wandering in distant parts.'[13] Pushkin took the epigraph from the thirteenth-century Persian poet Sadi via a French translation of Thomas Moore's *Lalla Rookh*, where it is included. The second half of the epigraph recurs in the final stanza of *Onegin*, almost certainly applying, among others, to the fallen and exiled Decembrists, as the authorities were quick to suspect. Indeed, Vyazemsky was rapped over the knuckles by the authorities for quoting these lines in an article. *The Fountain* recounts a Romantic tale of a Polish princess captured and loved unrequitedly by a Crimean Khan and murdered by his hitherto favourite, Zarema. Putting her to death in turn, the Khan erects a 'fountain of tears' in memory of the Polish princess. Pushkin on his visit to the Crimea found the once gorgeous palace of Bakhchisaray deserted and the fountain rusted over. In *Onegin's Journey* he imagines it still working.

The narrative poem *Ruslan and Lyudmila* (1817–20) was written, apart from its Introduction and Epilogue, before his exile and encounter with Byron's 'Southern' poems. Its light-hearted tone links it much more with the later Byron of *Don Juan*, which prompted the writing of *Onegin*. Belonging to the exuberant tradition of mock-epic going back via Voltaire to Ariosto in the Renaissance, it is set in Kievan Russia, cradle of Russian civilization, in the reign of the Grand Duke Vladimir (*c.* 978–1015). Yet it is shot through with ironic references to contemporary St Petersburg, echoing Pushkin's three wild years

there after leaving school. The poem ensured Pushkin's fame.
Nothing like it had ever been heard before. Essentially a fairy
tale, with some historical elements, it tells of the abduction of
Lyudmila from her bridal bed by the wicked dwarf magician,
Chernomor, and how her bridegroom, Ruslan, outwits and
defeats three rivals to rescue her. It is to this playful atmosphere
that Pushkin returns after three years of exile in 'accursed
Kishinev', putting behind him his Romantic poems (except for
The Gipsies) and introducing a new hero:

> Friends of Ruslan and of Lyudmila,
> Let me acquaint you with this fellow,
> The hero of my novel, pray,
> Without preamble or delay:
> My friend Onegin was begotten
> By the Neva, where maybe you
> Originated, reader, too
> Or where your lustre's not forgotten
>   (Chapter I, stanza 2)

The old Romantic hero is brought back to St Petersburg and
placed in the social context he has deserted. While he bears the
scars of his predecessors, he is now the subject of irony.

5

Started in 1823 in Kishinev, *Onegin* was completed eight years
later in the village of Tsarskoye Selo, which housed both the
imperial summer palace and Pushkin's *lycée*. Pushkin finished
Chapter I in 1824 in Odessa on the Black Sea, to which he was
transferred after Kishinev, and published it separately in 1825.
Chapter II he wrote in the same year in Odessa together with
part of Chapter III, which he completed in the following year,
1825, on the family estate at Mikhailovskoye in north-west
Russia and his last place of exile. Here, from 1825 to 1827, he
wrote Chapters IV to part of VII, which he finished in
St Petersburg in 1828. Chapter VIII he wrote in Boldino, his

father's estate in the province of Nizhny Novgorod, south-west of Moscow, in 1830, revising it and adding Onegin's letter in Tsarskoye Selo in 1831. By then he was thirty-two.

It will be seen from this trajectory that the romantic involvements of the four characters largely coincide with Pushkin's stay in Mikhailovskoye. The countryside described in these chapters – the cornfields stretching out from Onegin's manor house, the fields, valleys and woods where Tatiana wanders – reproduce the surroundings of Pushkin's family estate. Exile was lonely here, forbidding the dissipations enjoyed in Kishinev and Odessa, but it allowed him to write the central chapters of *Onegin* and the magnificent historical drama *Boris Godunov*. And, as happened when the Rayevskys passed through Kishinev, so here in the neighbouring estate of Trigorskoye Pushkin found a hospitable family with attractive, intelligent daughters to engage his affections and his poetry. To one of the Rayevsky daughters has been ascribed the famous digression on little feet in Chapter I. Pushkin wrote his final tragic and bitter St Petersburg chapter in Boldino, where on his engagement to Natalia Goncharova he had received 200 serfs from his father and so become a landowner. His most creative times were spent in Boldino, but his desire to settle there foundered on the demands of his wife and the Tsar, both of whom wanted him in the capital. While Pushkin was now at the height of his powers, his popularity started to wane as an indifferent, bourgeois reading public emerged and populist journalists began attacking aristocratic literature. Pushkin's growing isolation left its tone on much of the last chapter. Even the critic Vissarion Belinsky, his champion in the next generation, called him a poet of the landowning class. Belinsky, a commoner, strove for an embattled and critical literature that would replace what he saw as Pushkin's resigned acceptance of the status quo. Nevertheless, he described *Onegin* as an 'encyclopedia of Russian life'.[14] In the new intellectual world of Russia, divided into opposing camps, especially the Westernizers and Slavophiles, it was not possible to repeat Pushkin's universality, at least not in verse, and in prose not before Tolstoy. Pushkin's many-sidedness did indeed depend on the pivotal position of the minor nobility and the momentary hope for national unity that inspired its most remarkable members. It also required a reading public for which poetry was still the most meaningful literary idiom. *Eugene Onegin* generated themes and characters for subsequent writers, but as a form it remained unique. One or two poets, notably Mikhail Lermontov, attempted something similar, but without success. Pushkin himself uses the *Onegin* stanza again in a small fragment, *Yezersky* (1832), in which he laments the decline of the old nobility. The hero, descendant of an ancient lineage, is now a civil servant, so anticipating the deliberately named Eugene of *The Bronze Horseman* (1833), who, no longer a nobleman, is destroyed by one of the recurrent floods that invade Peter the Great's historic city.

The original Chapter VIII was meant to describe Onegin's journey between leaving his estate and returning to St Petersburg. Chapter IX would have been the present Chapter VIII. In 1853, Pavel Katenin, writing to Pavel Annenkov, Pushkin's biographer, suggested a political reason for the chapter's exclusion:

> Concerning the eighth chapter of *Onegin*, I heard from the late poet in 1832 that besides the Nizhny market and the Odessa port, Eugene saw the military settlements organized by Count Arakcheyev, and here occurred remarks, judgements, expressions that were too violent for publication and he decided were best assigned to eternal oblivion. Therefore, he discarded the whole chapter from his tale – a chapter that after cancellation has become too short and, so to speak, impoverished.[15]

The aim of these military establishments, established by Alexei Arakcheyev in 1817, was to reduce the cost of a standing army during peacetime by dragooning government peasants into labour camps, where they would combine military service with working on the land under punitive discipline. One of these settlements outside Odessa might have attracted the attention of Onegin as it did that of the Decembrist leader, Pavel Pestel, who hoped to break into it at the time of the planned revolt and incite the detainees to mutiny. As it stands, the published

Fragment resembles a travelogue punctuated by the hero's cries of 'ennui', as he moves restlessly from one place to another. Critics have noticed a similarity with Byron's *Childe Harold's Pilgrimage*, which continued to fascinate Pushkin and which he attempted to translate as late as 1836.

He wrote and burned Chapter X in Boldino shortly after finishing the present Chapter VIII and *Onegin's Journey*, but left a coded copy of the stanzas published in this volume, which have been the subject of different readings and orderings. Only two of the stanzas are almost complete. I have followed the presentation by Boris Tomashevsky, the leading Pushkin textologist of the Soviet era. While using the same stanzaic form, the chapter is entirely different from the rest of the novel, reading more like a chronicle. The content of the chapter is politically explosive, starting with a scathing satire on Alexander I and ending with an ironic history of the Decembrist movement. It also includes a sceptical hope in stanza 7, where every other line begins with 'maybe', that Nicholas I will reunite the Siberian exiles with their families. None of the characters in the previous chapters makes an appearance here. However, a Captain Yuzefovich reported Pushkin saying to him: 'Onegin will either perish in the Caucasus or join the Decembrist movement.'[16]

The internal chronology of the novel varies from between four and seven years' distance from the occasions of writing it. This temporal proximity emphasizes Pushkin's closeness to his characters, in particular Onegin. The time-frame of the story (1819–24) is only just out of kilter with the length of Pushkin's exile (1820–25). From internal evidence we can work out the ages of the characters. Pushkin himself is twenty-one when he meets Onegin, Onegin is twenty-six, Lensky eighteen, Olga sixteen, Tatiana seventeen, and nineteen when she rejects Onegin. The poem is an epitaph to youth, including Pushkin's. Tatiana marries, but after two years she is childless. 'It is sad to think we're given/Our youth to be enjoyed in vain', Pushkin reflects in his last chapter (stanza 11).

The passage of the seasons shapes this chronology, forming the backdrop not only of the novel, but of Pushkin's generation and life as such:

> Alas! each generation must
> By Providence's dispensation
> Rise, ripen, fall, in quick succession,
> Upon life's furrows
> > (Chapter II, stanza 38)

The seasons intertwine with the characters. Tatiana naturally falls in love in spring, while Onegin's belated passion is compared with the 'cold and ruthless' storms of autumn. Pushkin balances Tatiana's heady feelings as she waits for Onegin at the end of Chapter III with down-to-earth similes from nature:

> So a poor butterfly will flutter
> And beat an iridescent wing,
> Caught by a schoolboy, frolicking;
> So a small winter hare will shudder
> On seeing in the distant brush
> A hunter crouched behind a bush.
> > (Stanza 40)

As an example of what literary criticism could get up to at the time, Pushkin was ridiculed by his chief enemy, the government spy Faddei Bulgarin, for introducing a beetle in Chapter VII:

> Evening arrived. The sky has darkened.
> The beetle whirrs. The waters flow.
> > (Stanza 15)

Was the beetle a new character, he asked. This apparently inane hostility to the ordinary in *Onegin* – and other works – was based on Pushkin's mixing of the 'low' with the 'high'. It was a social as well as literary attack. Something of the sort was experienced by early Wordsworth for similar reasons, but the criticism of him was mild by comparison.

NOTES

1. *Carbonari*: Literally, 'charcoal burners', a group of secret societies in France, Italy and Spain that aimed to overturn the forces of Restoration after the defeat of Napoleon.

2. *I am writing now . . . into my head*: A. S. Pushkin, *Sobranie Sochinenii*, vol. 9, Letters 1815–1830 (Moscow: GIKhL (Gosudarstvenoye Izdatel'stvo Khudozhestvennoi Literatury), 1963), p. 77.

3. *a weak imitator . . . Lord Byron*: (Written in French: 'un faible imitateur d'un original très peu recommandable'), letter from Vorontsov to Count Nesselrode, Minister of Foreign Affairs, *Eugene Onegin: A Novel in Verse by Aleksandr Pushkin*, translated from the Russian, with a Commentary by Vladimir Nabokov (London: Routledge and Kegan Paul, 1964), vol. 3, p. 194.

4. *No one respects Don Juan . . . introduction*: Letter of 24 March 1825, Pushkin, *Sobranie Sochinenii*, vol. 9, p. 144.

5. *the only poetic figure in Russian history*: Letter to his brother, L. S. Pushkin, first half of November 1824, Pushkin, *Sobranie Sochinenii*, vol. 9, p. 119.

6. *It was as if in those generations . . . write in prose*: Edmund Wilson, *The Triple Thinkers* (Harmondsworth: Penguin, 1962), p. 57.

7. *precision and brevity . . . vanished youth*: A. S. Pushkin o Literature (Moscow: GIKhL, 1962), p. 23.

8. *Between these two types . . . engulfs everything*: *Russian Views of Pushkin*, ed. and trans. D. J. Richards and C. R. S. Cockrell (Oxford: William A. Meeuws, 1976), p. 23.

9. *as Nabokov has shown*: See his Commentary, *Eugene Onegin: A Novel in Verse*, vol. 2, pp. 387–9.

10. *to depict that indifference . . . nineteenth century*: A. S. Pushkin, *Stikhotvoreniya*, vol. 1 (Leningrad: Sovetsky Pisatel', 1955), p. 677.

11. *Ah freedom . . . he embraced*: Ibid., p. 157.

12. *You want freedom for yourself alone*: Ibid., p. 257.

13. *Many, like myself . . . distant parts*: Ibid., p. 213.

14. *encyclopedia of Russian life*: V. G. Belinsky, *Polnoye sobraniye sochinenii* (Moscow: Academy of Sciences, USSR, 1953–7), vol. 7, p. 503.

15. *Concerning the eighth chapter . . . impoverished*: N. L. Brodsky,

Evgeny Onegin Roman A. S. Pushkina (Moscow: Gosudarstven-
noye Uchebno-Pedagogicheskoye Izdatel'stvo Ministerstva Pros-
veshcheniya RSFSR, 1957), p. 337.

16. *Onegin will either perish ... Decembrist movement*: Yu. M.
Lotman, *Roman A. S. Pushkina Evgeny Onegin Kommentarii*
(Leningrad: 'Prosveshcheniye, 1983), p. 316.

Further Reading

The following selection is confined to books in English and excludes many excellent articles on *Eugene Onegin* in scholarly journals. (Some of these are indicated in *The Companion to Pushkin*, see below.) An extensive bibliography of critical literature, in English, Russian and other European languages, is to be found in the study below by Sally Dalton-Brown. This also lists another eleven English translations of Pushkin's novel.

Biographies

Binyon, T. J., *Pushkin* (London: HarperCollins, 2002)

Feinstein, E., *Pushkin* (London: Weidenfeld & Nicolson, 1998)

Vickery, Walter N., *Pushkin, Death of a Poet* (Bloomington and London: Indiana University Press, 1968)

Vitale, Serena, *Pushkin's Button* (London: Fourth Estate, 1999)

Critical Works on *Eugene Onegin*

Briggs, A. D. P., *Eugene Onegin*, Landmarks of World Literature Series (Cambridge: Cambridge University Press, 1992)

Clayton, J. D., *Ice and Flame: Aleksandr Pushkin's 'Eugene Onegin'* (Toronto: University of Toronto Press, 1985)

Dalton-Brown, S., *Pushkin's 'Evgenii Onegin'* (London: Bristol Classical Press, 1997)

Hoisington, S. S. (ed.), *Russian Views of Pushkin's 'Eugene Onegin'*, trans. S. S. Hoisington and W. Arndt (Bloomington: Indiana University Press, 1988)

Studies of Pushkin with discussion of *Eugene Onegin*

Bayley, John, *Pushkin: A Comparative Commentary* (Cambridge: Cambridge University Press, 1971)

Bethea, D. (ed.), *Pushkin Today* (Bloomington: Indiana University Press, 1993).

Greenleaf, M., *Pushkin and Romantic Fashion: Fragment, Elegy, Orient, Irony* (Stanford: Stanford University Press, 1994)

Hoisington, S. S. (ed.), *A Plot of Her Own: The Female Protagonist in Russian Literature* (Evanston, IL: Northwestern University Press, 1995). Includes chapter by Hoisington on 'Tatiana'

Kahn, Andrew (ed.), *The Cambridge Companion to Pushkin* (Cambridge: Cambridge University Press, 2006). Includes chapter on *Onegin* by Marcus Levitt

Sandler, S., *Distant Pleasures: Alexander Pushkin and the Writing of Exile* (Stanford: Stanford University Press, 1989)

Tertz, Abram (A. Sinyavsky), *Strolls with Pushkin* (New Haven and London: Yale University Press, 1993)

Vickery, Walter, *Alexander Pushkin*, revised edn (New York: Twayne Publishers, 1992)

Studies of Russian literature with discussion of *Eugene Onegin*

Andrew, Joe, *Writers and Society during the Rise of Russian Realism* (London: Macmillan, 1980)

Fennell, J., *Nineteenth-Century Russian Literature: Studies of Ten Russian Writers* (London: Faber and Faber, 1973)

Freeborn, R., *The Rise of the Russian Novel: Studies in the Russian Novel from 'Eugene Onegin' to 'War and Peace'* (Cambridge: Cambridge University Press, 1973)

Todd, W. Mills, *Fiction and Society in the Age of Pushkin: Ideology, Institutions, and Narrative* (Cambridge, MA, and London: Harvard University Press, 1986)

Wilson, Edmund, *The Triple Thinkers* (New York: Oregon

Books, 1977). Twelve essays on literary subjects including 'In Honour of Pushkin'

Woodward, James B., 'The Principle of Contradictions in *Evgeniy Onegin*' in *Form and Meaning: Essays on Russian Literature* (Columbus, OH: Slavica, *c.* 1993)

Other Writings on Pushkin

Bethea, David, *Realizing Metaphors: Alexander Pushkin and the Life of the Poet* (Madison, WI: University of Wisconsin Press, 1998)

Clarke, Roger, *Eugene Onegin and Four Tales from Russia's Southern Frontier: A Prisoner in the Caucasus, The Fountain of Bachchisaray, Gipsies, Poltava* (Herts: Wordsworth Classics, 2005). Translated into English prose with an Introduction and Commentary

Fennell, J., *Selected Verse with Introduction and Prose Translations* (Bristol: Bristol Classical Press, 1991)

Lukács, G., *Russian Realism in World Literature* (London: Merlin Press, 1970). Includes 'Pushkin's Place in World Literature'

Richards, D. J. and Cockerell, C. R. S., *Russian Views of Pushkin* (Oxford: Willem A. Meeuws, 1976)

Wolff, Tatiana, *Pushkin on Literature* (London: Methuen, 1971)

A Note on the Translation

The *Onegin* stanza looks like a sonnet, but lacks the sonnet's traditional antithesis of octet and sestet. It is more a mixture of contrasts of the kind listed in the Dedication. Antithesis and repetition are its building blocks. Pushkin's poetry has been called a 'poetry of grammar'.[1] In *Onegin*, more than elsewhere, the poet plays with a language that is just settling into a standard form. If Pushkin sought a 'nakedness' in prose,[2] he uses the bare elements of grammar – adverbs, conjunctions, interrogatives – to construct the *Onegin* stanza. Stanza 22 in Chapter I, for example, turns on five repetitions of 'still', cut off by a single 'already' in the final couplet:

> Still cupids, devils, snakes keep leaping
> Across the stage with noisy roars;
> And weary footmen still are sleeping
> On furs at the theatre doors;
> There's coughing still and stamping, slapping,
> Blowing of noses, hissing, clapping;
> Still inside, outside, burning bright,
> The lamps illuminate the night;
> And still in harness shivering horses
> Fidget, while coachmen round a fire,
> Beating their palms together, tire,
> Reviling masters with their curses;
> Already, though, Onegin's gone
> To put some new apparel on.

Pushkin's 'stills' initiate the lines, which I was unable to follow. Only Nabokov, in his literal translation, reproduces Pushkin's syntax exactly, which is a useful exercise for showing how the poetry depends on the deployment of grammar, but makes no pretence to be poetic. Repetition and contrast of primary words form an armature for the *Onegin* stanza. But such words or particles are usually more open-throated than their English equivalents. The Russian conjunctions 'i' and 'a', for example, meaning 'and' and 'but', can be repeated melodically, whereas the repetition of their equivalents in translation will be rebarbative. The same holds for the interrogatives 'when', 'what', 'which', all ending in consonants, where their Russian equivalents terminate in vowels: 'kogda', 'shto', 'kakoi/kotory' and can take any number of repetitions. For this reason the structure of the *Onegin* stanza can easily fall apart in translation.

The iambic tetrameter is an octosyllabic line with a weak and strong beat repeated four times (as in 'The boy stood on the burning deck'). This is the so-called 'masculine line', which has a strong stress on the final syllable. The 'feminine line' adds an unstressed syllable ('The boy stood on the burning vessel'). The Onegin stanza is made up of eight masculine lines and six feminine. It is a succinct line, which can be used more flexibly in Russian because of the greater variety of long and short words. English is more monosyllabic. Any stanza of my translation will have used on the average a third more words than the original. This may be an argument for employing the pentameter (five stresses) instead. It is after all the classic verse of English poetry just as the tetrameter is of Russian. But to do so would miss the cadences of the original and the lightness of Pushkin's line. One danger of the tetrameter in English is that it can easily degenerate into a jingle as it did in the *vers de société* of the eighteenth and early nineteenth centuries.

There is another technical problem – the 'feminine', or unstressed, ending (e.g. 'rapture'), for which there are relatively few rhymes in English compared with what Russian's inflected vocabulary offers, so that the translator is too often reduced to using the 'shon' words – 'machination', 'domination' – to which I, too, plead guilty. Instead I have allowed myself near-rhymes:

'Lyudmila'/'fellow', 'service'/'impervious', 'Latin'/'smattering'.
While feminine rhyming is more problematic, I have also used
near or half-rhymes for many 'masculine' (stressed) endings,
where I thought an exact rhyme would constrain the meaning:
'live'/'love', 'face'/'peace', 'Muse'/'joys'. These two practices
have been customary in English poetry since at least the start
of the last century. I have noticed an excess of padding and
distortion in previous translations that keep resolutely to exact
rhyming. But not every half-rhyme is euphonious, and in the
end I've had to rely on my ear. In the metre too I have introduced
the irregularity of a trochee (strong beat/weak beat) at the
beginning of a line, again in common with poetic usage, cer-
tainly since Shakespeare. Although I am familiar with previous
translations, at no point in my own did I consult them, but
from Nabokov's literal version I borrowed several phrases.

My translation succeeds the earlier Penguin version by
Charles Johnston,[3] which was the first to put Pushkin's poem
on the map in English-speaking countries, inspiring Vikram
Seth's *The Golden Gate* and other imitations. Yet its aura is
old-fashioned like those autumnal productions of Chekhov that
once flourished on the British stage. The first major translator
of *Onegin*, Oliver Elton (1937),[4] mourned the 'nobleness' that
had vanished from English literature by 1880 and found most
nineteenth-century Russian writers unhealthy and repellent.
Pushkin was an oasis for him – light, gay and authentically
religious, unlike Dostoyevsky and Tolstoy. But there is little
lightness about his translation, which is full of eighteenth- or
early nineteenth-century phraseology – 'thou', 'thee', 'tis',
'twas', 'fain', 'nay' and many inversions and contortions. It
might perhaps be argued in favour of such a diction that, since
Onegin is about the squirearchy and nobility at the beginning
of the nineteenth century, a period flavour is appropriate. How-
ever, Pushkin's language is modern by comparison with Elton's
and is felt to be modern in Russia today.[5]

Elton, a professor of English who taught himself Russian,
had family roots in the landed gentry, and Johnston was a
diplomat married into the Russian aristocracy. The latter's verse
novella *Talk About the Last Poet* (1981) recalls a vanishing

idyll set in France during the collapse of the Roman Empire in
the West. In his Preface he insists that he feels no nostalgia
about the more immediate demise of the British Empire, and
yet, with evident approval, quotes a 'distinguished critic' who
describes him as its 'last poet'. Does not a similar hankering
take him to *Onegin*, likewise an idyll destroyed? Johnston is
not as backward-looking as Elton but, like him, though cer-
tainly not to the same extent, he poeticizes Pushkin's language,
blurring its precision.

The critic John Bayley, who introduced Johnston's transla-
tion, had already reinforced this eighteenth-century image of
Pushkin in 1971 in his *Pushkin: A Comparative Commentary*,[6]
where, in order to familiarize anglophone readers with the
Russian poet, he had aligned him with Jane Austen and Laur-
ence Sterne, pointing out perceptively that all three authors
shared a pre-modern, pre-professional, pre-realist mode of writ-
ing. But whether their work relies purely on convention and
artifice, as he argues, is another matter. Pushkin adored Sterne,
whom he read in French, and *Onegin*'s devious manner of
storytelling may remind us of him. But Bayley's comparison is
really more formalist than historical, since he finds a similar
use of convention and artifice in a long range of writers from
Chaucer to Joyce and owes much of his interpretation to the
Russian Formalist Viktor Shklovsky, who, in 1923, described
the novel as a Sternean game with the plot.[7] Today, in Western
academic circles, this tradition, now more complex and innov-
ative, has become the prevailing wisdom. Avant garde critics in
Russia have now gone further, crowning Pushkin as the first
Russian postmodernist.

This development was anticipated in 1964 by Vladimir
Nabokov who asserted that Pushkin's characters were no more
than stylized impersonators of figures in Western literature and
that the only Russian element of importance in the novel was
the language. His translation is a hybrid of 'period' and artifice.
For every historically specific word in the original he finds or
invents a corresponding archaism or neologism ('mollitude',
'dulcitude', 'juventude', 'ancientry', 'buttsome') which few, if
any, readers will have encountered. In this aestheticizing of

the past Nabokov anticipates the postmodern translation of the American Douglas Hofstadter.[9] While Nabokov still holds the text sacrosanct, apart from his bizarre archaisms, Hofstadter turns it into a quarry of personal interpolations and alterations, retaining only stanza, rhyme and metre, all, he assures us, in a Pushkinian sense of fun.

I have attempted in my translation to write in a contemporary idiom that avoids the antiquarian or the modern/postmodern. As far as the period translation is concerned, I am at one here with the American James Falen, who remarked of his admirable 1995 version of *Onegin* that he aimed 'to adapt the rhythms of the poem to the rhythms of English speech' today and to avoid 'the sorts of inversions and verbal contortions'[10] that in his view marred the earlier translations. Only in a few cases have I introduced dated words like 'ere', 'o'er', 'midst', and then for metrical reasons. The rhyming and metrical format of *Onegin* declares that it is a historical work. It is not a form that is common today. We rhyme much less today. There is no need to imitate poets of the past in order to give a historical sense to *Onegin*. I was once counselled in Russia to render Pushkin's various styles into equivalents from English poetry, but that would have turned the translation into a Nabokovian artefact. It is very tempting to adopt the manner of Byron's *Don Juan*, especially since it was Byron's poem that set Pushkin going. But it would miss the lyrical depth and what an acquaintance once described to me as the 'homeliness' of Pushkin, who in any case, soon turned against the English poet. It would also miss Pushkin's classical compactness. On the other hand, it is extremely difficult to render the multiplicity of styles in *Onegin*, which are embedded in history, and which require a commentary. Pushkin helps by parodying these styles and so bringing them into relief. The same is true of the constant epithets accompanying his characters. These are convenient stepping-stones for a translator. In present-day syntax they will stand out and evoke the flavour of the original without lapsing into the archaic. Best of all is to be able to reproduce Pushkin's simplicity, tangibility and precision, then the problem falls away and he appears as our contemporary.

The idea for my translation originated in a series of seminars held in the Literature Department of the University of Essex in 1966, when Pushkin was much less known in Britain than he is now and considered untranslatable for some of the reasons given above. A group of us, questioning this and the notion of untranslatability as such, undertook a collective translation of *Eugene Onegin*. Our poet-professor, Donald Davie, was to provide the verse. The project failed and Davie died, but without his initiative I should never have embarked, many years later, on the present version, of which I'll remark, adapting Pushkin's lines:

> I've scrutinized it all for any
> Discrepancies – and there are many,
> But any wish to change them now
> My publisher will not allow.

(see Chapter One, stanza 60)

NOTES

1. *poetry of grammar*: See Roman Jakobson, *Verbal Art, Verbal Sign, Verbal Time* (Oxford: Basil Blackwell, 1985), pp. 37–47.

2. *'nakedness' in prose*: Pushkin talks of 'the charm of naked simplicity', *Polnoye sobranie sochinenii, izd. AN SSSR* (1937–50), vol. 11, p. 121.

3. *Eugene Onegin*, trans. Charles Johnston (Harmondsworth: Penguin, 1977).

4. *Evgeny Onegin*, trans. Oliver Elton (London: The Pushkin Press, 1943).

5. A. D. Briggs produced a 'revised translation' in 1995, which does not essentially change the nature of Elton's version (Alexander Pushkin, *Yevgeny Onegin*, edited with revised translation by A. D. P. Briggs, based on a translation by Oliver Elton, illustrated by M. V. Dobujinsky (London: Everyman, 1995)).

6. John Bayley, *Pushkin: A Comparative Commentary* (London: Cambridge University Press, 1971).

7. Viktor Shklovsky, *Ocherki po poetike Pushkina, Evgeny Onegin (Pushkin i Stern)* (Berlin: Epokha, 1923), pp. 199–220.

8. *Eugene Onegin: A Novel in Verse*, translated from the Russian with a Commentary by Vladimir Nabokov (London: Routledge and Kegan Paul, 1964).

9. *Eugene Onegin: A Novel in Verse*, trans. Douglas Hofstadter (New York: Basic Books, 1999).

10. *to adapt the rhythms ... verbal contortions*: James E. Falen, *Alexander Pushkin: A Novel in Verse* (Oxford: Oxford University Press, 1995), p. xxviii.

A NOTE ON THE MAP

The suggested location of the characters' estates is imaginary, but the descriptions of Onegin's estate in the first stanza of Chapter II and stanza 15 of Chapter VII (when Tatiana visits his manor house) reflect Pushkin's family estate at Mikhailovskoye. For an alternative location see Nabokov's Commentary, *Eugene Onegin*, vol. 2, p. 31 and vol. 3, pp. 111–12.

Kishinev, Odessa, Mikhailovskoye, Moscow, St Petersburg and Boldino were the main places where Pushkin wrote *Onegin* (see Introduction).

Moscow, Nizhny Novgorod, Astrakhan, the Caucasus and the Crimea are the stages of Onegin's journey.

N

Gulf of Bothnia

Gulf of Finland

• St Petersburg

• Novgorod

• Pskov

★ Mikhailovskoye

• Opochka

River Volga

River Kama

Ural Mountains

Nizhny Novgorod •

• Kazan

• Moscow

• Boldino

River Dnieper

Uralsk •

• Voronezh

River Ural

• Kiev

River Don

River Volga

River Dniester

BESSARABIA

• Kishinev

• Odessa

• Rostov

Sea of Azov

Astrakhan •

CRIMEA

• Simferopol

• Stavropol

• Mineralinye Vody

Caspian Sea

Black Sea

Caucasus Mountains

• Tiflis

★ Suggested location of characters' estates in *Eugene Onegin*

TURKEY

0   150 miles

0   300 kilometres

European Russia in the 1820s

EUGENE ONEGIN

A Novel in Verse

Pétri de vanité il avait encore plus de cette espèce d'orgueil qui fait avouer avec la même indifférence les bonnes comme les mauvaises actions, suite d'un sentiment de supériorité, peut-être imaginaire.

Tiré d'une lettre particulière.[1]

Dedication[1]

Tired of amusing proud society,
Grown fonder of my friends' regard,
I would have wanted with due piety
To offer you a pledge, dear bard,
More worthy of your soul's perfection,
Full of a holy reverie,
Of poetry and clear reflection,
Of high thoughts and simplicity;
But so be it – let your affection
Accept these chapters and their rhymes,
Half-comic and half-melancholic,
Ideal and down-to-earth bucolic,
The careless fruit of leisure times,
Of sleepless nights, light inspirations,
Of immature and withered years,
The intellect's cold observations,
The heart's impressions marked in tears.

CHAPTER I

And it hurries to live and it hastens to feel.
Prince Vyazemsky[1]

I

My uncle is a man of honour,
When in good earnest he fell ill,
He won respect by his demeanour
And found the role he best could fill.
Let others profit by his lesson,
But, oh my God, what desolation
To tend a sick man day and night
And not to venture from his sight!
What shameful cunning to be cheerful
With someone who is halfway dead,
To prop up pillows by his head,
To bring him medicine, looking tearful,
To sigh – while inwardly you think:
When will the devil let him sink?

2

Reflecting thus, a youthful scapegrace,
By lofty Zeus's[2] will the heir
Of all his kinsfolk, in a post-chaise,
Flew headlong through the dusty air.
Friends of Ruslan and of Lyudmila[3]
Let me acquaint you with this fellow,
The hero of my novel, pray,
Without preamble or delay:

My friend Onegin was begotten
By the Neva, where maybe you
Originated, reader, too
Or where your lustre's not forgotten:
I liked to stroll there formerly,
But now the North's unsafe for me.[4]

3

Having retired from noble service,
His father lived on borrowed cash,
He gave three balls a year, impervious
And lost all in a final crash.
Eugene was saved by fate's decision:
Madame took on his supervision,
Then to *Monsieur* passed on her trust.[5]
The child had charm, though boisterous.
Monsieur l'Abbé, a threadbare Frenchman,
Made light of everything he taught
For fear of getting Eugene fraught;
Of stern morality no henchman,
He'd mildly check a boyish lark
And walked him in the Summer Park.[6]

4

But when young Eugene reached the morrow
Of adolescent turbulence,
Season of hopes and tender sorrow,
Monsieur was straightway driven hence.
Behold my Eugene's liberation:
With hair trimmed to the latest fashion,
Dressed like a London *dandy*, he
At last saw high society.
In French, which he'd by now perfected,
He could express himself and write,
Dance the mazurka, treading light

And bow in manner unaffected.
What more? Society opined:
Here was a youth with charm and mind.

5

We've all learned through our education
Some few things in some random way;
Thank God, then, it's no tribulation
To put our knowledge on display.
Onegin was to many people
(Who judged him by the strictest scruple)
A pedant, yet an able lad.
He was by fortune talented
At seeming always to be curious,
At touching lightly on a thing,
At looking wise and listening,
When argument became too serious,
And, with a sudden epigram,
At setting ladies' smiles aflame.

6

Custom no longer favours Latin:
The truth, therefore, was plain enough –
That he was able with a smattering
To puzzle out an epigraph,
To talk of Juvenal[7] or set a
Concluding *vale* to a letter;
From the *Aeneid*[8] a verse or two,
Not without fault, he also knew.
He did not have the scholar's temper
In dusty chronicles to trace
The story of the human race:
But anecdotes he did remember
Of bygone times, which he'd relay,
From Romulus until this day.

7

The lofty passion not possessing,
That sacrifices life to rhyme,
He could, no matter how we pressed him,
Not tell a trochee from an iamb,
Homer,[9] Theocritus[10] he rubbished,
But Adam Smith[11] instead he relished,
And was a great economist.
That is, he knew how states subsist,
Acquire their wealth, and what they live on
And why they can dispense with gold,
When, in the land itself they hold
The simple product[12] ready given.
His father could not understand,
And mortgaged, therefore, all his land.

8

What Eugene knew of in addition
I have no leisure to impart,
But where he showed true erudition,
More than in any other art,
What from his early adolescence
Had brought him bliss and painful lessons,
What all day long would occupy
His aching inactivity –
This was the art of tender passion,
That Ovid[13] sang and paid for dear,
Ending his brilliant, wild career
In banishment and deportation
To far Moldavia's steppes, where he
Pined for his native Italy.

[9][14]

10

How soon he learned the skill of feigning,
Of seeming jealous, hiding hope,
Inspiring faith and undermining,
Appearing sombre and to mope,
Now acting proud and now submissive,
By turns attentive and dismissive!
How languid, when no word he said,
How fiery, when he spoke, instead,
In letters of the heart how casual!
Loving one thing exclusively,
How self-forgetting he could be!
How rapid was his look and bashful,
Tender and bold, while off and on
With an obedient tear it shone.

11

What talent for appearing novel,
Causing with feigned despair alarm,
Jesting to make the guileless marvel,
Flattering to entertain and charm,
Pouncing upon a moment's weakness,
Subduing innocence and meekness
With passion and intelligence,
Expecting certain recompense,
Begging, demanding declarations,
Eavesdropping on the heart's first sound,
Chasing his love, and, in a bound,
Snatching clandestine assignations . . .
And later in tranquillity
Giving her lessons privately!

12

How soon he knew how to bedevil
The heart of a professed coquette!
Or, to annihilate a rival,
How bitingly he would beget
A train of malice, spite and slander!
What snares he'd set to make him founder!
But you, blest husbands, you remained
His friends and kept him entertained:
The cunning spouse, a Faublas[15] pupil,
Was eager to become his man,
So, too, the wary veteran,
And the grand cuckold, without scruple,
Forever satisfied with life,
His dinner and adoring wife.

[13, 14]

15

Sometimes, when still in bed he drowses,
Notelets are brought to greet the day –
What? Invitations? Yes, three houses
Inviting him to a soirée:
A ball here, there a children's evening,
For which will my young scamp be leaving?
With which begin? It matters not:
He'll be wherever on the dot.
Meanwhile, apparelled for the morning
And, donning a broad bolivar,[16]
Onegin to the boulevard
Drives out and strolls, at leisure swanning,
Until Bréguet[17] with watchful chime
Rings out that it is dinner time.

16

It's dark: into a sleigh he settles.
The cry resounds: 'Away, away';[18]
Upon his beaver collar, petals
Of frostdust form a silver spray.
Off to Talon's:[19] he's sure that therein,
Waiting for him, he'll find Kaverin.[20]
He enters: cork to ceiling goes
And comet wine[21] spurts forth and flows,
Bloody roast beef[22] is there to savour,
And truffles, young men's luxury,
The bouquet of French cookery,
And Strasbourg pie, that keeps forever,[23]
Between a golden ananas[24]
And Limburg cheese's living mass.[25]

17

Thirst still replenishes the beakers
To down hot cutlets one by one,
But Bréguet tells the pleasure seekers
Of a new ballet that's begun.
The theatre's heartless legislator,
Fickle adorer and spectator
Of actresses, who are the rage,
An honoured citizen backstage,
Onegin flies off to the theatre,
Where liberty's admirers[26] are
Prepared to clap an entrechat,
To hiss off Cleopatra, Phaedra,
Call for Moëna[27] (in a word,
Make sure their voices can be heard).

18

Enchanting world! There shone Fonvizin,[28]
Bold king of the satiric scene,
A friend of liberty and reason,
And there shone copycat Knyazhnín.[29]
There, Ozerov[30] shared the elation
Of public tears and acclamation
With young Semyonova; there our
Katenin[31] reproduced the power
Of Corneille's genius; there the scathing
Prince Shakhovskoy[32] delivered his
Resounding swarm of comedies;
There was Didelot,[33] in glory bathing;
There, in the wings that gave me shelter,
My youthful days sped helter-skelter.

19

My goddesses! Where now? Forsaken?
Oh hearken to my call, I rue:
Are you the same? Have others taken
Your place without replacing you?
When shall I listen to your chorus,
Behold in soul-filled flight before us
Russia's Terpsichore[34] again?
Or will my mournful gaze in vain
Seek a known face on dreary stages,
And, with my disabused lorgnette
Upon an alien public set,
Indifferent to its latest rages,
Shall I in silence yawn and cast
My mind back to a bygone past?

20

The house is full; the boxes brilliant;
Parterre and stalls – all seethe and roar;
Up in the gods they clap, ebullient,
And, with a swish, the curtains soar.
Semi-ethereal and radiant,
To the enchanting bow obedient,
Ringed round by nymphs, Istomina[35]
Stands still; one foot supporting her,
She circles slowly with the other,
And lo! a leap, and lo! she flies,
Flies off like fluff across the skies,
By Aeolus[36] wafted hither thither;
Her waist she twists, untwists; her feet
Against each other swiftly beat.

21

Applause all round. Onegin enters,
Treading on toes at every stall,
Askew, his double eyeglass centres
On ladies whom he can't recall;
At boxes, at the tiers he gazes;
With all the finery and faces
He's dreadfully dissatisfied;
Bows to the men on every side
And, in profound abstraction pacing,
Looks at the stage, then turns away –
And yawns, exclaiming with dismay:
'The whole damn lot there need replacing.
I've suffered ballets long enough,
And even Didelot's boring stuff.'[37]

22

Still cupids, devils, snakes keep leaping
Across the stage with noisy roars;
And weary footmen still are sleeping
On furs at the theatre doors;
There's coughing still and stamping, slapping,
Blowing of noses, hissing, clapping;
Still inside, outside, burning bright,
The lamps illuminate the night;
And still in harness shivering horses
Fidget, while coachmen round a fire,
Beating their palms together, tire,
Reviling masters with their curses;
Already, though, Onegin's gone
To put some new apparel on.

23

Shall I attempt to picture truly
The secret and secluded den
Where fashion's model pupil duly
Is dressed, undressed and dressed again?
Whatever trinket-dealing London
To satisfy our whims abundant
Exports across the Baltic flood,
Exchanging it for tallow, wood;
Whatever Paris, in its hunger,
Having made taste an industry,
Invents for our frivolity,
For luxury and modish languor –
These graced, at eighteen years of age,
The study of our youthful sage.

24

Pipes from Tsargrad,[38] inlaid with amber,
Bronzes and china on a stand,
Perfumes[39] in crystal vials to pamper
The senses of a gentleman;
Combs, little files of steel, and scissors,
Straight ones and curved, and tiny tweezers,
And thirty kinds of brush to clean
The nails and teeth, and keep their sheen.
Rousseau[40] (I'll note with your permission)
Could not conceive how solemn Grimm[41]
Dared clean his nails in front of him,
The madcap sage and rhetorician.
Champion of rights and liberty,
In this case judged wrong-headedly.

25

One still can be a man of action
And mind the beauty of one's nails:
Why fight the age's predilection?
Custom's a despot and prevails.
My Eugene, like Chaadaev,[42] fearful
Of jealous censure, was most careful
About his dress – a pedant or
A dandy, as we said before.
At least three hours he spent preparing
In front of mirrors in his lair,
And, stepping out at last from there,
Looked like a giddy Venus wearing
A man's attire, who, thus arrayed,
Drives out to join a masquerade.

26

Having diverted you concerning
The latest taste in toiletry,
I could regale the world of learning
With his sartorial repertory;
An enterprise that's bold, I know it,
Yet, after all, I am a poet:
But *pantalons*, *frac* and *gilet*[43]
Are still not Russian words today.
Indeed, I offer my excuses,
Since my poor style, such as it is,
Could well forgo the vanities
Of foreign words and like abuses,
Though I dipped into, formerly,
The Academic Dictionary.

27

But to continue with our story:
We'd better hurry to the ball
To which Onegin in his glory
Has sped by coach to make his call.
Through sleeping streets, past houses darkened
Twin carriage lamps pour out a jocund
Illumination row on row,
Projecting rainbows on the snow;
With lampions around it scattered,
A splendid house is brightly lit,
Past whole-glass windows shadows flit
And profiled heads are silhouetted
Of ladies, and outlandish men –
Fashion's most recent specimen.

28

Behold our hero at the doorway;
Past the hall porter like a dart
He flies, ascends the marble stairway,
Flicking his straying hair apart,
Enters. The ballroom's full to brimming;
The music now is tired of dinning;
Mazurkas entertain the crowd;
The room is packed, the noise is loud;
The spurs of Chevalier Gardes[44] jangle,
The little feet of ladies fly;
Their charming tracks are followed by
Glances that fly from every angle,
And jealous female whisperings
Are deafened by the howling strings.

29

In days of revelries and passions
I'd go insane about a ball:
For billets doux and declarations
There's no securer place at all,
Respected husbands! May I offer
My service to you lest you suffer;
I beg you, note my every word,
I want you always on your guard.
And you, mammas, pay more attention,
Observe your daughters' etiquette
And keep a hold on your lorgnette!
Or else . . . you'll need God's intervention!
I'm only writing this to show
That I stopped sinning long ago.

30

Alas, much life I have neglected
For every pastime thinkable,
Yet were my morals not affected,
I to this day would love a ball.
I love the youthfulness and madness,
The crush, the glitter and the gladness,
The care with which the women dress;
I love their little feet, yet guess
You'd be unlikely to discover
Three shapely pairs of women's feet
In all of Russia. Long indeed
Have two small feet caused me to suffer . . .
Sad, cold, I still recall their smart,
And in my sleep they stir my heart.

31

To what far desert will you wander,
Madman, to overcome their sting?
Ah, little, little feet! I wonder
Where now you crush the flowers of spring?
Born to the softness of the orient,
On our sad snows you left no imprint:
You loved the sumptuous feel instead
Of rugs that yielded to your tread,
You lived in luxury, refinement.
For you how long ago did I
Forget renown and eulogy,
My native land and my confinement?
The happiness of youth has passed
Like your light trace on meadow grass.

32

Diana's[45] breast, the cheeks of Flora,[46]
Are charming, friends, I do agree,
But somehow what enchant me more are
The small feet of Terpsichore.
To all who gaze on them magnetic,
Of priceless recompense prophetic,
Their classic gracefulness inspires
A wilful swarming of desires.
I love them, dear Elvina,[47] under
A lengthy tablecloth or pressed
On grass in spring or when they rest
In winter on a cast-iron fender,
Upon the parquet floors of halls,
Beside the sea on granite walls.

33

Once by the sea, a storm impending,
I recollect my envy of
The waves, successively descending,
Collapsing at her feet with love.
Oh how I wished to join their races
And catch her feet in my embraces!
No, never did I in the fire
Of my ebullient youth desire
To kiss with so much pain and hunger
A young Armida's[48] lips or seek
The rose upon a flaming cheek
Or touch a bosom full of languor;
No, never did a passion's squall
So rend and tear apart my soul.

34

Another memory comes, revealing
A cherished dream in which I stand
Holding a happy stirrup . . . feeling
A tiny foot inside my hand.
Imagination seethes, excited,
Once more its contact has ignited
The blood within my withered heart,
Once more I love, once more I smart! . . .
But why should I think it my duty
To praise these proud ones with my lyre,
Who don't deserve the passions or
The songs engendered by their beauty.
Their charming words and glances cheat
As surely as . . . their little feet.

35

But my Onegin? Home to bed he
Drives sleepily through city streets,
While restless Petersburg already
Is wakened by the drummer' beats.
The merchant's up, the hawker's calling,
And to his stand the cabman's crawling,
The Okhta[49] girl, her jug held tight,
Crunches the snow in hurried flight.
The early-morning noise is cheering,
Shutters unlock, in columns high
Blue chimney smoke ascends the sky,
The baker, punctual German, wearing
His cotton cap, already has
Opened and shut his vasisdas.[50]

36

But, turning morning into nighttime,
Exhausted by the ballroom's din,
The child of luxury and pastime
In blissful shade sleeps quietly in.
He'll wake past noon, and till next morning
His selfsame life will go on turning
In its unchanging, motley way,
Tomorrow just like yesterday.
And yet how happy was my Eugene –
A free man in the bloom of years
'midst splendid conquests and affairs,
'midst daily pleasures to indulge in?
Was it in vain that, feasting, he
Displayed such health and levity?

37

No: soon a coldness numbed his feeling;
The social hubbub left him bored;
The fair sex ceased to be appealing,
To dominate his every thought.
Betrayals no more entertained him,
While friends and friendships simply pained him,
Since he, not always, it was plain,
Could drink a bottle of champagne,
To down a Strasbourg pie and *beef-steaks*,
And scatter caustic words of wit,
While thinking that his head might split;
And he, a fiery rake, his leave takes
Of that exhilarating life
Of sabre, lead and martial strife.

38

A malady, whose explanation
Is overdue, and similar
To English spleen – the Russian version,
In short, is what we call *khandra* –[51]
Possessed him bit by bit; not tempted,
Thank God, to shoot himself, but, emptied
Of all attachment to this life,
He, like Childe Harold,[52] would arrive
In drawing rooms, dejected, languid;
Neither the worldly gossiping,
Nor game of boston,[53] then in swing,
Immodest sighs or glances candid,
Naught touched Onegin to the core
He noticed nothing any more.

[39, 40, 41]

42

Capricious ladies of society!
You were the first ones he forswore,
And, in our years, *bon ton*,[54] propriety
Have, it is true, become a bore;
While you may find a dame among them,
Elucidating Say and Bentham,[55]
Their conversation, all in all,
While harmless, is nonsensical;
On top of that, they are so gracious,
Majestic and intelligent,
So full of pious sentiment,
So circumspect, precise and precious,
So inaccessible to men,
The sight of them brings on the spleen.[56]

43

And even you, young beauties, gracing
The droshkies that career away,
Over the city's pavements racing
From late at night to break of day,
You, too, he left in equal measure.
An apostate from stormy pleasure,
He locked himself inside his den,
Yawning, he reached out for a pen,
He wished to write – but could not manage
The pain of persevering toil,
Nothing proceeded from his quill,
Nor did he join that cocky parish
Or guild of which I'll speak no wrong,
Since it's among them I belong.

44

And once more given to inaction,
Empty in spirit and alone,
He settled down – to the distraction
Of making other minds his own;
Collecting books, he stacked a shelfful,
Read, read, not even one was helpful:
Here, there was dullness, there pretence;
This one lacked conscience, that one sense;
All were by different shackles fettered;
And, past times having lost their hold,
The new still raved about the old.
Like women, books he now deserted,
And mourning taffeta he drew
Across the bookshelf's dusty crew.

45

Disburdened of the world's opinions,
Like him, disdaining vanity,
At that time we became companions.
I liked his personality,
The dreams to which he was addicted,
The oddness not to be depicted,
The sharp, chilled mind and gloomy bent
That rivalled my embitterment.
We both had known the play of passions,
By life we both had been oppressed;
In each the heart had lost its zest;
Each waited for the machinations
Of men, and blind Fortuna's gaze,
Blighting the morning of our days.

46

He who has lived and thought can never
Help in his soul despising men,
He who has felt will be forever
Haunted by days he can't regain.
For him there are no more enchantments,
Him does the serpent of remembrance,
Him does repentance always gnaw.
All this will frequently afford
A great delight to conversations.
Initially, I was confused
By Eugene's speech, but I grew used
To his abrasive disputations,
His humour halfway mixed with bile
And epigrams in sombre style.

47

How often did the summer court us,
When skies at night are limpid, bright[57]
And when the cheerful, glass-like waters
Do not reflect Diana's light;
Recalling former years' romances,
Recalling love that time enhances,
With tenderness, with not a care,
Alive, at liberty once more,
We drank, in mute intoxication,
The breath of the indulgent night!
Just as a sleepy convict might
Be carried from incarceration
Into a greenwood, so were we
Borne to our youth by reverie.

48

Leaning upon a ledge of granite,
His soul full of regrets and woes,
Eugene stood pensively (the Poet[58]
Himself appears in such a pose).
All round was silent, save a sentry
Hailing another, or the entry,
With sudden clip-clop from afar,
Of droshkies in Millionaya.[59]
Upon the sleeping river, gliding,
Sailed one lone boat with waving oars,
Bold song and horn from distant shores
Charmed us . . . but what is more delighting
Than on a merry night to hear
Torquato's octaves drawing near!

49

O Adriatic waves, o Brenta![60]
Nay, I shall see you and rejoice,
With inspiration new I'll enter
And hearken to your magic voice!
To grandsons of Apollo sacred,
I know it well, to me it's kindred
From Albion's proud poetry.[61]
The nights of golden Italy
I'll spend with a Venetian daughter,
Now talkative, now mute; with her
In a mysterious gondola
Voluptuously through the water
My lips will study how to move
In Petrarch's[62] tongue, the tongue of love.

50

My hour of freedom, is it coming?
I call to it: it's time, it's time!
Above the sea, forever roaming,[63]
I beckon every sail and clime.
Mantled by storms, with waves contending,
Upon the sea's free crossway wending,
When shall I start my freedom's flight?
Dull shore that gives me no delight,
It's time to leave you for the ocean,
That swells beneath a Southern sky,
And in my Africa[64] to sigh
For sombre Russia, for the portion
Of love and suffering I incurred
And where I left my heart interred.

51

Onegin was prepared to travel
To foreign parts with me, but fate
Was soon to part us and unravel
Our plans until a future date.
His father died upon the instant.
Before Onegin an insistent
Brigade of creditors appeared,
Each wanting something different cleared:
Eugene, detesting litigation,
Contented with his lot, at once
Abandoned his inheritance,
In this perceiving no privation,
Or was it that he could foretell
His ageing uncle's death as well?

52

Indeed, quite suddenly the steward
Reported uncle gravely ill
And on his deathbed, looking forward
To bidding Eugene a farewell.
No sooner had he finished reading
This woeful note than to this meeting
Upon a post-chaise Eugene sped,
And yawned, as he prepared ahead
For sighs and boredom and deception
For money' sake (and it was here
My novel started its career);
But he, instead of this reception,
Found uncle on a table laid,
Earth's tribute ready to be paid.

53

He found the grounds full of attendants;
Arriving from all sides to call,
Friends, enemies were in attendance,
All lovers of a funeral.
The dead man buried, feasting followed,
The priests and guests imbibed and swallowed,
And, gravely, afterwards dispersed
As if some business they'd rehearsed.
Now our Onegin, country dweller,
Of land, wood, water, factory
Is master (former enemy
Of order and a wasteful fellow),
And very glad to change his lot
For something new, no matter what.

54

For two whole days the lonely meadows,
The bubbling brook's tranquillity,
The oak wood's leafy cool and shadows,
Appeared to him a novelty;
The third day he could no more muster
Delight in grove or hill or pasture;
Already they put him to sleep;
Clearly he saw he could not keep
Out boredom in a country setting,
Though not a palace, street or ball
Or cards or verse were there at all.
Khandra was there, on guard and waiting,
And dogged him like a faithful wife
Or shadow fixed to him for life.

55

But I was born for peaceful pleasures,
For country quiet: there I thrive:
There sounds the lyre with clearer measures.
Creative dreams are more alive.
In innocent pursuits I wander,
By a deserted lake I ponder
And *far niente* is my law.
I wake each morning ready for
Sweet comfort and a free existence:
I sleep a great deal, little read,
To wanton glory pay no heed.
Casting my mind into the distance,
Did I not spend my happiest days
In idleness and shaded ways?

56

O flowers, country, love, inaction,
O fields! I am your devotee!
I always note with satisfaction
Onegin's difference from me,
Lest somewhere a sarcastic reader
Or publisher or such-like breeder
Of complicated calumny
Discerns my physiognomy
And shamelessly repeats the fable
That I have crudely versified
Myself like Byron, bard of pride,
As if we were no longer able
To write a poem and discuss
A subject not concerning us.

57

Poets, I'll note, in this connection
Are friends of amorous reverie.
It used to be my predilection
To dream of objects dear to me;
My soul retained their secret image
Until the Muse gave them a language:
Carefree, I'd sing of my ideal,
Maid of the mountains, and of all
The captive maids of Salgir's[65] waters.
Now, friends, I hear you put to me,
The question not infrequently:
For whom among these jealous daughters
Sighs most your lyre? To which of these
Did you devote its melodies?

58

'Whose gaze, exciting inspiration,
Rewarded with caressing eyes
Your pensive song and adoration?
Whom did your verses idolize?'
Friends, not a single one, believe me!
Love's mad alarms will not deceive me,
I've been through them with little joy.
Happy is he who can alloy
Them with a fevered rhyme: he doubles
The poet's sacred frenzy, strides
In Petrarch's footsteps, and besides
Relieves the heart of all its troubles,
And captures glory's palm to boot;
But I, in love, was stupid, mute.

59

Love passed, the Muse resumed dominion
And cleared the darkness from my mind,
Free now, I seek again the union
Of feelings, thoughts and magic sound.
I write, my heart's no longer pining,
My pen no longer wanders, making
Sketches of female heads or feet
Alongside verses incomplete.
Dead ashes cannot be replenished,
I'm sad still, but the tears are gone,
And soon, soon when the storm is done
And in my soul all trace has vanished,
Then will I start a poem – oh,
In cantos, twenty-five or so.

60

I have a plan already for it,
And how the hero will be known;
But for the moment I'll ignore it,
Having completed Chapter One.
I've scrutinized it all for any
Discrepancies – and there are many,
But I've no wish to change them yet;
I'll pay the censorship my debt;
My labour's fruits I shall deliver
To the reviewers to devour;
Depart then, newborn work this hour,
Off to the banks of Nevsky river
And earn for me the prize of fame:
Falsification, noise and blame!

CHAPTER II

O rus!
Horace

O Rus'!

1

The country place where Eugene suffered
Was a delightful little spot;
The innocent might there have offered
Blessings to heaven for their lot.
The manor house stood in seclusion,
Screened by a hill from wind's intrusion,
Above a stream. Far off, there stretched
Meadows and golden cornfields, patched
With dazzling, multi-coloured flowers;
Small hamlets could be glimpsed around,
Herds wandered through the meadow ground,
And, in its thick, entangled bowers
A vast, neglected garden nursed
Dryads, in pensive mood immersed.

2

The noble castle was constructed
As castles should be: solid-based,
Designed for comfort, unaffected,
In sensible and ancient taste,
With lofty rooms throughout the dwelling
A salon damasked floor to ceiling,
Portraits of Tsars upon the walls
And stoves with multi-coloured tiles.

Today all this is antiquated,
I really cannot fathom why;
My friend, however, walked right by,
Unable to appreciate it,
Since he would yawn, indifferent to
An old interior or a new.

3

Into that very room he settled,
Where, forty years, till his demise,
With housekeeper the old man battled,
Looked through the window, swatted flies.
All was quite simple; oaken floorboards,
Table, divan of down, two cupboards,
And not an ink stain anywhere;
He opened up the cupboards there:
The first housed an expenses manual,
The second rows of fruit liqueurs
And eau-de-pomme in jugs and jars
Beside an 1808 annual:
The old man, by much work perplexed,
Consulted not another text.

4

Alone among his acquisitions,
Merely to while away the time,
At first, our Eugene made provisions
To introduce a new regime.
A sage in rural isolation,
He eased the peasant yoke, replacing
The old *corvée* with light quit-rent;
The serf blessed fate for what it sent.

But Eugene's thrifty neighbour, flurried,
Sat sulking; in his corner he
Envisaged some catastrophe;
Another slyly smiled, unworried,
But they were all unanimous:
Here was a crank most dangerous.

5

At first, they all rode up to greet him;
But at the back porch every day
A stallion from the Don would meet him
As soon as on the carriage way
Their country carts could be detected,
When off he'd gallop, undeflected.
Outraged by this behaviour, they
Withdrew their friendship straightaway.
'Our neighbour is a boor, as mad as
A freemason, a crack-brained ass;
Drinks only red wine by the glass;
Won't stoop to kiss the hands of ladies;
It's "yes" and "no", not "yes, sir", "no,
sir".' All agreed this was *de trop*.

6

A new landowner, at that moment,
Had driven down to *his* estate
And offered equal cause for comment
And stringent neighbourhood debate.
By name Vladimir Lensky, wholly
Endowed with Göttingenian soul,[1] he
Was handsome, in his youthful prime,
A devotee of Kant[2] and rhyme.
He brought with him the fruits of learning
From mist-enveloped Germany:
Those dreams extolling liberty,

That fervent spirit, oddly yearning,
That language with its ardent flair
And curling, shoulder-length black hair.

7

By chill corruption not yet blighted,
Not having fallen yet from grace,
In friendly greetings he delighted
And in a maiden's sweet embrace.
Of heart's affairs he had no knowledge,
Hope nursed his feelings, gave him courage,
And worldly noise and glitter still
Lent his young mind a novel thrill.
With a sweet fancy he would cradle
His doubting heart's uncertainty;
For him our life and destiny
Appeared as an enticing riddle,
To solve which he would rack his mind,
Suspecting wonders of mankind.

8

He thought that he should be united
With a congenial soul, that she
Would pine, whenever he departed,
And keep awaiting him each day;
He thought that friends would, in like manner,
Don fetters to defend his honour,
And that their hands would never spare
The vessel[3] of his slanderer;
That there were some whom fate had chosen,
Blest comrades of humanity;
That their immortal family
Would in a future time emblazon
Us all with overwhelming rays
And grace the world with blissful days.

9

Compassion, righteous indignation,
Pure love directed to the good,
And fame's sweet pain, inebriation
Had stirred from early days his blood.
He with his lyre roamed ever further;
Beneath the sky of Schiller, Goethe,[4]
In sudden flame his soul burst forth,
Kindled at their poetic hearth,
And, happy one, without degrading
The art's exalted Muses, he
Nursed proudly in his poetry
Exalted feelings, never fading,
Surges of virgin reverie,
And charms of grave simplicity.

10

He sang of love, to love obedient,
His song possessed the clarity
Of simple maidens' thoughts, of infant
Slumber and of the moon, when she
Shines in the sky's untroubled spaces,
Goddess of sighs and secret places;
He sang of parting and despond,
Of *something* and the *dim beyond*,
He sang, too, of romantic roses;
He sang of distant lands, those spheres
Where he had long shed living tears,
Where silently the world reposes;
He sang of life's decaying scene,
While he was not yet quite eighteen.

11

Where only Eugene in their desert
Could judge his gifts and quality,
He had no appetite to hazard
His neighbours' hospitality;
He fled their noisy conversations:
Their sensible deliberations
Regarding haymaking, the wine,
The kennels and their kith and kind
Were not, of course, lit up with feeling,
Poetic fire, perceptive wit,
Intelligence, nor with the art
That made society appealing;
The talk, though, of their spouses dear
Was far less meaningful to hear.

12

Lensky, a wealthy youth and handsome,
Was looked upon as marriageable;
Such in the country was the custom;
All daughters were eligible
To court their *semi-Russian neighbour*;
When he arrived, the guests would labour
At once, by hinting, to deplore
The dull life of a bachelor;
The samovar's inviting Lensky.
And Dunya pours him out a cup,
They whisper to her: 'Watch, look up!'
They bring in a guitar, too, then she
Begins to shrill (good God!) and call:
Oh come into my golden hall . . .

13

But Lensky, not, of course, intending
To wear the ties of marriage yet,
Looked forward warmly to befriending
Onegin, whom he'd newly met.
Not ice and flame, not stone and water,
Not verse and prose are from each other
So different as these men were.
At first, since so dissimilar,
They found each other dull, ill-suited;
Then got to like each other; then
Each day met riding. Soon the men
Could simply not be separated.
Thus (I'm the first one to confess)
People are friends from idleness.

14

But friendship even of this order
We cannot boast of. Having fought
All prejudices, we consider
Ourselves the ones, all others nought.
We all aspire to be Napoleons;
Two-legged creatures in their millions
Are no more than a tool for us,
Feelings we find ridiculous.
While fairer in his preconceptions
Than many, Eugene was inclined
In toto to despise mankind,
But (as each rule has its exceptions)
Some individuals he spared,
And feelings, too, by him unshared.

15

He heeded Lensky with indulgence.
The poet's fervent talk and mind,
Still hesitant in forming judgements,
His look of inspiration blind –
All this was novel to Onegin;
He tried to stop his lips from making
A chilling comment, and he thought:
I'd really be a fool to thwart
His moment's bliss with my rejection;
His time, without me, will arrive;
But for the moment let him thrive,
Believing in the world's perfection;
Forgive the fever of the young,
Their ardour and their raving tongue.

16

All things promoted disputations
And led them to reflect: they would
Discuss the pacts of vanished nations,
The fruits of learning, evil, good,
And centuries-old prejudices,
The secrets of the grave's abysses,
And life and destiny in turn –
All these were subjects of concern.
The poet, heatedly contending,
Recited in a reverie
Fragments of Nordic balladry,
And Eugene, gently condescending,
While little grasping what he heard,
Attended to his every word.

17

More often, though, it was the passions
That occupied my anchorites.
Free from their stormy depredations,
Onegin sighed with some regrets
As he recounted their abatement.
Happy who tasted their excitement
And in the end could leave it, but
Happier still who knew it not,
Who cooled his love with separation,
Hostility with calumny,
Who yawned with wife and company,
Immune to jealousy's invasion,
And who ensured he did not lose
His fortune to a crafty deuce.

18

When to the banner we've foregathered
Of sensible tranquillity,
When passion's flame at last is smothered,
And we as an absurdity
Consider its caprices, surges,
Belated repetitions, urges –
Resigned, but not without a tear,
We sometimes like to lend an ear
To tales of other people's passions,
And hearing them stirs up our heart.
Thus an old soldier takes delight
In eavesdropping on the confessions
Of young, mustachioed blades who strut,
While he's forgotten in his hut.

19

But flaming youth is quite unable
To hide a feeling or a thought
And ever is prepared to babble
Love, hatred, joy and sorrow out.
Himself by passion invalided,
With solemn mien Onegin heeded
The poet who confessed his heart
With love and using all his art;
A simple soul, not seeking glory,
He laid his trusting conscience bare.
Eugene with ease discovered there
The poet's young, romantic story
With its abundant feelings that
To us have long since been old hat.

20

He loved, ah, as we cannot know it,
Today such love's anomalous,
Only the mad soul of a poet
Is still condemned to loving thus:
Always and everywhere one vision,
One customary, single mission,
One customary, single grief.
Not cooling distance's relief,
Nor lengthy years of separation,
Nor hours devoted to the Muse,
Nor foreign beauties he could choose,
Nor merry noise, nor meditation
Had changed in him a soul whose fire
Was lit by virginal desire.

21

Mere boy, by Olga captivated,
Not knowing a tormented heart,
He witnessed, tenderly elated,
Her childish merriments and sport.
In leafy shade, by oaks protected,
He shared the games that she selected;
Their fathers – friends and neighbours, they –
Destined the children's wedding day.
Beneath a backwoods porch the maiden,
In girlish innocence and grace,
Blossomed beneath her parents' gaze,
A lily of the valley, hidden
In densest grass, unnoticed by
The passing bee or butterfly.

22

By her the poet first was given
His youthful dream of ecstasy,
And thoughts about her would enliven
His pipe's first moan of melody.
Farewell to golden games, forever!
He took instead to groveland cover,
Seclusion, stillness and the night,
The stars and heaven's brightest light,
The moon amid her constellation,
The moon, to whom when evening nears,
We dedicated walks and tears,
Our secret sorrow's consolation . . .
But now we only see in her
A substitute for lamplight's blur.

23

Forever modest and submissive,
Forever merry as the day,
As charming as a lover's kisses,
As artless as the poet's way,
Her eyes as azure as the heaven,
Her flaxen curls, her smile so even,
Her voice, her slender waist and stance
These made up Olga . . . but just glance
At any novel at your leisure,
You'll find her portrait there – it's sweet,
Once I myself found it a treat,
But now it bores me beyond measure.
Reader, I shall, if you'll allow,
Turn to the elder sister now.

24

Her elder sister was Tatiana . . .
This is the first time that we grace
A tender novel in this manner
With such a name, so out of place.
What of it? It is pleasing, resonant;
I know, of course, that it is redolent
Of memories of ancientness
Or maids' rooms! We must all confess:
That even in the names we're given
There's very little taste on show
(We will not mention verses now);
Enlightenment we don't believe in,
We've simply utilized it for
Mere affectation – nothing more.

25

And so then she was called Tatiana.
Lacking her sister's beauty, poise,
Her rosy freshness, in no manner
Would she attract a person's gaze.
A wayward, silent, sad young maiden,
Shy as a doe, in forest hidden,
She seemed inside her family
A stranger, an anomaly.
She could not snuggle up to father
Or mother; and herself a child,
By children's games was not beguiled
To skip or play, but often, rather,
Would at a window silently
Sit on her own throughout the day.

26

Of contemplative disposition
Beginning with her cradle days,
She coloured with a dreamy vision
The idle flow of rural ways.
Her slender fingers knew not needles;
Embroidery seemed made of riddles;
With silken patterns she was loath
To animate a linen cloth.
A sign of the desire to govern,
The child with her obedient doll
Rehearses for the protocol
Of etiquette and worldly canon,
And to her doll with gravity
Imparts mamma's morality.

27

But even in those years Tatiana
Possessed no doll nor made pretence
To tell it in an adult manner
About town fashions and events.
And childish escapades were foreign
To her: in winter, tales of horror,
Told in the darkness of the night,
Gave to her heart much more delight.
Whenever nurse, obeying Olga,
Brought all her little playmates down
To play upon the spacious lawn,
She found the games of catch too vulgar,
The ringing laughs and jollity
Were boring to her equally.

28

Upon her balcony, preceding
The rising of the dawn, she loved
To watch the dancing stars receding
That on the pale horizon moved,
When earth's fine edge is softly glowing,
The wind that heralds morn is blowing,
And by degrees the day grows bright.
In winter when the shade of night
Possesses half the world much longer,
And longer, too, the lazy East,
In moonlight overcome by mist,
Continues to repose in languor,
Awakened at her usual time,
By candlelight from bed she'd climb.

29

Fond early on of reading novels,
For which all else she would forgo,
She grew enamoured of the marvels
Of Richardson[5] and of Rousseau.
Her father was a decent fellow,
Of the preceding age and mellow,
Who saw no harm in books, which he,
Not having read at all, would see
As empty playthings, unengrossing,
And did not care what secret tome
Lay until morning, in his home,
Beneath his daughter's pillow dozing.
As for his wife, she'd also gone
Quite crazy over Richardson.

30

Her love for him was not connected
With having read her Richardson,
Nor was it that she had rejected
A Lovelace for a Grandison.[6]
But in the past Princess Alina,
Her Moscow cousin, when she'd seen her,
Had talked about these gentlemen.
Her husband was her fiancé then,
A bond to which she'd not consented;
She sighed after another one
Who, with his heart and mind, had won
Her liking more than her intended:
This Grandison was smart at cards,
A fop and Ensign in the Guards.

31

Like him, she dressed to match the fashion
In keeping with good taste, well bred;
But all at once without discussion
The girl was to the altar led.
And, to dispel her dreadful sorrow,
Her husband wisely left, the morrow,
Taking her to his country seat,
Where God knows whom she was to meet.
At first, she strained and sobbed and ranted,
All but divorced her husband, too,
Then turned to household matters, grew
Acclimatized, became contented.
Habit is heaven's gift to us:
A substitute for happiness.

32

Habit allayed the grief she suffered,
That nothing else could remedy;
A thing of note she soon discovered
That gave her equanimity:
Between domestic work and leisure
She ascertained the perfect measure
For governing her husband's life,
And then became a proper wife.
She drove out to inspect the farmers,
She pickled mushrooms, saved and spent,
She shaved the conscripts' foreheads,[7] went
On Saturdays to use the bathhouse,
Beat servant girls who got her cross –
She, not her husband, was the boss.

33

Time was, she would have written in a
Shy maiden's album with her blood,
Praskov'ya she'd have called Polina
And made a song of every word.
She'd wear tight stays to suit convention,
A Russian N just like a French one
She'd learned to utter through her nose;
But all this soon came to a close:
Stays, album, the Princess Alina,
The sentimental verselets, all
She now forgot, began to call
'Akul'ka' formerly 'Selina',
And finally appeared becapped
Inside a quilted housecoat wrapped.

34

But heartily her husband loved her,
On her designs he did not frown,
In all, he cheerfully believed her,
While dining in his dressing-gown;
His life rolled on without a hazard;
At eventide, sometimes, there gathered
A group of kindly neighbours, who,
Informally, arrived to rue
And tittle-tattle, who confided
And chuckled over this and that.
Hours passed – time that the tea was set,
They summoned Olga to provide it.
Then supper came and close of day,
And so the guests would drive away.

35

Their peaceful lives went on, retaining
The customs of antiquity;
At Shrovetide they'd be entertaining
With Russian pancakes (or *bliny*);
They fasted twice a year for sinning,
They loved round swings that sent them spinning,
The choral dances, guessing songs.
On Trinity, among the throngs
Of yawning peasants at thanksgiving,
They touchingly shed tears, three drops
Upon a bunch of buttercups;[8]
They needed *kvas*[9] like air for living;
And at their table guests were served
With dishes, as their rank deserved.

36

And thus the two of them grew older
Until the grave invited down
The husband, squire and erstwhile soldier,
And he received a second crown.[10]
He died an hour before his dinner,
Mourned by the neighbour of the manor,
By children and a faithful wife,
More candidly than many a life.
He was a simple, kindly *barin*,[11]
And there, above his last remains,
A solemn monument proclaims:
The humble sinner, Dmitry Larin,
Slave of the Lord and Brigadier
Beneath this stone reposeth here.

37

To his penates[12] now returning,
Vladimir Lensky visited
His neighbour's humble gravestone, mourning,
With sighs, the ashes of the dead;
Long was his heart with grief afflicted,
'Poor Yorick,' he declared, dejected,
'He used to hold me in his arms.
How, in my childhood, oftentimes,
I played with his Ochakov medal![13]
He destined Olga for my bride,
Shall I be here that day . . . ? he said.'
True sadness put him on his mettle,
Vladimir straightway felt a call
To write a gravestone madrigal.

38

And there, in tears, he wrote another
To mark the patriarchal dust
Of both his father and his mother . . .
Alas! each generation must
By Providence's dispensation
Rise, ripen, fall, in quick succession,
Upon life's furrows; in its wake
Others the selfsame journey take.
So, our light-headed tribe, now roaming,
Grows up, gets animated, seethes,
Sees off its ancestors with wreaths.
But our time, too, is coming, coming,
And one fine day our grandsons will
Bundle us out with equal zeal!

39

Meanwhile, enjoy, friends, till it's ended,
This light existence, every dram!
Its nullity I've comprehended
And little bound to it I am;
I've shut my eyelids now to phantoms;
But distant hopes appear and sometimes
Continue to disturb my heart.
I'd find it sad now to depart
The world without some recognition.
Not courting praise, I live and write,
But still, it seems, I should delight
In glorifying my sad mission,
In having just a single sound
Recall me, like a friend that's found.

40

And someone's heart it will awaken;
And this new strophe that I nurse
Will not in Lethe[14] drown, forsaken,
If destiny preserves my verse.
Perhaps some future ignoramus
(A flattering hope!), when I am famous,
Will point to my illustrious portrait
And say: now that man was a poet!
I offer *you*, then, my oblations,
Admirer of Aonia's maids,[15]
O you, whose memory never fades
And saves my volatile creations,
Whose hand, that favours my renown,
Will pat the old man's laurel crown![16]

CHAPTER III

Elle était fille, elle était amoureuse.
Malfilâtre[1]

I

'Where now? How very like a poet!'
'Onegin, I must go, goodbye.'
'By all means, but (I'd like to know it),
Where do you spend your evenings?' 'Why,
I see the Lárins.' 'That's amazing.
Mercy, does it not drive you crazy
To murder every evening thus?'
'Not in the least.' 'I am nonplussed.
From here I picture the occasion:
First (listen, am I right?), I see
A simple, Russian family,
Concern for guests and their provision,
Jam, endless chatter with regard
To rain and flax and cattle-yard . . .'

2

'I do not see why that's so shocking.'
'It's boring, that is why, dear man.'
'I hate your fashionable mocking;
I'm happy with a homely clan,
Where I . . .' 'An eclogue's bound to follow!
For God's sake, that will do, good fellow.
But now, you're off; I'm sorry. Say,
Could you devise for me a way

Of seeing for myself your Phyllis,
The object of your thoughts from far,
Your tears, pen, rhymes, etcetera.
Present me.' 'But you're joking.' 'Promise.'
'I'll gladly.' 'When?' 'Why, now's all right.
They will receive us with delight.'

3

'Let's go, then.' At their destination
They're met with the formality,
The sometimes onerous ministration
Of old-world hospitality.
The order of the fare's habitual:
Jam in small dishes[2] starts the ritual,
Then lingonberry juice is brought
And set upon an oil-cloth board.[3]

....
....
....
....
....
....

4

Returning home, the two are flying
At high speed by the shortest way.
Now let us condescend to spying
On what our heroes have to say.
'You yawn, Onegin, what's the matter?'
'A habit, Lensky – all that chatter.'
'But you seem worse.' 'The same old thing.
But look, the light is vanishing.
Faster, Andryushka, hasten, hasten!
What silly places all these are!
Oh, by the way, your Larina

Is simple, but a dear old person;
I fear the lingonberry juice
May cause my stomach some abuse.

5

'Please tell me which one was Tatiana.'
'Oh, she's the sister who appeared
All sad and silent like Svetlana,[4]
And by the window sat and stared.'
'But surely you don't love the younger?'
'Why not?' 'Were I like you a singer,
I'd choose the other for my wife.
In Olga's looks there's no more life
Than Van Dyck has in his madonnas:
Her countenance is round and fair
Just like the daft moon shining there
Above the daft horizon on us.'
Vladimir answered icily
And all the way sat silently.

6

Meanwhile, Onegin's visitation
Had made on all the Larin folk
A most significant impression
And given neighbours cause for talk.
Conjecture followed on conjecture,
All started furtively to lecture,
To joke, to judge, not without spite
And view Tatiana as a bride;
Some, going further still, asserted
That wedding plans had all been made
And simply had to be delayed
Till modish rings had been located.
And as for Lensky's wedding, they
Had long ago arranged the day.

7

Tatiana listened with vexation
To gossip of this kind; but she,
With inexplicable elation,
Kept thinking of it secretly;
And in her heart the thought was live;
The time had come, she fell in love.
So will a seed that's fallen in
The earth be quickened by the spring.
For long had her imagination,
Consumed with pain and lassitude,
Yearned to assay the fatal food;
For long a heartsick enervation
Constrained her youthful breast; her soul
Waited . . . for somebody to call,

8

And was requited . . . Eyes asunder,
She said: 'It's he! He's made his call.'
And now, alas, her hot, lone slumber,
And every day and night were full
Of him; by some enchanted force
All objects seemed without a pause
To speak of him; how tedious
The kind entreaties and the fuss,
The watchful looks of worried servants!
Enveloped in despondency,
She paid no heed to company
And cursed their leisurely observance
Of custom and the sudden way
They would arrive and overstay.

9

Now with what eager concentration
She reads delicious novels through,
With what enlivened fascination
She drinks deception's honeydew.
In fantasy she visualizes
The characters that she most prizes:
The lover of Julie Wolmar,[5]
Malek Adhel[6] and de Linar,[7]
And Werther,[8] martyr to his passion,
And Grandison[9] the consummate
Who dulls us like an opiate –
All these in her imagination
Were in a unique shape expressed,
All in Onegin coalesced.

10

The authors that she loves so seize her,
She feels herself their heroine,
She *is* Julie, Delphine,[10] Clarissa;[11]
Alone, Tatiana roams within
The silent woods, armed with a novel
In which she seeks and finds some marvel:
Her secret glow, her dreamy mood,
Her heart's abounding plenitude;
She breathes a sigh and, taking over
Another's grief or ecstasy,
Whispers by heart, unconsciously
A letter for her hero lover . . .
But he, whatever else he'd done,
Was certainly no Grandison.

11

His manner gravely elevated,
The fervent author in times gone
Showed us a hero dedicated
To perfect aims – a paragon.
To him, forever persecuted
Iniquitously, he committed
A tender soul, intelligence
And an attractive countenance.
Nursing the flame of purest passion,
The hero, always rapturous,
Was ready for self-sacrifice,
And, in the novel's closing action,
Vice was forever beaten down
And virtue gained a worthy crown.

12

But nowadays all minds are clouded,
A moral brings on somnolence,
Vice in the novel, too, is lauded
And there has gained pre-eminence.
The British Muse's tales[12] intrude on
The slumber of our Russian maiden,
And now she's ready to adore
Either the pensive vampire[13] or
The vagrant Melmoth,[14] restless, gloomy,
The Wandering Jew[15] or the Corsair[16]
Or the mysterious Sbogar.[17]
Lord Byron's whim most opportunely
Clothed even hopeless egotism
In woebegone romanticism.

13

My friends, this makes no sense, I know it.
Perhaps by heavenly decree
I shall no longer be a poet,
A demon new will enter me;
And having scorned the threats of Phoebus,
I'll settle to prosaic labours;
A novel of the ancient kind
Will occupy my blithe decline.
There, not the secret pangs of villainy
I shall in grim relief narrate,
But simply, friends, to you relate
The legends of a Russian family,
Love's charming dreams in former days
And ancient Russia's rural ways.

14

I shall record the plain orations
When fathers or old uncles met,
The children's chosen assignations
By ancient limes, by rivulet;
The jealous agonies of lovers,
Partings, and tears as love recovers;
I'll have them quarrel once again
And lead them to the altar then . . .
I shall recall the tender feeling,
Love's aching words upon my tongue,
Impassioned speeches made when young
And courting a fair mistress, kneeling
And uttering an ardent vow
From which I'm disaccustomed now.

15

Tatiana, dear Tatiana, vanquished!
Together with you, now I weep;
Your fate already you've relinquished
Into a modish tyrant's keep.
You'll perish, dear; but till we lose you
The dazzling light of hope imbues you:
You'll summon up a sombre bliss,
Discover life's felicities,
Imbibe the magic bane of yearning,
Daydreams will court your every pace,
And you'll imagine in each place
A tryst to which you're always turning;
In front of you and everywhere
You'll see your fateful tempter there.

16

Tatiana seeks the garden bowers
To grieve in, chased by aching love,
But soon her lifeless eyes she lowers
And loses the desire to rove.
Her bosom lifts, her features redden,
A sudden flame consumes the maiden,
Upon her lips her breath has died,
Her ears with sound, her eyes with light
Are filled . . . Night comes, the moon's patrolling
The distant space of heaven's dome,
The nightingale sings in the gloam
Of trees, its sonorous accents calling.
Tatiana does not go to bed
But quietly talks to nurse instead:

17

'I can't sleep here, nurse, it's so airless!
Open the window, sit by me.'
'Why, Tanya, what is it?' 'I'm cheerless,
Let's talk of how things used to be.'
'Tanya, what things? Once I was able
To keep a store of every fable,
Old tales that, true or false, I'd tell
Of maidens and of spirits fell;
But now my mind's grown dark and woolly:
I can't recall a thing. Alas,
It's all come to a sorry pass!
I am confused' . . . 'Nurse, tell me truly
About those years, can you recall
Whether you were in love at all?'

18

'Tanya, my dear! We never even
Knew what love was in my young day;
Else mother-in-law would have driven
Me out in no uncertain way.'
'How did you marry, then?' 'Oh, Tanya,
It seemed to be God's will. My Vanya
Was even younger then than me,
And I was just thirteen, you see.
Two weeks a matchmaker kept coming
To all my kinsfolk, finally
My father blessed me. Bitterly
I wept for fear of what was looming;
While they untwined my braid they wept,
And chanted while to church I crept.

19

'Into an unknown family taken . . .
But you're not listening now, I fear.'
'Oh nurse, nurse, I'm unhappy, aching,
I'm sad and sick at heart, my dear.
I'm on the verge of crying, sobbing!'
'You are not well.' 'My heart is throbbing.'
'Save us, O Lord, have mercy, pray!
What would you like, you've but to say . . .
Let's sprinkle you with holy water,
You're all aflame' . . . 'I'm not unwell:
I am . . . in love, nurse . . . can't you tell?'
'May the good Lord protect his daughter!'
Her ancient hand raised in the air,
She crossed the girl and said a prayer.

20

'I am in love,' again she whispered
To the old woman mournfully.
'You are unwell,' her nurse persisted.
'I am in love, go, let me be.'
Meanwhile, the moon was radiating
A languid light, illuminating
Tatiana's graces, pale with care,
Her loosened and unruly hair,
Her tears and, there before her sitting,
Upon a bench, the ancient dame
With kerchiefed head, her feeble frame
Into a bodywarmer fitting;
And all beneath the tranquil night
Dozed in the moon's inspiring light.

21

And now Tatiana's heart was soaring
As she looked out and watched the moon . . .
A sudden thought came, overpowering . . .
'Nurse, leave, I want to be alone.
Just let me have a pen, some paper.
The table, too. I'll lie down later.
Goodbye.' And she's alone at last.
All's quiet. For her the moon has cast
Its light. Upon her elbow leaning,
She writes, with Eugene on her mind,
And in a letter undesigned
There breathes a guileless maiden's yearning.
The letter's ready, folded, who . . .
Tatiana! Is it written to?

22

I've known fair beauties unapproachable,
The chaste, the cold, the wintry kind,
Implacable and irreproachable,
Unfathomable to the mind;
I've marvelled at their modish manner,
Their inborn virtue, sense of honour,
And, to be frank, from them I fled,
And, terror-stricken, thought I read
Above their brows hell's admonition:
Abandon hope for evermore.
The joys of loving they forswore,
To frighten people was their mission.
Perhaps you've seen by the Neva
Fair ladies who are similar.

23

Amidst admirers acquiescent
I've seen like women in my days,
Conceited, haughty and indifferent
To sighs of passion or to praise.
But what did I, amazed, discover?
That they, despite their stern behaviour,
Frightening to a timid swain,
Could make his love return again,
At least by showing some compassion,
At least, by a more tender word
That they permitted to be heard,
And, blinded in his naive fashion,
The lover with new energy
Once more pursued sweet vanity.

24

Why blame Tatiana, then? For having
Not known in her simplicity
Deceit or falsehood and for craving
Her chosen dream so fervently?
For loving without double-dealing,
Obedient to the bent of feeling?
For being predisposed to trust,
For being by the heavens blest
With turbulent imagination,
Intelligence, a lively will,
A wayward spirit, never still
And with a tender heart's vibration?
Will you then not forgive her, when
She follows passion's weathervane?

25

Coquettes are cool in their decisions.
Tatiana loves in earnest, she
Gives up herself without conditions
Like a small child, defencelessly.
Of love she says not: let's postpone it
To raise its value when we own it,
To trap it more assuredly;[18]
First let us puncture vanity
With hope, then introduce confusion
To rack the heart, and when we tire,
Revive it with a jealous fire;
Or else, fatigued by joy's profusion,
The cunning captive day or night
May from his prison-house take flight.

26

I can foresee another matter:
Saving the honour of my land,
I must translate Tatiana's letter,
Without a doubt you'll understand.
Russian she knew, but very badly,
She did not read our journals, sadly;
And in her native tongue she could
With difficulty write a word.
And so in French she penned this version . . .
What's to be done? Once more I say
A lady's love up to this day
Has not expressed itself in Russian,
Up to this day our proud tongue shows
It's still not used to postal prose.

27

Some would have women reading Russian,
A frightful prospect, if applied;
Imagine females in discussion
With *The Well-Meaner*[19] at their side!
I turn to you, my poets, teach us;
Is it not true: those charming creatures
For whom, to expiate your wrongs,
You wrote, in secret, verse and songs,
To whom you pledged your heart's affection,
Did they not try, with much travail,
Our Russian speech, to no avail,
Yet using such a sweet inflection
That on their lips a foreign tongue
Became their native one ere long?

28

The Lord forbid my ever meeting
A bonneted scholar at a ball
Or seminarist with a greeting
As she departs in yellow shawl.[20]
Like rosy lips unused to smiling,
Russian, I find, is unbeguiling
Without grammatical mistakes.
Perhaps (my head already aches)
A crop of exquisite new creatures
Will heed the journals, set up school
And make us bow to grammar's rule:
Verse will acquire more useful features;
But I . . . what matters this to me,
I shall respect antiquity.

29

An incorrect and careless patter,
An inexact delivery
Will generate a heartfelt flutter
Within my breast as formerly.
I've not the strength to be repenting,
Since Gallicisms are as tempting
As bygone sins of youth, no worse
Than Bogdanovich's[21] in verse.
But stop. It's time now I translated
The letter of my maiden dear,
I gave my word, and what? I fear
My wish to do so has abated.
I know that tender Parny's[22] ways
Are out of fashion nowadays.

30

Bard of *The Feasts*[23] and languid sorrow,
If you had still remained with me,
I would have troubled you, dear fellow,
With a request, immodestly:
That you transpose the foreign diction
Of an impassioned maid's affliction
Into enchanting melodies.
Where are you? Come: my rights I raze
And, with a bow, place in your keeping . . .
But in a land of mournful stone,
His heart forgetting praise, alone,
Beneath the Finnish sky escaping,
He wanders, and his soul hears not
My grief for his unhappy lot.

31

Before me is Tatiana's letter;
Religiously, I treasure it,
I read it with a secret shudder
And cannot get my fill of it.
Who could have taught such tender writing,
Such words so carelessly delighting,
Who taught her that affecting rot,
Mad conversation of the heart,
A captivating, harmful mixture?
I cannot tell. But now you'll meet
My version, feeble, incomplete,
Pale copy of a vivid picture,
Or as *Der Freischütz*[24] might be played
By girlish pupils, still afraid.

Tatiana's Letter to Onegin

I write to you – what more is needed?
What else is there that I could say?
It's in your power, I concede it,
To punish my naiveté.
But if you've even slightly pitied
The dismal lot that I endure,
You won't abandon me, I'm sure.
At first, I did not want to vex you.
Believe me: you'd have never known
The shame I've suffered all alone,
Had I been hopeful to expect you
Here in our home, where we could speak,
If only seldom, once a week,
Enough to listen to your greeting
And say a word to you, and then
For days and nights to wonder when
I could enjoy another meeting.

They say, though, you're unsociable;
You treat our world with condescension,
And we're . . . in no way fashionable,
But welcome you without pretension.

Why ever did you visit us?
Lost in the village where I languish
I never would have known you, thus
I never would have known this anguish;
Time would have taught me to extinguish
My naive longings (but who knows?);
I would have found a friend for life,
Would have become a faithful wife
And virtuous mother, if I chose.

Another! . . . No, I'd not have given
My heart to anyone on earth!
It has been foreordained in heaven . . .
I was marked out for you from birth;
My life has been a precondition
For our encounter – which I crave;
I know you're sent by God's provision,
And you're my guardian till the grave . . .
You came in dreams that soon abounded,
Even unseen, I treasured you.
Your wondrous glances pierced me through,
Long in my soul your voice resounded . . .
No, this was not a dream for me!

I knew you on your first appearing;
All faint and numb, aflame and fearing,
I uttered inwardly: it's he!
Wasn't it you that I was hearing
When in the stillness I'd depart
To help the poor folk? Weren't you nearing
Each time I prayed in hope of cheering
The anguish of my troubled heart?

And even at this very second,
Wasn't it you, dear vision, beckoned
And slipped through night's transparency,
Inclining gently at my bedhead,
You, who with joy and love persuaded
And whispered words of hope to me?
Who are you: guardian angel, mentor,
Or, if not, a perfidious tempter?
Resolve my doubts, my wavering,
Perhaps my feelings are misguided,
An artless soul's imagining!
And something else has been decided . . .
But let that be! My fate is sealed,
I place it now in your safekeeping,
I beg of you, become my shield,
If you were here, you'd see me weeping . . .
Imagine what it's like for me,
Alone, not understood and ailing,
I'm frightened that my reason's failing,
That I shall die here silently.
I wait for you: you can inspirit
My hoping heart with just one glance
Or interrupt this heavy trance
With censure, which alas I merit!

I close! I dread to read this through . . .
I'm faint with shame and fear . . . However,
I boldly put my trust in you,
Whose honour is my pledge forever.

32

By turns, Tatiana's moaning, sighing,
The letter trembles in her hand,
Upon her fevered tongue lies drying
The rosy seal,[25] a paper band.

Her head sinks downward to her shoulder,
Her light chemise that won't enfold her
Slips to expose her shoulder's charm . . .
But now the radiance of the calm
And moonlit sky grows dim. A valley
Is outlined through the mist of dawn,
Streams silver; and a shepherd's horn
Wakes villagers to rise and rally.
It's morn, all bustle here and there,
But my Tatiana does not care.

33

The rising dawn does not affect her;
Sitting with lowered head and still,
She does not set upon the letter
Her monogram and graven seal.
But now the door has opened quietly,
Grey-haired Filipyevna treads lightly,
Carrying tea upon a tray.
'It's time, my child, to greet the day.
But look, my pretty one, you're ready!
Aren't you my early little bird!
Oh, last night I was so afeard!
But thank the Lord, you're well and steady!
There's not a trace of last night's fret,
Your face is now all poppy red.'

34

'Oh nurse, I need a favour, listen.'
'Of course, dear, I'm at your command.'
'Don't think . . . who knows? . . . perhaps suspicion . . .
But don't refuse, please understand.'
'My dear, I vow by the Almighty.'
'Well, send your grandson very quietly –

Give him this note for O . . . for that . . .
Our neighbour . . . Tell him not to chat
To anybody or to dawdle
And not to mention me by name . . .'
'To whom, then?' asked the ancient dame.
'Oh, nowadays my head's a muddle.
Neighbours are many in this part,
I cannot think of where to start.'

35

'Oh really, nurse, you are slow-witted!'
'I'm old, I'm very old, my heart,
The mind grows dull, you must admit it,
But way back I was very smart,
And if the master once requested . . .'
'Oh nurse, nurse, I'm not interested.
What you were like then I don't care,
What matters is this letter here:
It's for Onegin.' 'Oh the letter.
Do not be cross with me, my soul,
You know, I make no sense at all.
But you look pale again, not better.'
'It's nothing, nurse, but don't delay,
Please send your grandson on his way.'

36

The day flowed by, there came no letter
Nor anything the following day.
Since morning dressed, pale as a spectre,
Tatiana waits for a reply.
Olga's adorer drove up. 'Tell us,
Where's your companion?' came the zealous
Inquiry from the châtelaine.
'He has forgotten us, that's plain.'

Tatiana trembled, flushed, uneasy.
'He promised that today he'd come.'
Lensky replied to the old dame:
'No doubt the post has kept him busy.'
Tatiana cast a downward look,
As though she'd heard a harsh rebuke.

37

It darkened: on the table, gleaming,
The evening samovar now hissed,
On it the Chinese teapot, warming;
Light vapour eddied under it.
Poured out by Olga's hand, the steady,
Dark flow of fragrant tea already
Into the cups ran, in a stream;
A household boy served up the cream;
Tatiana, though, preferred to linger
Before the window, breathing on
The frosted panes; and, pensive one,
She wrote, with a beguiling finger,
In windowpane calligraphy,
A monogram: an O and E.

38

And, meanwhile, still her soul is aching,
And tears have filled her languid gaze.
A thud of hoofs! . . . Her blood is shaking.
Closer! Into the yard they race.
Eugene! Tatiana, lighter than a
Shadow, is leaping through the manor,
She flies, flies from the porch outside
Into the garden, mortified;

Without a backward look she scurries
Past borders, little bridges, lawn,
The lake's approach, the copse; has torn
Down lilac bushes as she hurries;
Through flowers to the brook she flies,
Where, halting, out of breath, she sighs

39

And falls upon a bench . . . exclaiming:
'Here's Eugene! God, how will I cope?
What will he think?' With torment flaming,
Her heart retains a dream of hope.
She trembles, burns and looks behind her,
Wondering if he'll come to find her;
Hears nothing. In the orchard, maids
Were picking berries in brigades
And singing by decree a merry,
Collective song (aimed to prevent
A cunning servant girl intent
On eating, secretly, a berry
Belonging to her lord – a ruse
Which landed folk are pleased to use!)

Song of the Girls[26]

Come, you maidens beauteous,
Dear companions, near to us,
Frolic, if you're timorous,
Have your fling, my darling ones.
Let us sing a song we know,
One that we all cherish so,
Let us lure a fine young lad
To our dance as round we go.
When we lure this fine young lad,
When we see him distantly,
Let us scatter, darling ones,

Pelt him with our cherries, dears,
Cherries bright and raspberries,
Currants red we'll also throw,
Do not come and eavesdrop on
Songs we cherish secretly,
Do not come and spy upon
Games we girls play privately.

40

Tatiana hears with scant attention
Their ringing voices, while she waits
Impatiently until the tension
That agitates her heart abates,
Until her cheeks desist from burning.
But in her breast there's still the yearning,
Nor do her cheeks give up their glow,
But ever brighter, brighter grow . . .
So a poor butterfly will flutter
And beat an iridescent wing,
Caught by a schoolboy, frolicking;
So a small winter hare will shudder
On seeing in the distant brush
A hunter crouched behind a bush.

41

Tatiana sighed and, though still yearning,
Rose from her bench in calmer state:
Set off, but just as she was turning
Into the avenue, there straight
Before her Eugene stood, eyes blazing,
Like some forbidding phantom gazing,
And she, as if by fire seared,
Stayed rooted to the spot, and feared.
But to detail the consequences

Of this unlooked-for tryst, dear friends,
I've no more strength. I'll make amends;
Meantime, I need my recompenses
For so much talk – an interlude
Of strolls and rest, then I'll conclude.

CHAPTER IV

La morale est dans la nature des choses.
Necker[1]

[1, 2, 3, 4, 5, 6]

7

The less we love a woman, woo her,
The more disposed to us she gets,
And thus more surely we undo her
And catch her in our tempting nets.
Time was, when cool debauch was lauded
And as the art of love rewarded.
Blowing its trumpet far and wide,
It fed a loveless appetite.
But this grand game, once so paraded
In our forefathers' vaunted day,
Is one for ancient apes to play:
The fame of Lovelaces has faded
As have their famed red heels affixed
And their majestic periwigs.

8

Who is the man not bored by feigning,
Repeating things in other ways,
In all solemnity maintaining
What people think in any case,
By hearing all the same objections,
By undermining predilections,

Such as a girl of mere thirteen
Is free from and has always been!
Who will not tire of the denials,
The threats, the vows, the put-on fear,
The notelets of six pages sheer,
The gossip, rings, the tears, betrayals,
Surveillances by mothers, aunts
And husbands with their friendly stance!

9

My Eugene drew the same conclusions.
In his first youth he'd fallen prey
To stormy errors and delusions
And passion's unrestricted play.
Spoiled by the life he had been granted,
By one thing for a while enchanted,
Another disenchanting him,
Thwarted desire tormenting him,
Tormented, too, by quick successes,
Hearing amid the noise and lull
The timeless mutter of the soul,
A yawn with laughter he suppresses:
Precisely so, eight years he killed,
His prime thus passing, unfulfilled.

10

Beauties no longer claimed his passion,
He wooed them with insouciance;
Refusal was a consolation,
Betrayal a deliverance.
He sought them with no great affection
And left them, feeling no connection,
Barely recalled their love and spite.
Just so a casual guest one night

Will visit friends for some distraction;
Sits down to whist; concludes the game:
He sets off on the journey home,
Falling asleep with satisfaction,
And, in the morning, does not know
Himself that evening where he'll go.

11

But, on receiving Tanya's letter,
Onegin was profoundly stirred;
The girlish daydreams that beset her
Roused thoughts in him he'd long interred;
And he recalled the mournful manner
And pale complexion of Tatiana;
And plunged into a reverie,
A sweet and sinless fantasy.
Perhaps a glow of old emotion
Returned to him in his decline,
But he'd no wish to undermine
Her trustfulness, her pure devotion.
We'll fly now to the garden where
Tatiana met him, in despair.

12

For two long minutes they were quiet,
Onegin then approached her, said:
'You wrote to me, do not deny it.
The letter that you sent I've read.
I read a trusting soul's confession,
A pure, effusive declaration;
Your openness appeals to me;
It roused into activity

A heart that long ago turned heartless;
But I've no wish to praise you; I
Shall recompense your candour by
My own confession, just as artless;
Listen to my avowal now;
And to your judgement I shall bow.

13

'If I had wanted life restricted
To living in domestic bliss;
If I, by kindly fate conscripted,
Were destined to be father, spouse,
If I could ever without stricture
Be charmed by a familial picture,
I'd doubtless choose no other bride
Than you to cherish at my side.
I'd say, without poetic glitter,
That I had found my past ideal,
With you my destiny I'd seal
And cleave to you when times were bitter,
A pledge of beauty and the good,
And would be happy . . . if I could!

14

'But happiness I never aimed for,
It is a stranger to my soul;
Alas, the virtues you are famed for,
I do not merit them at all.
Upon my conscience: do believe me,
Wedlock would make you want to leave me.
Once used to you, I'd cease to love
The bride I could not love enough;

The tears that surely you'd be shedding
Would fail to touch my heart and would
Only infuriate my mood.
Judge, then, what roses for our wedding
Would Hymen pluck, how many more
To mark the days we have in store.

15

'What in a family's more depressing
Than when a poor wife wastes her tears
Over a spouse who keeps her guessing
And day and evening disappears;
Where this dull man, pleased with his treasure
(Yet cursing fate in equal measure),
Is always silent, angry, grim
And coldly jealous. I'm like him.
And is it this you were awaiting
With such impassioned innocence,
When you with such intelligence
And such simplicity were writing?
Is this the lot that you deserve,
That fate keeps for you in reserve?

16

'Our dreams and years we can't recover,
I shall not renovate my soul . . .
I love you like an elder brother
And, it may be, more gently still.
So, don't be angry with me, listen:
A youthful maid will always hasten
From dream to dream, she no more grieves
Than when a sapling sheds its leaves,
Exchanging them each spring for fresh ones,
Heaven no doubt has ruled it so.
You'll fall in love again, I know,

But . . . learn to govern your confessions;
Not all, like me, will understand,
Naiveté risks a dangerous end.'

17

Thus Eugene preached. Tatiana, crying,
Saw nothing through her tears, but she,
Scarce breathing and without replying,
Listened to Eugene's homily.
He gave his arm with some compassion.
Mechanically (the word in fashion)
She leaned upon it, silent, sad,
Bending her languid little head;
Returning round the kitchen garden,
Together they arrived, and none
With disapproval looked thereon:
The country has its rules regarding
A person's liberty and rights
No less than haughty Muscovites.

18

You will agree with me, my reader,
Our friend respected Tanya's plight
And was not tempted to mislead her;
His soul showed here in noble light
Not for the first time; though ill-wishers
Were unreservedly malicious,
Finding him wholly dissolute:
His enemies, and friends to boot,
(Perhaps there's not so great a difference)
Upbraided him that way and this.
I fear those friends who seek to please.
Oh give me enemies in preference!
What friends are these, if friends at all,
Whom for good reason I recall!

19

What then? Oh nothing. I'm just laying
Empty and gloomy dreams to rest;
It's only by the by I'm saying
That once a slander gets expressed
By some foul liar in a garret
To whom the *monde* awards a carrot,
That there is no absurdity,
No epigram's vulgarity,
That those good folk whom you've befriended
Would not repeat a hundred times,
With errors and distasteful rhymes,
And smile with malice unintended;
Yet they are yours through thick and thin,
They love you . . . like your kith and kin.

20

Hm! Hm! I ask you, noble reader,
Are all your kindred healthy, well?
Allow me: you perhaps may need a
Lesson from me on how to tell
Just what is meant by kinsfolk really.
By kinsfolk, then, is meant ideally:
The folk whom we do not neglect,
But love and cosset with respect,
And, following the rules obtaining,
At Christmas visit or, if not,
By post congratulate the lot,
So that throughout the year remaining
They will not think of us . . . and may
God grant them life for many a day!

21

The love you get from tender beauties
Is surer than from kin or friend:
However turbulent its duties,
Your rights are honoured in the end.
That's so. But then there's whirling fashion
And nature's wayward disposition,
And what the *monde* thinks is enough . . .
And our sweet sex is light as fluff.
And then, it is to be expected
That virtuous wives will all be true
To husbandly opinions, too;
Your faithful mistress has defected
Before you know it: love's a joke
That Satan plays on gentlefolk.

22

Whom then to love? Whom to have faith in?
Who can there be who won't betray?
Who'll judge a deed or disputation
Obligingly by what we say?
Who'll not bestrew our path with slander?
Who'll cosset us with care and candour?
Who'll look benignly on our vice?
Who'll never bore us with his sighs?
Oh, ineffectual phantom seeker,
You waste your energy in vain:
Love your own self, be your own man,
My worthy, venerable reader!
A worthwhile object: surely who
Could be more lovable than you?

23

What followed on from the encounter?
Alas, it is not hard to guess!
Love's pangs continued to torment her,
Continued to inflict distress
Upon a young soul craving sadness;
No, in her passion near to madness
Still more does poor Tatiana burn;
Sleep shuns her bed, will not return;
Health, bloom of life that sweetly flowers,
Smile, virginal repose and peace –
All, like an empty echo cease.
On Tanya's youth a darkness lowers;
Thus does the shadow of a storm
Enshroud a day that's scarcely born.

24

Alas, Tatiana's fading, waning;
Grows pale, is wasting, does not speak!
There is no joy for her remaining,
Nothing to make her soul less bleak.
Shaking their heads, the neighbours gather,
Whispering gravely to each other:
'It's high time that we married her!'
But that will do. I much prefer
To cheer up the imagination
With pictures of a happy love,
And from this sad one take my leave.
I cannot help, though, my compassion;
Forgive: I love Tatiana so,
It's hard for me to let her go.

25

From hour to hour with still more rapture
For Olga, young and beautiful,
Vladimir to delightful capture
Surrendered now with all his soul.
He's constantly beside her, whether
In darkness in their room together
Or in the garden, arm in arm,
Wandering in the morning calm.
What then? By love intoxicated,
Bewildered by a tender shame,
He only dares from time to time,
By Olga's smile invigorated,
To play with an unravelled tress
Or kiss the border of her dress.

26

He sometimes takes and reads out for her
An edifying novel on
The state of nature, which the author
Knows better than Chateaubriand,[2]
Meanwhile omitting certain sections
(Inanities or pure confections
Too dangerous for Olga's age),
And blushes as he turns the page.
Sometimes, all company forsaking,
They settle to a game of chess
And, leaning on a table, guess
What move the other may be making,
And Lensky with a dreamy look
Allows his pawn to take his rook.

27

At home or homewards, at all stages
He's with his Olga occupied,
Upon an album's fleeting pages
He sketches pictures for his bride –
Of rural prospects, small and simple,
A gravestone, Aphrodite's temple,
Or draws a dove atop a lyre
With pen and wash she might admire;
On pages meant for recollections,
Beneath the names already signed,
He leaves a tender verse behind,
Mute monument of his reflections,
Of sudden thought the drawn-out trace,
Still, after many years, in place.

28

Of course, you've more than once encountered
The album of a country miss,
Where all her girlfriends will have entered
Their messages in every space.
With orthographic imprecision,
Unmetered verses, by tradition,
In shortened or in lengthened line
Betoken friendship's loyal sign.
Upon the first leaf you'll be meeting
Qu'écrirez-vous sur ces tablettes?
And signed with *toute à vous, Annette;*[3]
And on the last you will be reading:
Whoever loves you more than I,
Let them append here how and why.

29

You'll find here, doubtless, on some pages
Two hearts, a torch and tiny flowers;
You're bound to read here all the pledges
Of love until the final hours;
Some army poet here has scribbled
A verselet, villainously ribald.
In such an album, I confess,
I, too, am glad to pen a verse,
Secure in my presupposition
That any zealous rot of mine
Will merit a regard benign,
And not the solemn inquisition
Of those, who, with their wicked smile,
Appraise my nonsense by its style.

30

But you, O miscellaneous volumes
From every devil's library,
Magnificent, resplendent albums,
A voguish rhymester's calvary,
In which Tolstoy[4] with nimble touches
Has plied his wonder-working brushes
Or Baratynsky lent his lyre,
May God consume you with His fire!
Whenever, holding her in-quarto,
Some brilliant lady comes to me,
I shake with animosity,
An epigram I'd fain resort to,
Already stirring in my soul,
But all they want's a madrigal![5]

31

It is not madrigals that Lensky
In Olga's album writes to please,
His pen breathes love, his tender entry
Refrains from frosty pleasantries;
Olga alone holds his attention,
All that concerns her, every mention:
And, river-like, his elegies
Flow forth aglow with verities.[6]
Just so indeed, with like elation,
Your heart, Yazykov,[7] finds the room
To sing of someone, God knows whom,
And when the precious compilation
Of all your elegies appears,
They'll show how fate has shaped your years.

32

But hush! I hear an awesome critic[8]
Cry: 'Drop your wreath of elegies,
So miserable and pathetic,'
And to us rhymesters bellow: 'Cease
Your whimpering and endless croaking
About those times you keep invoking,
Regretting what is past, what's gone:
Enough! Sing us another song!'
'You're right and you will surely steer us
To trumpet, dagger and the mask,
And with each one set us the task
Of resurrecting dead ideas.
Is that not so, friend?' 'Not a bit!
No, gentlemen, write odes, that's it,

33

Like those that praised our mighty nation,
Like those established long ago . . .'
'You mean an ode for each occasion?
Oh come, friend, does it matter so?
Remember in *The Other Version*⁹
The satirist's animadversion.
Or has that versifier's guile
Replaced our rhymesters' gloomy style?'
'But elegies don't have a moral,
They're aimless – that's what makes one weep –
Whereas an ode's majestic sweep
Is noble and . . .' 'Here's cause to quarrel,
But I'll restrain myself before
I make two ages go to war.'

34

To fame and freedom dedicated,
Vladimir, when his spirits flowed,
Could turn out something elevated,
But Olga would not read an ode.
When tearful poets have been suffered
To read their work to a beloved
And gaze into her eyes – they say
There is no greater prize today.
But blest is he with modest passion,
Who reads to her for whom he longs,
The object of his love and songs –
A pleasant, languid belle in fashion!
Blest, too . . . though, maybe, while he reads,
She's occupied with other needs.

35

When I want somebody to read to,
To match a dream with tuneful phrase,
It is my nurse that I pay heed to,
Companion of my youthful days,
Or, following a boring dinner,
A neighbour comes in, whom I corner,
Catch at his coat tails suddenly
And choke him with a tragedy,
Or (here I am no longer jesting),
Haunted by rhymes and yearning's ache,
I roam beside my country lake
And scare a flock of wild ducks resting:
Hearing my strophes' sweet-toned chants,
They fly off from the banks at once.

[36]¹⁰

37

But where's Onegin? By the way,
Brothers! I must entreat your patience:
I shall describe without delay
His daily life and occupations.
A hermit underneath God's heaven
In summer he was up by seven
And, lightly clad, would set off till
He reached the river by the hill;
The singer of Gulnare¹¹ repeating,
Across this Hellespont he swam,
Then drank his coffee, while through some
Disreputable journal flitting,
And dressed . . .¹²

[38]

39

A book, sound sleep, a fine excursion,
The purl of streams, the woodland shade,
A fresh, young kiss for his diversion
From dark-eyed, fair-complexioned maid,
A fiery steed with trusty bridle,
A fancy meal at which to idle,
A bottle of resplendent wine,
Seclusion, quiet – thus, in fine,
The life Onegin lived was sainted;
And to it he by slow degrees
Surrendered, the fair summer days
Never, in carefree languor, counted,
Forgetting both the town and friends,
The boring feasts and latest trends.

40

But summer in our North is merely
A Southern winter's counterfeit,
It's glimpsed and gone: we know this, clearly,
Although we won't acknowledge it.
The sky already breathed with autumn,
The sun already shone more seldom.
The day was getting shorter now,
And with a melancholy sough
The forest lost its secret awning,
Mist settled on the fields, the peace
Was broken by the screech of geese
Migrating south: already dawning,
A dullish season lay in wait;
November stood outside the gate.

41

A chill, dark dawn presages winter;
No labour's heard upon the fields;
A wolf and hungry she-wolf enter
The road to find out what it yields;
Sensing the pair, a road horse, nearing,
Snorts – and the traveller goes tearing
Uphill, relieved to be alive;
No longer does the herdsman drive
His cows abroad while night is clinging,
No more at noontime does he sound
His horn to gather them around;
A maiden in her small hut, singing,
Spins by the crackling splintwood light,
A friend to every winter's night.

42

And crackling frost already settles
And silvers midst the fields and leas,
(You've guessed the rhyme to come is 'petals',[13]
So take it, reader, quickly, please!).
The ice-clad river sheds a lustre
That fashion's parquet cannot muster.
The merry sound of boys on skates,
Cutting the ice, reverberates;
A heavy goose steps out with caution,
Plants its red feet upon the ice,
And plans to swim, but in a trice,
Slips and falls over in mid-motion;
The first snow flickers gaily round,
Falling in stars upon the ground.

43

What pastime can you find that's pleasing
Out in the backwoods? Walking? Try.
For all the countryside is freezing,
The naked flatness tires the eye.
A gallop in the bitter prairie?
The very mount you ride is wary
In case its blunted shoe should catch
Against a sudden icy patch.
Under your lonely roof take cover,
Let Pradt and Scott[14] divert your mind
Or check expenses, if inclined,
Grumble or drink, somehow or other
Evening will pass, the morrow too:
With ease you'll see the winter through.

44

Childe Harold to a T, Onegin
Lapsed into pensive indolence:
Enjoyed a bath with ice on waking,
And then, alone in residence,
Absorbed in household calculations,
Armed with a blunted cue, he stations
Himself at billiards, starts to play
With just two balls till close of day.
The evening comes, the game is ended,
The cue's forgotten in the shade,
Before the fire a table's laid,
Onegin waits: here's Lensky, splendid!
A troika of roan horses wheel
Into the yard – quick, start the meal!

45

At once, a Veuve Cliquot or Moët,
That most revered and blessed wine,
Is brought to table for the poet,
In a chilled bottle, as they dine.
Like Hippocrene it sparkles, flashes
And pours in playful, frothy splashes
(A simile for – please invent).
It once enraptured me: I spent
My last poor penny on its solace.
Dear friends, do you remember that?
Its magical cascades begat
No dearth of silliness and follies,
Verses and jokes in endless streams
And arguments and cheerful dreams.

46

But now its noisy effervescence
Betrays my stomach, and instead
I much prefer Bordeaux's quiescence
Which spares the stomach and the head.
Aï[15] I can no longer savour;
Aï is like a woman's favour,
Ravishing, gay, mercurial,
Impetuous and trivial . . .
If now Bordeaux is my addiction,
It's as a friend who's always there
To benefit us everywhere,
Partaking sorrow and affliction,
Sharing the leisure time we spend.
Long live Bordeaux, our precious friend!

47

The fire is out; ash barely covers
The golden coal; a tiny flow
Of vapour, just apparent, hovers;
The grate exhales the faintest glow.
And, up the chimney, pipe smoke rises.
Wine in the gleaming glass still fizzes
Among the empty dinner plates.
An evening gloom accumulates . . .
I like a friendly chat in quiet
Over a friendly bowl of wine,
Above all at that special time
'Between the wolf and dog'[16] (though why it
Should be so called, I've no idea).
But our two friends are talking here:

48

'How are the Larin girls, I wonder,
Tatiana, sprightly Olga, tell?'
'Pour me just half a glass or under . . .
Enough, dear chap . . . the family's well
And all of them send salutations.
But Olga, ah, what transformations!
Dear fellow, Olga's in her prime,
What shoulders, bosom, soul! . . . Some time,
Let's visit them, they'll be delighted;
Judge for yourself, my friend, it's clear:
You drop in twice, then disappear
And never show a nose. They're slighted.
But I'm a fool . . . for as I speak,
You are invited there next week.'

49

'I?' 'Yes. The family's celebrating
Tatiana's nameday, Saturday.
Mother and Olen'ka are waiting:
You've no good reason to gainsay?'
'But goodness knows what sort of rabble
I shall encounter, that's the trouble . . .'
'I'm sure nobody will be there,
It's just a family affair.
So let us go, do me the favour!'
'Well, yes; let's hope I'm entertained.'
'You're kind,' Vladimir said and drained
His glass, a toast to his fair neighbour,
Then started talking once again
Of Olga – such is love's refrain!

50

Cheerful he was – about to marry.
In just a fortnight he'd be wed.
The crown sweet love gave him to carry,
The mystery of the nuptial bed
Awaited Lensky's exaltations.
Hymen's concerns and tribulations,
The chilling train of yawns in store
He neither dreamed of nor foresaw.
While we whom Hymen will not capture
Perceive in home life but a show
Of tedious pictures row on row,
A Lafontaine[17] account of rapture . . .
Oh, my poor Lensky, he at heart
Was born to play this very part.

51

She loved him . . . or was she deceiving?
Why should a happy man suspect?
Blest he who's given to believing,
Who sets aside cold intellect,
Whose heart, enjoying bliss delightful,
Rests like a traveller drunk at nightfall
Or (gentler) like a butterfly
That settles on a flower nearby;
But sad is he who lacks illusion,
Whose head is steady, never stirred,
Who hates each impulse, every word,
Foreseeing always their conclusion;
Whose heart experience has chilled,
Whose urge to reverie is stilled.

CHAPTER V

Never know these fearful dreams,
You, O my Svetlana!

Zhukovsky[1]

I

Winter that year arrived belated,
The autumn weather not yet gone,
Impatient nature waited, waited,
Snow only fell in January, on
The third at night-time. Early waking,
Tatiana, from her window seeking,
Beheld at morn the whitened court,
The roof, the fence and flower plot,
Delicate patterns on the windows,
The trees in winter's silver frond,
Gay magpies gathering beyond,
And distant hills that were by winter's
Resplendent carpet softly bound.
The scene is bright and white all round.

2

Winter! . . . The peasant, celebrating,
Climbs on his sleigh and clears a spot;
Sniffing the snow and hesitating,
His nag then somehow starts to trot;
A daredevil kibitka[2] hurries,
Ploughing up fluffy snow in furrows;
The driver hurtles with panache
In sheepskin coat and crimson sash.

An impish household lad who's chosen
To seat a small dog on his sled,
And play the part of horse instead,
Already has a finger frozen.
He finds it fun, the pain he scorns,
His mother from her window warns . . .

3

But pictures with this kind of feature
Will not appeal to you, I fear,
They're nothing more than lowly nature,
You won't find much refinement here.
Warmed by the god of inspiration,
One poet,[3] rich in stylization,
Has painted early snow for us
In every nuance sumptuous;
He'll hold you fast, there's no denying,
Depicting in his fiery lay
Secret excursions in a sleigh;
But, in the meantime, I'm not trying
To fight with either him or you,
Whose *Finnish Maid*[4] I can't outdo.

4

Tatiana, knowing not the reason,
But being Russian to the core,
Adored the Russian winter season,
The frosty beauty that it wore,
Rime in the sun when days were freezing,
The sleighs, and, at late dawn, the blazing
Resplendence of the rosy snows,
And Twelfth Night evenings dark and close.

And in her household these occasions
Were celebrated as of old,
Young ladies heard their fortunes told
In servant girls' prognostications,
That promised them a husband from
The army with a march and drum.

5

Tatiana held to the convictions
Of ancient lore, believed in dreams,
In guessing cards and the predictions
Discernible in moonlight beams.
She was disturbed by every portent,
All objects held a secret content,
Proclaiming something to be guessed,
Presentiments constrained her breast.
The mincing tomcat, sitting, purring
Upon the stove would lift a paw
To wash its snout – in this she saw
A certain sign that guests were nearing.
Seeing the young moon's countenance
Two-horned, upon her left, at once

6

She'd turn quite pale, begin to tremble.
Or if a falling star should fly
Across the sombre sky and crumble,
Then Tanya hurried to be nigh,
To catch the star while still in motion
And, all her senses in commotion,
To whisper to it her desire.
If it should anywhere transpire
In her excursions from the manor
For her to meet a monk in black
Or see a swift hare cross her track,

All this so terrified Tatiana,
That she with sad presentiment
Expected some adverse event.

7

And yet – she found a secret pleasure
In very terror; surely we
Are creatures that you cannot measure,
We all are contradictory.
Yuletide is come with jubilation;
Immersed in blissful divination,
The young have nothing to regret,
Their life extends before them yet,
A radiant prospect, undiscovered;
Through spectacles old age divines
While to the gravestone it inclines
And nothing past can be recovered;
But does it matter? They'll believe
Their hopeful prattle till they leave.

8

With curious gaze Tatiana ponders
The wax that, sinking, leaves behind
A labyrinthine web of wonders,
Enchanting wondrously her mind.
Up from a brimming dish of water
Rings surface in successive order;
And, when her little ring appears,
A song is sung of bygone years:
The peasants there have all the riches,
They heap up silver with their spades;
We promise those who hear us maids
Glory and good! The tune is piteous,
Portending losses and mischance;
Maidens prefer the tomcat chants.[5]

9

A frosty night; a sky transparent;
A starry choir from heaven flows
In so serene and quiet a current . . .
In low-cut frock Tatiana goes
Into the spacious courtyard, training
A mirror on the moon,[6] complaining
That nothing in her darkened glass
Shows save the trembling moon, downcast . . .
But hark! . . . a crunch of snow . . . the maiden
Flies tiptoe to a passing man,
Her little voice more tender than
The sound of reed pipe gently played on:
'*What is your name?*' He looks; anon
He answers: it is Agafon.[7]

10

Instructed by her nurse, Tatiana
Arranged a séance all night through;
And in the bathhouse of the manor
Ordered a table laid for two.
But sudden fear assailed Tatiana . . .
And I – remembering Svetlana –
Felt fear as well[8] – but that will do . . .
We won't tell fortunes all night through.[9]
Her silken girdle she unknotted,[10]
Undressed and settled into bed,
Lel[11] hovering above her head,
While underneath her pillow slotted
Lies a young maiden's looking glass.
All's hushed. Sleep overtakes the lass.

11

A wondrous dream she has: she's taken
A path across a snow-filled glade.
Gloomy and dismal, sad, forsaken;
Snowdrifts rear up before the maid,
And through them runs a seething torrent,
A dark, untamed and age-old current,
With thundering, whirring, churning waves;
Glued by the ice, two flimsy staves
Are set above the rushing water –
A perilous and tiny bridge
That oscillates from edge to edge.
This and the roaring chasm thwart her;
Perplexed, not knowing what to think,
She halts there at the very brink.

12

As at a vexing separation,
Tatiana murmured at the tide,
Saw neither man nor habitation
To call to on the other side.
But soon a drift began to quiver
And who appeared beside the river?
A burly bear with ruffled fur;
Tatiana cried, he roared at her,
Stretched out a paw, sharp claws protruding;
She braced herself, with trembling hand
She leaned on it and scarce could stand;
They reached the bank, where she, concluding
That she was safe, walked on ahead,
Then . . . what was that? . . . a bear-like tread!

13

The shaggy footman is behind her,
She dares not look, strains every limb
In hope the creature will not find her,
But there is no escaping him.
The odious bear comes grunting, lumbering;
A wood's before them; pines are slumbering
In frowning beauty, boughs hang low,
Weighed down with heavy flocks of snow;
And, seeping through the topmost summits
Of aspens, birches, lindens bare,
The starry rays invade the air.
The shrubs, the path and where it plummets
Are covered by the blizzard's sweep
And in the snowfall buried deep.

14

Bear in pursuit, Tatiana dashes
Into the wood, up to her knee
In powdery snow; a long branch catches
Her by the neck, then forcefully
Wrenches away her golden earrings;
Tatiana, wholly without bearings,
Leaves in the snow a small, wet boot,
Pulled from her charming little foot;
She drops her handkerchief, foregoing
To pick it up, the bear is nigh,
Her hand is trembling, yet she's shy
To raise the dress around her flowing;
She runs, and he pursues her still,
Then she abandons strength and will.

15

She falls into the snow; and nimbly
The bear retrieves and carries her;
She yields insensibly and limply,
She does not breathe, she does not stir;
Along a forest path he rushes,
And suddenly through trees and bushes
A hut appears; all's wild around
And sad snow covers roof and ground,
A window sheds illumination
And noise and shouting blast the ear;
The bear declares: 'My gaffer's here:
It's warm inside his habitation.'
And, quickly, opening the door,
He lays the maiden on the floor.

16

Tatiana, coming to, looks round her:
The bear has gone: beyond the hall
Shouting and tinkling glass astound her
As if there's some big funeral;
Making no sense of this she quietly
Peers through a chink . . . the scene's unsightly,
No fancy could imagine it:
Around a table monsters sit,
One with a dog's face, horned, abnormal,
Another with a cockerel's head,
A witch with bearded goat cross-bred,
A skeleton, august and formal,
A small-tailed dwarf, and what is that,
Apparently half-crane, half-cat?

17

More wondrous, more intimidating,
Astride a spider sits a crab,
Upon a goose's neck, rotating,
A skull is perched with scarlet cap,
And there a crouching windmill dances,
Waving its snapping vanes like lances;
Barks, laughter, whistles, song, applause,
Men's talk and horses stamping floors!
What could Tatiana do but marvel
To see among this company
The man she loved so fearfully,
The hero of our present novel!
Onegin steals a quick look for
Whoever may be at the door.

18

He gives a sign – they spring to action,
He drinks – they shout and drink a round.
He laughs – they roar with satisfaction,
He knits his brow – there's not a sound.
It's obvious that he's the master:
And Tanya no more fears disaster,
And curious to find out more
She opens gingerly the door . . .
A sudden gust of wind blows, lashing
The flaming lamps that light the night;
The goblins cower at the sight;
Onegin, from his chair, eyes flashing,
Rises with clatter; they all rise:
And swiftly to the door he flies.

19

A terrified Tatiana hastens
To flee Onegin and his team;
Not possible; and, in impatience,
She scurries round and wants to scream,
But Eugene pulls the door wide open
And she's exposed to the misshapen
And hellish spectres; savage cries
Of laughter resonate; their eyes,
Their curved proboscises, moustaches,
Their hooves, horns, tusks and tufted tails,
Their bony fingers, sharp like nails,
Their bloody tongues – all these mismatches
At once towards the girl incline
And all cry out: 'She's mine! She's mine!

20

'She's mine,' Onegin spoke out grimly,
And suddenly the pack was gone;
In frosty darkness Tanya dimly
Confronted Eugene all alone.
Towards a corner seat he takes her,
Upon a shaky bench he lays her
And, bending downward, rests his head
Upon her shoulder; when a tread
Discloses Olga, then Vladimir;
A sudden light, and in alarm
Onegin stands with upraised arm,
His eyes roam wildly seeing *him* here,
He chides the uninvited pair;
Tatiana's lying in despair.

21

The argument grows louder quickly,
Onegin snatches up a knife,
Frightening shadows gather thickly,
Onegin's taken Lensky's life.
A piercing cry, the hut is shaking,
Tatiana, terror-stricken, waking,
Looks round her room, already bright,
As through a frozen pane the light
Of crimson dawn's already playing;
The door stirs. Olga flies to her,
Aurora-like but rosier,
And lighter than a swallow, saying:
'What did you dream, whom did you see?
Oh, Tanya, tell, who can it be?'

22

But she, not noticing her sister,
Lay leafing through a book in bed;
Page after page kept turning faster,
And to her sister nothing said.
The book that claimed her rapt attention
Wanted the poet's sweet invention,
No saws or pictures could be seen,
But neither Virgil nor Racine,
Not Seneca, not Scott, not Byron,
Not even *Ladies' Fashion*[12] could
Engross so much a woman's mood:
What now enticed her like a siren
Was Martin Zadek,[13] Chaldee sage,
Who solved your dreams on every page.

23

This weighty tome a passing trader
Had brought to Tanya's solitude,
And finally managed to persuade her
To buy it, if he could include
A few odd volumes of *Malvina*;[14]
She paid three rubles, one poltina,
He also put into the scales
A book containing vulgar tales,
Two Petriads,[15] a Russian grammar
And volume three of Marmontel.[16]
Once Martin Zadek casts his spell,
Tanya surrenders to his glamour . . .
He brings her solace when she grieves,
He sleeps with her and never leaves.

24

The dream disturbs her. In confusion,
Not knowing what it presages,
She seeks a meaningful solution
To all its monstrous images.
Arranged in alphabetic order,
The index gives the words that awed her:
A bear, a blizzard, little bridge,
Dark, fir, a forest, hedgehog, witch
And so on. Tanya's reservations
A Martin Zadek won't dispel,
And yet her nightmare does foretell
A multitude of sad occasions.
For several days thereafter she
Keeps thinking of it anxiously.

25

But lo, her crimson hand extending,[17]
Daybreak, from valleys large and small,
Leads forth the folk who'll be attending
A merry nameday festival.
From morn the Larin home's abounding
With neighbours from estates surrounding;
Whole families have made their way
On britska,[18] coach, kibitka, sleigh.
There's jostling as the hall is filling,
In the salon new faces, hugs,
Girls' smacking kisses, barking pugs,
Noise, laughter, crush as more folk spill in,
Guests make their bows and shuffle by,
Wet-nurses shout and children cry.

26

Together with a spouse well nourished,
There entered portly Pustyakov;[19]
Gvozdin, a splendid lord who flourished
On peasant farmers badly off;
Then the Skotinins, grey-haired, prospering
With their innumerable offspring
From thirty-odd right down to two;
And Petushkov, our fop, came, too;
Then my first cousin, one Buyanov,
In pointed cap and cloaked with fluff
(But you must know him well enough);
And councillor-in-retirement, Flyanov,
A scandalmonger, seasoned cheat,
And bribe-taker who loved to eat.

27

The family of Kharlikov[20] had
Monsieur Triquet within its fold;
A noted wit, late from Tambov, clad
In reddish wig, bespectacled.
Triquet, in truly Gallic manner,
Had brought a stanza for Tatiana,
Set to a children's melody:
Réveillez-vous, belle endormie.[21]
This stanza saw its publication
In a decrepit almanac;
Triquet, a poet with a knack,
Redeemed it from disintegration,
And in the place of *belle Nina*
He boldly put *belle Tatiana*.

28

And now from an adjacent quarter
A company commander came,
The idol of each ripened daughter
And district mothers, all aflame.
He entered . . . ah now, what's he saying?
The regimental band is playing,
The colonel has arranged it all,
What fun! There is to be a ball!
The young things skip, anticipating;
But dinner being served brings calm,
All go to table, arm in arm,
The grown-up girls near Tanya waiting,
The men *en face*; a buzz goes round;
All cross themselves as seats are found.

29

A sudden ceasing of the chatter;
Mouths chew; and, meanwhile, all about,
Crockery, plates and covers clatter
And clinking wine-glasses ring out.
But soon the guests by small gradations
Revive their deafening conversations.
They shout, laugh, argue through the meal,
Nobody listens, ladies squeal.
The doors fly open, Lensky enters,
With him Onegin. 'Lord, at last!'
Cries out Dame Larina, and fast
The guests make room, as each one ventures
To move a cover or a chair;
They seat the two young friends with care.

30

They sit right opposite Tatiana;
She, paler than the moon at morn,
More agitated in her manner
Than hunted doe, stays looking down
With darkening eyes; a glow pervades her,
A surge of passion suffocates her;
She does not hear from our two friends
The salutation each extends;
About to cry, poor thing, she's ready
To fall into a swoon or faint;
But will and reason bring restraint;
Clenching her teeth, remaining steady,
She quietly utters just a word
And from the table has not stirred.

31

With tragi-nervous demonstrations,
With maidens' fainting fits and tears
Eugene had long since lost all patience:
He'd had enough of them for years.
Finding himself at this huge banquet,
The oddball was already angry.
But noticing the languid maid's
Disquiet, he, with lowered gaze,
Fell sulking and, with indignation,
Swore he would madden Lensky and
Avenge himself on every hand.
Rejoicing in anticipation,
He in his soul began to sketch
Caricatures of every guest.

32

Of course, it was not just Onegin
Who could detect Tatiana's plight,
But at that moment all were taking
Cognizance of a pie[22] in sight
(Alas, too salty for the throttle).
Meanwhile, inside a pitch-sealed bottle
Between the meat and blanc-manger[23]
Tsimlyansky[24] wine goes on display,
Followed by long and narrow glasses,
So like your waist, Zizi,[25] so small,
The crystal pattern of my soul,
The object of my guiltless verses,
The vial of love's enticing brew –
How often I got drunk on you!

33

The damp cork pops, the bottle's emptied,
The glasses fizz with ancient wine;
Then, by his stanza long tormented,
Triquet with ceremonial sign
Stands up; and all the guests before him
Are still. Unable to ignore him,
Tatiana's scarce alive; Triquet,
Holding a paper, turns her way
And starts his song, off-key. He's fêted
With shouts and calls, the guests clap hard,
She owes a curtsey to the bard;
The poet, great but underrated,
Is first to drink her health, and she
Accepts his stanza gracefully.

34

Homage, congratulations greet her;
In turn Tatiana thanks each guest.
Then, as Onegin comes to meet her,
The maiden's air, her lack of zest,
Her discomposure, tired expression
Engender in his soul compassion:
He simply bows, yet in his eyes
Tatiana catches with surprise
A look miraculously tender.
Whether indeed he feels regret
Or plays with her like a coquette,
This wondrous look appears to mend her:
True tenderness in it she sees,
It puts Tatiana's heart at ease.

35

The chairs are pushed back in a clatter,
The drawing-room receives the crowd,
So bees from honied hives will scatter
To cornfields in a noisy cloud.
Contented with their festive labours,
The locals snuffle to their neighbours;
Ladies sit by the chimney-place;
Girls whisper in a corner space;
The men unfold the green baize tables,
Boston and ancient omber[26] call
The ardent players to their thrall,
Whist too, still one of players' staples –
But what a dull consortium,
All sons of avid tedium!

36

Whist's gallant heroes have completed
Eight rubbers; and as many times,
Having changed places, are reseated;
Now tea is served. We hear no chimes:
I like to time repasts at leisure
With dinner, supper, tea my measure.
We countryfolk make little fuss
Without Bréguet to govern us:
Our stomach is our faultless timer;
And, by the way, I like to talk
As much of dishes, feasts and cork,
In my capacity as rhymer,
As you did, Homer, bard divine
Whom thirty centuries enshrine.

[37, 38]

39

But tea is brought; the dainty maidens
Have scarce their saucers in their hand,
When from the hall they hear the cadence
Of flute, bassoon – the army band.
By music's thunder animated,
His tea-and-rum cup relegated,
Our Paris of the towns about,
Our Petushkov seeks Olga out,
Then Lensky Tanya; Kharlikova,
A seasoned maid, not married off,
Falls to our poet from Tambov,
Buyanov whirls off Pustyakova,
And all have spilled into the hall,
And in full glory shines the ball.

40

When I began this composition
(My Chapter One you will recall),
I wanted with Albani's[27] vision
To paint a Petersburgian ball.
But, by an empty dream's deflection,
I got engrossed in recollection
Of once-familiar little feet
Along whose narrow tracks so neat
I swear I'll go no more a-roving![28]
With youth betrayed, its time for me
To learn to live more sensibly,
My deeds and diction need improving,
And this Fifth Chapter I shall cleanse
Of its digressions, when it ends.

41

Monotonous and madly whirling,
Like young life's whirl, when spirits soar,
The waltz revolves, the music swirling,
The couples flick across the floor.
The moment for revenge arriving,
Onegin, chuckling and reviving,
Approaches Olga. Rapidly,
He twirls her near the company,
Then seats her on a chair, proceeding
To talk to her of this or that;
One or two minutes spent on chat,
And they rejoin the waltz, unheeding;
The guests are taken by surprise,
Poor Lensky can't believe his eyes.

42

Now the mazurka has resounded.
Once, when you heard its thunder peal,
A giant ballroom shook and pounded,
The parquet cracking under heel.
The very window-frames vibrated;
Today, like ladies, understated,
We glide across the lacquered boards;
But in small towns and country wards
There the mazurka thrives, retaining
Its pristine charms: the leap and dash,
The play of heel, and the moustache;
These have not changed at all, remaining
Immune to wanton fashion's sway,
The Russian sickness of today.

[43]

44

My irrepressible Buyanov
Took Olga and Tatiana then
To meet Eugene, who promptly ran off
With Olga to the ball again.
He guides her, nonchalantly gliding,
And in a whisper, bends, confiding
A madrigal, the merest slush,
Squeezes her hand – her rosy flush
Takes on a brighter coloration,
Infusing her complacent face.
My Lensky, watching this take place,
Flares up with jealous indignation
And by the long mazurka vexed,
Solicits the cotillion next.

45

It isn't possible, she tells him,
Eugene already has her word.
Not possible? Ah, she repels him,
She could . . . good God, what has he heard?
Scarce out of swaddling, always mild,
Now a coquette, a giddy child!
Already versed in artful play,
She's learned already to betray!
The blow's too much for Lensky; cursing
The sex's tricks, he leaves the hall,
Calls for a horse, and, full of gall,
Gallops away, in thought rehearsing:
A brace of pistols, bullets two –
Enough for fate to take its due.

CHAPTER VI

La, sotto i giorni nubilosi e brevi,
Nasce una gente a cui 'l morir non dole.[1]

Petrarch

1

On noticing his friend had vanished,
Onegin stayed at Olga's side,
Pensive, again to boredom banished,
Content with vengeance satisfied,
Now Olen'ka like him was yawning,
Her eyes in search of Lensky turning,
While the cotillion's endless stream
Oppressed her like a grievous dream.
But it has ended. Supper's ready.
The beds are made. The guests are all
Assigned their place from entrance-hall
To housemaids' quarters. All are needy
Of restful sleep. Alone Eugene
Drives home from this domestic scene.

2

All's calm: from the salon ascended
The snores of heavy Pustyakov,
Beside his heavy wife extended.
Gvozdin, Buyanov, Petushkov
And Flyanov (somewhat over-sated)
Were on the dinner chairs located,
And on the floor Monsieur Triquet
In vest and ancient nightcap lay.

The rooms of Olga and Tatiana
Were full of sleeping girls. Alone
And sad, Tatiana shone,
Illuminated by Diana;
To sleep, poor thing, she could not yield
And gazed upon the darkened field.

3

Tatiana to her soul is riven
By Eugene's unexpected call,
The sudden tender look he'd given,
His strange approach to Olga – all
Distresses her and makes her wonder,
To understand him's quite beyond her:
A jealous anguish makes her start,
As if a cold hand pressed her heart,
As if a chasm, black and frightful,
Had opened, roaring, under her.
'I'll die,' she says, but does not stir,
'To die from him will be delightful.[2]
I shan't complain, for I confess
He cannot bring me happiness.'

4

But onward, onward with my story!
Another character arrives.
Five versts away from Krasnogorye
(Lensky's estate) there lives and thrives
In philosophical seclusion
Still to this day, without intrusion,
Zaretsky, once a brawler and
The hetman[3] of a gaming band,

Chieftain of rakes, a pub declaimer,
But now, benign and simple, he
Maintains a bachelor family;
A steadfast friend, a squire grown tamer,
He's even honest – thus our age
Improves itself at every stage.[4]

5

Time was, he stood upon a pedestal,
Society flattered him with praise:
He was a maestro with a pistol
Who could at twelve yards hit an ace,
And once, engaged in actual battle,
Enraptured, he displayed his mettle
By falling from his Kalmuck steed
Into the mud at daring speed;
Drunk as a swine, this precious hostage
Surrendered to a Gallic squad,
A modern Regulus,[5] honour's god,
Prepared to yield again to bondage,
To drain on credit two or three
Carafes each morning chez Véry.[6]

6

To tease was once his recreation,
He'd dupe a fool or stupefy
A man of educated station,
In public gaze or on the sly,
Although some tricks he perpetrated
Did not remain uncastigated,
And sometimes, like a simple chap,
He'd fall himself into a trap.

He could dispute and be amusing,
Respond with answers, smart or dumb,
At times judiciously keep mum
Or be judiciously abusing,
Encourage two young friends to strife
And set them duelling for their life,

7

Alternatively reconcile them,
Arrange a breakfast for the three,
And, later, secretly revile them
With merry jokes and braggartry.
Sed alia tempora![7] Audacity
(Like lover's dream, another vanity)
Departs when lively youth has fled.
And my Zaretsky, as I said,
Lives like a sage, discovering solace
Where bird cherry, acacia climb;[8]
Sheltered from storms, he spends his time
In planting cabbages, like Horace,[9]
And breeding ducks and geese, is free
To teach his kids their ABC.

8

He was not stupid; and, despising
The heart in him, Eugene admired
The spirit of his judgements, prizing
The sound opinions he'd acquired.
Eugene was always pleased to meet him
And so was not surprised to greet him
When, in the morning, Eugene saw
His neighbour standing at the door.

With salutations done, Zaretsky
Broke off the chat that they'd begun
And, eyes a-twinkle with the fun,
Passed on to him a note from Lensky.
Onegin to the window went
And read the note the poet sent.

9

It was a gentlemanly letter,
A challenge or cartel[10] he'd penned;
Polite and cold and to the matter
He sought a duel with his friend.
Eugene's immediate reaction
To this demand for satisfaction
Was swift enough. Discussion spared,
He said he'd 'always be prepared'.
Zaretsky rose without explaining,
Not wishing to prolong his stay,
For household business claimed the day,
He left forthwith; Eugene, remaining
Alone, encountering his soul,
Was not contented with his role.

10

Indeed, a strict examination
Before a secret, inner court
Engendered much self-accusation:
First, that he'd not the right to sport
Last evening in such casual fashion
With Lensky's timid, tender passion;
Then . . . why not let a poet play
The fool at eighteen, while he may.

Eugene, who loved him as a brother,
Might well have proved, by seeking peace,
To be no ball of prejudice
That's batted one way or another,
No fiery boy, no fighting kind,
But man of honour, with a mind.

11

He might have manifested feeling
Instead of bristling like a beast,
He should have set about the healing
Of Lensky's heart. Such thoughts soon ceased.
'Too late now, everything is settled,
Now this old duellist has meddled
In the affair, what's left to do?
He's vicious and a gossip, too.
The answer to his droll dominion
Should be contempt, of course, but then
The whispers, laughs of stupid men . . .'
And there it is – public opinion![11]
Our idol, honour's spring, which, wound,
Ensures our universe goes round.

12

Lensky, at home, with hatred blazing,
Awaits the answer fretfully;
His neighbour in the finest phrasing
Conveys it with solemnity.
This sets the jealous poet cheering;
The prankster might – so he'd been fearing –
Treat the occasion as a jest,
And by some ruse avert his breast

And duck the pistol by retreating.
These doubts resolved, tomorrow they
Must at the mill ere break of day
Embark upon their fateful meeting,
To raise the cock and, taking aim,
A temple or a thigh to claim.[12]

13

Detesting a coquette so cruel,
Still seething, Lensky sought to shun
A rendezvous before the duel,
He kept consulting watch and sun.
The wish to meet, though, was compelling,
Soon Lensky's at the sisters' dwelling.
Olga, he thought, would be upset
And agitated when they met;
But not a bit of it: on spying
The desolate bard, as in the past
She skipped down from the porch as fast
As giddy hope, towards him flying,
Light-hearted, free of care, serene –
In fact, as she had always been.

14

'Last night, why did you leave so early?'
Was what his Olen'ka first said.
His senses clouded, and he merely,
Without replying, hung his head.
Vexation, jealousy were banished,
Before her shining look they vanished,
Before her soft simplicity,
Before her soul's vivacity!

He gazes with sweet feeling, heartened
To see that he's still loved; and longs
Already, burdened by his wrongs,
To ask her whether he'll be pardoned,
He trembles, can't think what to say,
He's happy, almost well today . . .

[15, 16][13]

17

Pensive again, again dejected,
Vladimir, under Olga's sway,
Is not sufficiently collected
To speak to her of yesterday;
'I,' he reflects, 'will be her saviour.
I shall not suffer that depraver
To tempt a maiden's innocence
With fiery sighs and compliments;
Nor let a worm with venom slither
A lily's stalklet to enfold,
Nor see a flower two days old,
Half-opened still, condemned to wither.'
All this, friends, signified: I shall
Soon fire a bullet at my pal.

18

If he had known what wound was burning
My dear Tatiana's heart! If she
Had been aware, in some way learning,
If she'd been able to foresee
That Lensky, Eugene would be vying
To find a grave for one to lie in;

Who knows, her love perhaps might then
Have reconciled the friends again!
But no one had as yet discovered,
Even by chance, their angry feud.
On everything Eugene was mute,
Tatiana quietly pined and suffered;
The nurse might just have known of it,
But she, alas, was slow of wit.

19

All evening Lensky was abstracted,
Now taciturn, now gay. Somehow,
A person by the Muse protected,
Is always thus: with knitted brow,
To the clavier he'd wander, playing
A string of chords, no more assaying,
Or whisper, seeing Olga near,
'I'm happy, am I not, my dear?'
But it was late, his heart was aching,
He must depart, yet as he bade
Goodbye to her, his youthful maid,
His heart was on the point of breaking.
She looks at him: 'What is it?' 'Oh,
It's nothing, Olga, I must go.'

20

Arriving home, he first inspected
His pistols, ready for the fight,
Put them away, undressed, reflected
On Schiller's verse by candlelight.
But by one thought he's overtaken,
His melancholy does not slacken:

He sees before him Olga full
Of beauty inexplicable.
Vladimir closes Schiller's verses,
Takes up his pen and writes his own –
Nonsense to which a lover's prone;
It sings and flows. And he rehearses
His lines aloud, by fervour seized,
Like drunken Delvig[14] at a feast.

21

By chance his verse can still be read now,
I have it, ready for your gaze:[15]
'Whither, ah whither are you fled now,
My springtime's ever-golden days?
What is the coming day's decision?
Alas, it lies beyond my vision,
Enshrouded in the deepest night.
No matter, fate's decree is right.
Whether I'm piercèd by an arrow
Or whether it should miss – all's well:
A predetermined hour will tell
If we're to wake or sleep tomorrow:
Blest are the cares that day contrives,
Blest is the darkness that arrives!

22

'When daybreak comes with rays ascending
And sparkling day dispels the gloom,
Then I, perhaps – I'll be descending
Into the mystery of the tomb,
Slow Lethe will engulf forever
My young poetical endeavour;

I'll be forgot, but you'll return
To weep on my untimely urn,
And, maid of beauty, in your sorrow,
You will reflect: he loved me, sworn
To me alone in his sad dawn,
Bereft now of its stormy morrow! . . .
Come, heartfelt friend, come, longed-for friend,
I'll be your husband to the end.'

23

And so he wrote *obscurely, limply*
(Romantic[16] is the term we've coined,
Though what's Romantic here I simply
Have no idea; and what's the point?),
And finally, as night was ending,
His head towards his shoulder bending,
Vladimir dozed, while lingering still
Upon the modish word *ideal*;
But scarcely lost in sleep's enchantment,
He does not hear his neighbour, who
Enters the silent study to
Awaken him with a commandment:
'Time to get up, past six, we're late,
Onegin will not want to wait.'

24

But he was wrong: Eugene unheeding
Still sleeps a sleep that nought can mar.
Night's shades already are receding,
The cock salutes the morning star,
Onegin sleeps on at his leisure,
The sun climbs high into the azure,

A passing snowstorm overhead
Glitters and whirls. But from his bed
Our dormant hero has not started,
Sleep hovers still before his eyes.
At last he wakes, prepares to rise,
The curtains of his bed he's parted;
He looks outside – and sees, alack,
He should have started some time back.

25

He rings: his valet, French and chipper,
Reaches his chamber in a flash,
Guillot brings dressing-gown and slipper,
And hands him linen with panache.
Onegin hurries with his dressing,
Informs his man that time is pressing,
That he must take the duelling-case,
That they must leave, that they must race.
The sleigh is ready; Eugene, seated,
Flies to the mill, the horses strain.
He tells his valet to retain
Lepage's fatal tubes[17] till needed,
And have the horses moved to where
Two oaklings stand, and leave them there.

26

Leaning upon the dam stood Lensky
Who'd waited there impatiently,
While rural engineer Zaretsky
Surveyed the millstone critically.
Eugene arrives and makes excuses.
'That's very well, but where the deuce is

Your second, then?' Zaretsky cried.
In duels he took a pedant's pride,
Methodical by intuition:
To stretch out someone on the ground
Any old how was quite unsound,
One must obey a strict tradition
And follow rules of ancient days
(For which we should accord him praise).

27

'My second? Yes, let me present him,
He's here: Monsieur Guillot, my friend,
I do not see what should prevent him,
He's someone I can recommend.
Although he's not a well-known figure,
He is an honest guy and eager.'
Zaretsky bit his lip, appalled.
Onegin then to Lensky called:
'Shall we not start now?' 'If you're willing,'
Vladimir said. Behind the mill
They went. At some remove, meanwhile,
Zaretsky solemnly is sealing
A contract with the 'honest guy'.
The two foes stand with lowered eye.

28

How long since they from one another
Were parted by a thirst to kill?
How long since, each to each a brother,
They'd shared their leisure time, a meal
And thoughts? But now with grim impatience,
As in a feud of generations

Or frightful dream that makes no sense
Each, cool and silent, must commence
To wreak the other one's destruction . . .
Should they not stop and laugh instead
Before their hands have turned blood red,
Should they not spurn the duel's seduction? . . .
But what the world cannot abide
Are bogus shame and lack of pride.

29

The pistols glistened; soon the mallets
Resoundingly on ramrods flicked,
Through cut-steel barrels went the bullets,
The cock has for the first time clicked.
A greyish powder was decanted
Into the pan, and the indented,
Securely screwed-in flint raised high
Once more. Behind a stump nearby
Guillot was standing, disconcerted.
The foes cast off their cloaks, meanwhile
Zaretsky measured off in style
Thirty-two steps and then diverted
His friends towards the farthest pace,
Each took his pistol to the place.[18]

30

'Now march,' came the command. And readily,
As if the two had never met,
The erstwhile comrades slowly, steadily
Advanced four steps, not aiming yet,
Four fatal steps the two had taken.
And then, advancing still, Onegin

Raised by degrees his pistol first.
Five further paces they traversed.
And likewise Lensky calculated,
Closed his left eye, as he took aim –
But, with a sudden burst of flame,
Onegin fired . . . the moment fated
Had struck: the poet, with no sound,
Let drop his pistol to the ground.

31

His hand upon his breast he presses
Softly, and falls, as, misty-eyed,
His gaze not pain, but death expresses.
Thus, slowly, on a mountain-side
A mound of snow, already teetering,
Descends with sunny sparkles glittering.
Onegin, shuddering, swiftly flies
To where the young Vladimir lies,
He looks and calls . . . but there's no power
Can bring him back. The youthful bard
Has met an end untimely. Hard
The storm has blown, the finest flower
Has withered at the morning's dawn,
The fire upon the altar's gone.

32

He lay inert; uncanny-seeming,
A languid peace showed on his brow.
Beneath his breast the blood flowed, steaming,
The shot had gone right through him. How
One moment earlier inspiration
And love and hate, and aspiration

Had in this heart vibrated, churned,
How life had revelled, blood had burned;
But now, as in a house forsaken,
All it contains is dark and still,
A home forever silent, chill,
The windows shuttered, chalked and vacant,
The mistress vanished from the place
To God knows where, without a trace.

33

It's pleasant with a verse to chasten
A dunderheaded clown and foe,
Pleasant to watch the fellow hasten
With butting horns descending low
To view his image in a mirror
And turn from it in shame and horror;
More pleasant, friends, if he howls out:
'Oh look, that's me there!' like a lout;
Still pleasanter with quiet persistence
To plan a grave that lauds his name
And at his pallid brow take aim
From proper gentlemanly distance;
It's hardly pleasant, though, you'll find
To send him off to meet his kind.

34

What happens if your young companion
Is slaughtered by your pistol shot
For some presumptuous glance, opinion
Or repartee worth not a jot,
Insulting you while you were drinking,
Or if, in fiery pique, not thinking,

He calls you proudly to a duel,
Tell me the feelings that would rule
Your soul, when without motion lying
In front of you upon the earth,
Upon his brow the hue of death,
He slowly stiffens, ossifying,
When to your desperate appeal
He is insensitive and still?

35

With sharpening contrition growing,
Gripping the pistol in his hand,
Onegin watched Vladimir's going.
'Well then, he's dead, you understand,'
Pronounced the neighbour. Dead! Onegin,
Crushed by the utterance, walks off, quaking,
To call his people.[19] Straightaway,
Zaretsky gently on the sleigh
Settles the frozen corpse, escorting
The dreadful treasure to its home.
Sensing the corpse, the horses foam,
Wetting the steel bit, chafing, snorting,
But when they're ready to depart,
They fly as swiftly as a dart.

36

My friends, you're sorry for the poet:
Amid the bloom of hope, desire
From which the world will never profit,
And scarcely out of child's attire,
Gone! Where's the ardent agitation,
Where is the noble aspiration

Of youthful feeling, youthful thought,
Audacious, tender, highly wrought?
Where, too, is love's acclaimed impatience,
The thirst for knowledge, thirst for work,
The dread where vice and shame may lurk,
And you, most cherished ruminations,
You, phantoms of unearthly life,
You, dreams with sacred verses rife!

37

Perhaps he was for good intended
Or at the very least for fame;
His silenced lyre might have extended
Its sound through centuries to come
With ringing music. There awaited
Perhaps a special niche created
For him at an exalted site.
Perhaps his martyred shade in flight
Carried away a holy secret,
Remaining with him, and the joys
Are lost of an uplifting voice,
While from beyond the gravestone's remit
No hymn will rush to where he's laid,
Nor peoples come to bless his shade.

[38][20]

39

But then again the poet's portion
Might well have been quite commonplace.
The years of youth give way to caution,
Slowing the soul's impetuous pace.

Of poetry he might have wearied,
And, parting from the Muses, married;
A happy squire, with cuckold's crown,
Wearing a quilted dressing gown;
He might have learned life's true dimension,
At forty he'd have had the gout,
Drunk, eaten, moped, declined, got stout
And died according to convention
As children thronged and women cried
And village quacks stood by his side.

40

But, reader, we shall never know it;
Sufficient that upon a field
A youthful lover, dreamer, poet
Has by a friendly hand been killed!
A leftward path from the location
Where dwelt that child of inspiration
Leads to two pines with roots entwined,
Beneath which tiny currents wind
Out of the valley's brook they border.
The ploughman rests beside their brink
And female reapers come to sink
Their ringing pitchers in the water;
There, by the brook, in deepest shade,
A simple monument is laid.[21]

41

A herdsman to the tomb retreating
Sings (as the spring rain dots the grass)
Of Volga fishermen, while plaiting
His mottled sandals made of bast.
A young townswoman who is spending
Her summer in the country, wending

On horseback through the fields alone,
Rides headlong, comes upon the stone
And halts her steed, before it pausing,
As, tightening the leather leads,
She lifts her veil of gauze and reads
The plain inscription quickly, causing
A tear to dim her tender eyes
At Lensky's premature demise.

42

And, at a trot, she rides through meadows,
Sunk a long time in reverie,
Her soul pervaded by the shadows
Cast by the poet's destiny;
And wonders: 'How did Olga suffer?[22]
Was it for long she mourned her lover?
Or did she only briefly rue?
And where's her sister now? Where, too,
Is he, the fugitive, the hermit,
Of modish belles the modish foe,
Where did that gloomy oddball go,
The slayer of the youthful poet?'
I promise in due time I'll bring
A full account of everything,

43

But not today. Although my feeling
For Eugene has not changed a bit,
Though I'll return to him, unfailing,
Right now I am not up to it.
To Spartan prose the years are turning,
Coquettish rhyme the years are spurning;

And I – I with a sigh confess –
I'm running after her much less.
My pen has lost its former pleasures
Of daubing fleeting leaves, it seems,
Today, quite different, chilling dreams;
Quite different, unrelenting pressures,
In stillness or in social noise,
Disturb the sleep my soul enjoys.

44

I've come to know new aspirations,
I've come to know new sadness, too;
The former hold no expectations,
And earlier sadness still I rue.
Where are my dreams, the dreams I cherished?
What rhyme now follows, if not 'perished'?[23]
And is the garland of my youth
Withered at last, is this the truth?
Is it the truth, all plain, unvarnished,
Not in an elegiac cloak,
That (hitherto said as a joke)
The springtime of my days has vanished,
Can't be brought back and that I'm near
Already to my thirtieth year?[24]

45

The noontide of my life is starting,
Which I must needs accept, I know;
But oh, my light youth, if we're parting,
I want you as a friend to go!
My thanks to you for the enjoyments,
The sadness and the pleasant torments,

The hubbub, storms, festivity,
For all that you have given me;
My thanks to you. I have delighted
In you when times were turbulent,
When times were calm . . . to full extent;
Enough now! With a soul clear-sighted
I set out on another quest
And from my old life take a rest.

46

Let me glance back. Farewell, you arbours
Where, in the backwoods, I recall
Days filled with indolence and ardours
And dreamings of a pensive soul.
And you, my youthful inspiration.
Keep stirring my imagination,
My heart's inertia vivify,
More often to my corner fly.
Let not a poet's soul be frozen,
Made rough and hard, reduced to bone
And finally be turned to stone
In that benumbing world he goes in,
In that intoxicating slough
Where, friends, we bathe together now.[25]

CHAPTER VII

Moscow, Russia's favourite daughter,
Where is your equal to be found?

                    Dmitriyev

One can't but love one's native Moscow.

                    Baratynsky

  'Reviling Moscow! This is what
  You get from seeing the world!
  Where is it better, then?

  Where we are not.'

                    Griboyedov[1]

I

Chased by the vernal beams, already
Down the surrounding hills the snow
Has run in turbid streams that eddy
On to the flooded fields below;
Nature, not yet from sleep returning,
Greets with a smile the new year's morning.
The skies shine with a bluish sheen,
Transparent still, the woods turn green,
Lending the trees a downy cover,
The bee flies from its waxen comb,
Bringing the meadows' tribute home.
The dales dry out and colour over.
Herds low, the hush of darkness brings
The nightingale that newly sings.

2

How sad to me is spring's arrival,
Season of love, when all's in bud!
What languid tumult, what upheaval
Disturb my soul, disturb my blood!
With what a heavy, tender feeling
I revel in the season, breathing
The vernal wind that fans my face
In some secluded, rural place!
Or am I now estranged from pleasure,
Does all that gladdens, animates,
All that exults and radiates
Cast boredom, languor in like measure
Upon a soul long dead, does all
Seem dark to it, funereal?

3

Or, cheerless, when the leaves of autumn
Are resurrected by the spring,
We recollect a bitter fortune,
Hearing the woods' new murmuring;
Or we, in troubled contemplation
Compare with nature's animation
The withered years of our estate,
That nothing can resuscitate.
Perhaps in thought we may recover,
When caught in a poetic haze,
Some other spring of older days
That once more sets our hearts aquiver
With dreams of some far distant clime,
A wondrous night, a moon sublime . . .

4

It's time: good idlers, I beseech you,
Epicureans to the soul,
You, fortune's favourites, I entreat you,
You, fledglings of the Lyovshin[2] school,
You rural Priams[3] in your manors,
You, ladies blessed with gentle manners,
Spring calls you to the country soil,
Season of warmth, of flowers and toil,
Season of blissful walks and wandering,
Betokening seductive nights.
Quick, to the fields, the land invites
Your coaches, ponderously trundling;
By private horse or postal chaise,
Forsake the city gates, make haste!

5

You, too, my reader, ever gracious,
Into your foreign carriage climb,
Leave now the noisy city spaces
Where you caroused in winter time;
On my capricious Muse depending,
Let's hear the oak wood's sound ascending
Above a river without name,
Where my Eugene, the very same,
Reclusive, idle and dejected,
Spent winter only recently
In Tanya's close proximity,
My dreaming maid whom he rejected;
But now, no longer at his place,
He's left behind a dismal trace.

6

Midst hills in semi-circle lying,
Let us go thither where a brook,
By way of a green meadow plying,
Runs through a linden, forest nook.
The nightingale, through night's long hours,
Sings to the spring; the dog rose flowers,
And there is heard the source's sound –
There, too, a tombstone can be found
Beside two ancient pines umbrageous.
The inscription tells the passer-by:
'Vladimir Lensky doth here lie,
Who died a young man and courageous,
Aged such and such, in such a year.
Young poet, rest and slumber here.'

7

Upon a pine branch, low inclining,
Time was, there hung a secret wreath,
Rocked by the breeze of early morning
Over that humble urn beneath.
Time was, two girls in evening leisure
Would come to mourn this doleful treasure,
And, on the grave, in moonlight glow,
Embracing, they would weep . . . but now
The monument's forgot by people.
The trail to it is overgrown,
The wreath upon the bough is gone.
Alone, beside it, grey and feeble,
The shepherd sings still as before,
Plaiting his wretched shoes of yore.

[8, 9]

10

My poor, poor Lensky! Pining, aching,
Not long did his beloved weep,
Soon was the youthful bride forsaking
A grief that went not very deep.
Another captured her attention,
Another's flattering intervention
Restored the sufferer to calm,
A lancer wooed with practised charm,
And, by this lancer overpowered,
Already at the altar she
Stands with becoming modesty
Beneath the bridal crown, head lowered,
And, as her fiery eyes she dips,
A smile alights upon her lips.

11

Alas, poor Lensky! In the kingdom
Of distant, dark eternity,
Was he perturbed by vows reneged on,
Reports of infidelity,
Or, on the Lethe, lulled to slumber,
Where, blessedly, no thoughts encumber,
The poet is no more perturbed,
The earth is closed and no more heard?
Just so! An earth that will ignore us
Awaits us all beyond the grave.
The voice of lover, friend or knave
Breaks off. Alone, the angry chorus
Of heirs to the estate is raised,
Disputing in indecent haste.

12

Soon Olya's voice no more resounded
Inside her old environment,
The lancer, as his lot demanded,
Must take her to his regiment.
With tears of bitter sorrow flowing,
The mother at her daughter's going
Seemed almost ready now to die,
But Tanya simply could not cry,
Only a deathly pallor covered
The maiden's melancholy face.
When all came out to view the chaise
And, bustling, said goodbye and hovered,
Still holding back the newly wed,
Tatiana wished the pair God speed.

13

And after them, outside the manor,
Long did she gaze as through a mist . . .
Alone, alone now is Tatiana!
Alas, her sister, whom she missed,
Companion of so many seasons,
Her youthful little dove now hastens
To somewhere far off, borne by fate,
From her forever separate;
And, like a shade, she wanders, goalless,
Glances into the garden bare . . .
She finds no comforts anywhere
Nor anything to give her solace
For all the tears she has suppressed,
And torn asunder is her breast.

14

And in her cruel isolation
She feels more strongly passion's sway,
Her heart with greater perturbation
Speaks of Onegin far away.
She will not see him, maybe never,
She should abhor in him forever
The slayer of her brother. Woe,
The poet's dead ... already, though,
He is forgot, his bride has given
Herself already to be wed,
The poet's memory has fled
As smoke across an azure heaven,
There are two hearts yet, I believe,
That grieve for him ... but wherefore grieve?

15

Evening arrived. The sky has darkened.
The beetle whirrs. The waters flow.
Gone are the choirs to which we hearkened;
Across the river, smoking, glow
The fires of fishermen; and, dreaming
Under the silver moonlight streaming,
Out in the country, on her own,
Tatiana walks, walks on and on,
When suddenly, and with a quiver,
Below her, from her hill, she sees
A manor house, a village, trees,
A garden by a limpid river.
She gazes – and the heart in her
Starts beating fast and oftener.

16

She pauses now as doubts beset her:
Should she continue, does she dare?
He isn't here. They've never met her . . .
'Oh, just the house – and garden there.
I'll peep at them,' she says, advancing
Downhill, scarce breathing, round her glancing,
Bewildered as the house draws close . . .
And to the empty courtyard goes.
Dogs, barking, hurtle out toward her
And, hearing her alarming cry,
A noisy crowd of serf boys fly
From different entrances to guard her,
And, after fighting off each hound,
They leave the lady safe and sound.

17

'Please, can I see the house?' asked Tanya.
The children ran off speedily
To find the keeper of the manor
Who had with her the hallway key.
Anisya promptly came to meet her,
To open up the house and greet her.
She entered the deserted pile,
Our hero's recent domicile,
She looked: inside the hall, unheeded,
A cue lay on the billiard baize,
A riding crop upon a chaise
Dishevelled. She proceeded.
Here is the fireplace,' said the crone:
'Here master used to sit alone.

18

'He used to dine here in the winter
With neighbour Lensky, now deceased.
This way, I'll lead you. Here, we enter
The master's study, where he pleased
To sleep, take coffee, pay attention
To what the steward had to mention,
And read a book the morning through . . .
And the old master lived here, too.
Time was, on Sundays, by this casement,
He'd don his glasses and agree
To play "tomfoolery"[4] with me.
God save his soul, he was so patient,
And give his bones a peaceful berth
In his damp grave in mother-earth.'

19

With melting gaze Tatiana measures
The objects that surround her here,
All seem to her like priceless treasures,
All set her languid soul astir
With feelings joyful and half-anguished:
The desk, the lamp there, now extinguished,
The carpet-covered bed, the books,
The window over them that looks
Out on the moonlit dark unending,
And that pale half-light over all,
Lord Byron's portrait on the wall,
And, on a little column standing,
Arms crossed, a cast-iron statuette
With gloomy forehead and a hat.[5]

20

Tatiana long as in a vision
Stands in this fashionable cell.
But it is late. A cold wind's risen.
The valley's dark. The grove is still
Above the mist-enveloped river;
The moon behind the hill takes cover
And it is time, indeed high time
The pilgrim makes her homeward climb.
And Tanya, hiding her excitement,
Stifles a sigh before she starts
Out back to more familiar parts.
But first she asks whether she mightn't
Visit again the empty home
And read the books there on her own.

21

Tatiana and Anisya parted,
Beyond the gate. After two days –
In early morning now – she started
Towards that strange, deserted place.
And, in the study's silent setting,
Briefly the earth entire forgetting,
She was at last alone and free,
And wept a long time, copiously.
The books then called for her attention.
At first, she lacked the appetite,
But all the titles within sight
Appeared bizarre. With apprehension
She avidly began to read
And found a different world indeed.

22

Although, as we're aware, Onegin
Had long abandoned reading, still
There were some books he'd not forsaken
That earned a place in his goodwill:
The bard of *Juan* and the *Giaour*[6]
And two, three novels of the hour,[7]
In which the epoch was displayed
And modern man put on parade
And fairly faithfully depicted:
With his depraved, immoral soul,
Dried up and egotistical,
To dreaming endlessly addicted,
With his embittered, seething mind
To futile enterprise consigned.

23

There were preserved on many pages
The trenchant mark of fingernails,
With them the watchful girl engages
As if she were deciphering spells.
Tatiana saw with trepidation
What thought it was or observation
Had struck Onegin, what they meant,
To which he'd given mute consent.
And in the margins she encountered
His pencil marks by certain lines.
Throughout, his soul was by such signs,
Without his knowing it, expounded,
Whether by cross, by succinct word,
Or question mark, as they occurred.

24

And gradually my Tatiana
Begins to understand – thank God! –
More clearly now the true persona
To sigh for whom it is her lot,
By fate united to this stranger:
Eccentric, sad, exuding danger,
Creature of heaven or of hell,
This angel, this proud devil – well,
What is he then? An imitation,
A paltry phantom or a joke,
A Muscovite in Harold's cloak,
Of alien fads an explication,
Of modish words a lexicon,
A parody, when said and done?

25

Can she have solved Onegin's puzzle?
Can she have found the fitting 'word'?
The hours race on and in her tussle
Her journey home is long deferred.
Two neighbours there have met to chatter
About her. 'Well then, what's the matter?'
'She is no child now, if you please,'
Said the old lady with a wheeze.
'Why, Olen'ka is younger than her.'
'It's time that she was settled, yes,
But I feel helpless, I confess.
In such a curt and point-blank manner
She turns down everyone. And broods,
And wanders lonely in the woods.'

26

'Might she not be in love?' 'With whom, then?'
'Buyanov courted her – no fear.
And Petushkov – she left the room then.
A guest, hussar Pykhtin, was here,
And he found Tanya such a marvel,
Pursued her like the very devil!
I thought perhaps she'll take this one,
But no, once more the deal's undone.'
'My dear good woman, why not send her
To Moscow, to the bridal fair!
So many vacant places there.'
'Good sir, my income's much too slender.'
'Enough, though, for a winter's spree,
If not, then borrow – say, from me.'

27

The ageing lady was delighted
To hear this sensible advice;
She pondered – and at once decided
One winter would be worth the price.
And Tanya learns of her intention.
Unto the stringent *monde*'s attention
To offer up the clarity
Of countryside simplicity,
Its dated finery and dresses
And no less dated turns of phrase,
Sure to attract the mocking gaze
Of Moscow's popinjays and Circes![8]
God, no! Much better to remain
Secluded in the wood's domain.

28

Arising as the sun is dawning,
She hastens out; with melting eyes
Surveys the fields, and speaks in mourning
These words to all her rural ties:
'Farewell now, peaceful dales, farewell to
Familiar hilltops that I call to,
Farewell, familiar woods nearby;
Farewell, the beauty of the sky,
Farewell, glad nature that I cherish;
I am exchanging my dear peace
For noisy, glittering vanities . . .
Farewell, my freedom that must perish!
Whither and wherefore do I strive?
What can I hope for in this life?'

29

Her walks continue, lasting longer.
Now at a hillock, now a stream
Tatiana cannot help but linger,
Arrested by their special charm.
As with old friends Tatiana hastens
To carry on her conversations
With every meadow, grove in sight,
But short-lived summer's taking flight.
And golden autumn is arriving.
Nature, now pale and tremulous,
Is richly dressed for sacrifice.
Here is the North now, storm clouds driving,
It blows, it howls – and winter then,
The sorceress arrives again.

30

She's come, herself she scatters, weighting
The oaken boughs with flocks of snow;
Lies down in carpets undulating
Over the hills and fields below;
Spreads out a puffy shroud to cover
The trace of banks and frozen river;
Frost gleams. And we take pleasure in
Old Mother Winter's frolicking.
But Tanya finds her antics galling.
She shuns the winter, cannot bear
To take a breath of frosty air,
Or at the bath with new snow falling
To wash her face, her shoulders, breast.
Tatiana dreads this winter's quest.

31

Departure has been long extended,
The final date is almost gone.
The coach has been inspected, mended,
Recovered from oblivion.
The usual three kibitkas manage
The plethora of goods and baggage:
Pans, jars of jam, and chairs and chests
And feather beds and mattresses,
Roosters in cages, pots and basins,
Etcetera – for so much more
Is wrested from the family store.
And in the log hut, losing patience
The servants weep, farewell is hard:
And eighteen nags invade the yard.

32

They're harnessed to the master carriage,
The cooks prepare a lunch for all,
The three kibitkas teem with baggage,
While household women, coachmen brawl.
A bearded outrider is seated
Upon a jade, unkempt, depleted.
Up at the gate retainers vie
To bid their mistresses goodbye.
The venerable carriage, gliding,
Has crept beyond the gate. 'Farewell,
You peaceful places, hill and dell!
Farewell the refuge that I'd hide in!
When shall I see you all?' she cries,
And tears stream out of Tanya's eyes.

33

When we are free of the constrictions
Of our benign enlightenment,
In time (we're told, from the predictions
Of philosophic measurement,[9]
In some five hundred years) our highways
Will no more look like tawdry byways,
But surfaced roads on every hand
Will unify the Russian land,
And cast-iron bridges will support us
On wide arcs over waterways,
We'll part the mountains in the skies,
Dig daring tunnels under waters,
And Christendom will institute
A chain of inns on every route.

34

But now our roadways are decaying,
Our bridges, now forgotten, rot,
At stations fleas and bedbugs preying
Won't let a traveller sleep a jot.
There are no inns. In some cold cabin
There hangs for show a highfalutin'
And meagre menu to excite
An unrewarded appetite;
While rural Cyclopes take courage
Before a fire of little heat,
And with a Russian hammer treat
A slender European carriage,
And bless the ditches and the moats
That constitute our country's roads.

35

Yet in the chilly winter season
A drive is light and pleasant. Like
A voguish song devoid of reason,
Unruffled is the winter track.
We have automedons,[10] quick-witted,
And troikas tireless and intrepid,
And mileposts, like a fence, race by,
Diverting the lethargic eye.
But Larina drove none too fleetly,
Her transport all her own for fear
Post-chaises would have proved too dear,
And our young maid enjoyed completely
The road's monotonous delights:
They travelled seven days and nights.

36

But they are close now, and their horses
To white-stone Moscow gallop, as
They glimpse ahead the golden crosses
Glowing on ancient cupolas.
Brothers, there's nothing that can equal
My pleasure when a semi-circle
Of churches, belfries, gardens, halls
Opened to me inside the walls.
How often, sadly separated,
Fated to roam without resort,
Moscow, it was of you I thought!
Moscow, whose name reverberated
In every Russian heart! I heard
So many echoes in that word!

37

Here next, by leafy grove surrounded,
Petrovsky Castle[11] stands. Dark pride
In recent glory here resounded.
Here Bonaparte chose to reside
By Fortune's smile intoxicated,
He waited – but in vain he waited –
For Moscow on her bended knees
To yield to him old Kremlin's keys.
My Moscow spurned such self-abasement,
No gift, no feast day she declared,
A fiery welcome she prepared
To greet a hero so impatient.
From here he watched, in thought immersed,
The dreadful conflagration burst.

38

Farewell to you, Petrovsky Palace,
Witness of glory's first defeat,
Away now to the turnpike pillars[12]
Whitening on Tverskaya Street.
Across the pits the carriage flashes,
Past sentries, peasant women dashes,
Past street lamps,[13] shops and errand boys,
Past monasteries, gardens, sleighs,
Mansions, Bokharans,[14] small plantations,
Shacks, merchants, peasants selling wares,
Boulevards and Cossack messengers,[15]
Towers, pharmacies and stores with fashions,
Balconies, gates where lions curl,[16]
Crosses where flocks of jackdaws swirl.[17]

39, 40[18]

An hour or two they go on driving
In this exhausting marathon,
When at a gated house arriving,
They stop – just by St Khariton[19]
To see an aunt, who, with consumption
Some four years now, can hardly function.
To them the door is opened wide,
A grey-haired Kalmyk[20] stands inside,
Arrayed in torn kaftan and glasses,
And with a stocking in his hand.
In the salon, from her divan,
The cry they hear is the Princess's.
The two old ladies weep, embrace
And exclamations pour apace.

41

'Princesse, mon ange!' 'Pachette!'[21] 'Dear cousin
Alina!' 'Who'd have thought? It's been
So long. You'll stay? Well, stop this fussing,
Sit down – how wonderful, a scene
Out of a novel, just the manner.'
'But meet my daughter here, Tatiana.'
'Ah Tanya, come to me, my dear . . .
I'm getting quite deranged, I fear . . .
Our Grandison, do you remember?'
'What Grandison? Oh, Grandison!
Of course, I wonder where he's gone?'
'Lives near St Simeon's;[22] last December,
On Christmas Eve he called on me:
Married a son quite recently.

42

'The other one – a little patience . . .
Tomorrow, Tanya we shall show
To all her various relations.
Pity, I'm too infirm to go,
I scarce can drag my feet, the devils,
But you are weary from your travels;
Together let us take a rest,
Oh, I've no strength . . . my poor, tired chest . . .
Not even joy, not only sorrow
Is hard for me to bear, my dear.
I'm good for nothing now, it's clear.
Life in old age is such a horror.'
And, weeping, by exhaustion hit,
She breaks into a coughing fit.

43

Tatiana's touched by the good-hearted
Affection of the invalid,
And yet she is unhappy, parted
From her accustomed room and bed.
Round her a silken curtain closes,
Yet she can't sleep, when she reposes,
The church bells' early roundelay,
Precursor of the labouring day,
Arouses her, and in the shadows
She sits beside the window, sees
The darkness thinning by degrees,
But can't discern her fields, her meadows,
Before her lies a yard that's strange,
A stable, fence and kitchen range.

44

To daily dinners Tanya's taken
With her extended family,
But grandmas, grandpas cannot quicken
The girl's abstracted lethargy.
Relatives from a far location
Are welcomed with solicitation,
With exclamations and good cheer.
'How Tanya's grown! How long, my dear,
Since at your christening I dried you,'
'And since I held you – all those years!'
'And since I pulled you by the ears!'[23]
'And since with gingerbread I plied you!'
And grandmothers in chorus cry:
'Oh how our years go flying by!'

45

But nothing changes in their bearing,
Where age-old fashion is the rule;
The princess Aunt Yelena's wearing
Her ancient mobcap made of tulle;
Cerused still is Lukerya Lvovna,
Still telling lies Lyubov Petrovna,
Ivan Petrovich is inane,
Semyon Petrovich[24] just as mean;
Still Pelageya Nikolavna
Keeps Monsieur Finemouche[25] in her house
With Pomeranian dog[26] and spouse.
While he, the conscientious clubber,[27]
Is still the meek and deaf man who
Consumes and drinks enough for two.

46

Their daughters put their arms round Tanya.
These graces of young Moscow[28] now
Without a word observe Tatiana,
Surveying her from top to toe;
They find her somewhat unexpected,
Provincial and a touch affected,
A little pale, a little thin,
But passable for kith and kin;
And then, to nature's way submitting,
They take her to their rooms, make friends,
And kiss her, gently squeezing hands,
Fluff up her curls to look more fitting,
And in their singsong tones impart
Maids' secrets, secrets of the heart,

47

Conquests, their own and those of others,
Their hopes, their pranks, their reveries.
Their guileless conversation gathers,
Embellished by slight calumnies,
Then, to requite their indiscretion,
They sweetly ask for her confession
Of secrets of the heart she keeps.
But Tanya, just as if she sleeps,
Is hearing them without partaking,
And, understanding nothing, she
Protects her secret silently,
Her heart's fond treasure, blissful, aching,
The tears and joys she will not share
With anyone encountered there.

48

Tatiana seeks to be convivial,
To listen to what people say,
But in the drawing-room such trivial
And incoherent rot holds sway;
The people are so pale and weary,
Their very slander's dull and dreary.
Within this land of sterile views,
Interrogations, gossip, news,
Through four-and-twenty hours you'll never
Spot one lone thought, even by chance;
A languid mind won't smile or dance,
Even in jest the heart won't quiver.
We might to foolish jokes respond,
If you but knew some, hollow *monde*!

49

The archive boys[29] in congregation
Cast eyes on Tanya priggishly
And speak of her with denigration
In one another's company.
But there's one coxcomb in dejection
For whom she seems ideal perfection,
And, leaning on a doorpost, he
Prepares for her an elegy.
Once, Vyazemsky,[30] on meeting Tanya
At some dull aunt's, sat by the girl
And managed to engage her soul,
And near him, an old man,[31] who'd seen her,
Straightening out his wig, inquired
After this maiden he admired.

50

But where Melpomene[32] is uttering
Her loud, protracted wails, laments
And, with her gaudy mantle fluttering,
Confronts a frigid audience,
Where Thalia[33] is quietly napping,
Hearkening not to friendly clapping,
Where to Terpsichore alone
The young spectator now is drawn
(As was the case in years departed,
In your day and in mine the same),
At her no jealous ladies aim
Lorgnettes when once the ballet's started,
Nor modish experts train a glass,
From box or stall, to judge her class.

51

To the Assembly,[34] too, they bring her,
Where the excitement, crush and heat,
The tapers' glare, the music's clangour,
The flicker, whirl of dancing feet,
The light attire of pretty women,
The galleries with people brimming,
The arc of seats for brides-to-be
All strike the senses suddenly.
Here are inveterate fops, parading
Their waistcoats and impertinence,
And nonchalantly held lorgnettes.
Here are hussars on leave, invading,
Who, thundering through in great display,
Flash, captivate and fly away.

52

The night has many starry clusters,
And Moscow pretty women, too,
But, brighter far than all her sisters,
The moon shines in the airy blue.
But she – my lyre dares not disquiet her
With songs, I fear, that won't delight her –
Shines like the regal moon alone
Midst maids and ladies round her throne.
With what celestial pride she graces
The earth which by her is caressed,
What blissful feelings fill her breast,
How wondrous-languidly she gazes! . . .
But stop, enough, I beg of you,
To folly now you've paid your due.

53

Noise, laughter, galop, waltz, mazurka,
Bows, bustle . . . meanwhile from the dance
Tatiana hides – the capers irk her –
Beside a column, 'twixt two aunts,
She looks but does not see, detesting
The worldly tumult and the jesting,
She, stifling here, in fancy strains
To reach again her fields and lanes,
Her rural life: the tranquil bowers,
The poor folk, the secluded nook
Where flows a tiny, limpid brook,
Her novels and the country flowers,
And those tenebrous linden ways
Where *he* appeared in former days.

54

But while her mind is in the distance,
Forgetting *monde* and noisy ball,
A certain general of substance
Won't take his eyes off her at all.
The two aunts wink and in like manner
Both with their elbows nudge Tatiana,
And each one whispers in her ear:
'Look quickly to the left, my dear.'
'The left? But where? What is so special?'
'Well, never mind what it may be,
Just look . . . that group . . . in front, you see . . .
Those two in uniform, official . . .
Gone . . . Wait, his profile's in between.'
'Who? That fat general, you mean?'

55

But let's extend congratulations
To dear Tatiana, triumphing,
And change my course (entreating patience),
Lest I forget of whom I sing.
And by the way two words, updating:
'I sing a youthful friend, relating
His many eccentricities.
Please favour the felicities,
O epic Muse, of my exertions,
And, with your trusty staff, let me
Not wander on so waywardly.'
There, done! Enough! No more diversions!
Thus, classicism I placate:
An Introduction's here, though late.

CHAPTER VIII

Fare thee well, and, if for ever.
Still for ever fare thee well.[1]
                              Byron

I

In those far days, serene and careless,
The *lycée*'s[2] gardens saw me grow,
I read with pleasure Apuleius[3]
And disregarded Cicero[4],
In those far days, in dales mysterious,
In spring, when swans call out, imperious,
Near waters shining tranquilly,
The Muse began to visit me.
My student cell was inundated
With sudden light. She brought me there
A youthful feast, a merry fare
Of fancies that in song she fêted,
Sang, too, our glorious, ancient themes,
Sang of the heart that stirs our dreams.

2

And with a smile my Muse was greeted;
Our first success emboldened us,
We were by old Derzhavin[5] heeded
And blessed before he joined the dust . . .[6]

3

And I, who make the rule of passions
The only law I recognize,
Sharing my feelings with the fashions,
I led my frisky Muse to prize
The noise of feasts and fierce discussions,
Of watch-endangering excursions;[7]
And to these crazy feasts she brought
Her native gifts, began to sport
And gambol like a young bacchante,
And, over cups, to guests she'd sing,
And in a youthful gathering
Among the men she'd be the centre,
And in that amicable crowd,
My giddy mistress made me proud.

4

But I seceded from their union
And fled afar[8] . . . she followed me.
How often would she, fond companion,
Sweeten my mute trajectory
With secret tales and magic aura!
How often, moonlit, like Leonora,[9]
She'd gallop with me on a horse
Across the crags of Caucasus!
How often on the shores of Tauris[10]
She led me in nocturnal gloom
To listen to the sea's dull boom,
The Nereids'[11] unceasing chorus,
The waves profound, eternal choir
And hymn of praise to heaven's sire.

5

And then a change in her behaviour:
Forgetting feasts and opulence,
Amid the wastes of sad Moldavia[12]
She visited the humble tents
Of wandering tribes, and, living with them,
Grew wild and shared their daily rhythm,
Forgetting her Olympian speech
For strange, scant tongues the tribesmen teach,
For steppe-land song she found appealing . . .
Then suddenly this picture cleared
And in my garden she appeared
As a provincial miss, revealing
A thoughtful sadness in her look
And in her hands a small, French book.[13]

6

And, for the first time now, I'm taking
My Muse to join a worldly rout;
With jealous apprehension quaking,
I view the steppe-land charms she's brought.
Through solid rows aristocratic,
Of army fops, corps diplomatic
And past imperious dames she flits.
Now, looking quietly, she sits,
The noisy multitude admiring,
The flickering of dress and speech,
The guests who slowly try to reach
The young hostess, who waits untiring,
The men, who, like dark picture frames,
Surround the women and the dames.

7

She liked the hieratic order
Of oligarchic colloquies,
The chill of tranquil pride that awed her,
And ranks and years that mixed at ease.
But who in this august collection
Stands silently, with disaffection?
Not one of them appears to know.
Before him, faces come and go
Like ghosts in tedious succession.
What does his face show – spleen, hurt pride?
Why is this person at our side?
Who is he? Well, it's my impression
He's Eugene. Really? Yes, it's clear.
What wind is it that's blown him here?

8

Is he the same or more pacific?
Has he returned in novel style?
Or does he still play the eccentric?
What will he stage for us meanwhile?
As what will he appear now? Melmoth?
A cosmopolitan, a patriot,
A Harold, Quaker, Pharisee[14]
Or else some other *jeu d'esprit*
Or simply as a decent fellow,
Like you and me and everyone?
A fashion that is past and done
I say you should not try to follow.
We've had enough of all his show.
'You know him, then?' 'Well, yes and no.'

9

'Then tell me why you're so begrudging,
When talking of him. Might it be
Because we never tire of judging
The world around us ceaselessly,
Because a rash and fiery spirit,
To smug nonentities that near it,
Seems insolent and out of place, .
And men of wit constrain your space?
Because we're wont to talk forever
Instead of acting or because
Stupidity wins our applause?
Because grave men delight in trivia,
And only mediocrity
Will make us feel at liberty?'

10

Blest who in youth was truly youthful,
Blest who matured in proper time,
Who, step by step, remaining truthful,
Could weather, yearly, life's bleak clime,
To curious dreams was not addicted,
Nor by the social mob constricted,
At twenty was a blade or swell
And then at thirty married well;
Ridding himself, on reaching fifty,
Of debts and other bills to foot,
Then calmly gaining rank, repute
And money, too, by being thrifty;
Of whom the world's opinion ran:
NN's an estimable man.

11

How sad, however, if we're given
Our youth as something to betray,
And what if youth in turn is driven
To cheat on us, each hour, each day,
If our most precious aspirations,
Our freshest dreams, imaginations
In fast succession have decayed,
As leaves, in putrid autumn, fade
It is too much to see before one
Nothing but dinners in a row,
Behind the seemly crowd to go,
Regarding life as mere decorum,
Having no common views to share,
Nor passions that one might declare.

12

When noisy comments start to plague you,
You won't endure it (you'll agree),
If people of good sense should take you
For someone feigning oddity,
A melancholy, crazed impostor
Or maybe a satanic monster
Or even my own Demon.[15] Thus,
Onegin once more busies us.
He'd killed his friend; bereft of pleasure,
He lived with neither work nor goal
Till twenty-six, and still his soul
Languished in unproductive leisure;
He lacked employment and a wife
And any purpose in his life.

13

A restless spirit took him over,
A wish to travel, anywhere
(An inclination like a fever
Or cross that few will gladly bear).
And so he came to the conclusion
To leave the fields' and woods' seclusion,
Where every day a bloodstained shade
Appeared to him and would not fade,
And sallied forth without direction,
With one sensation in his mind;
And, as with all he'd left behind,
So travel, too fed his dejection.
He found his way back after all,
Like Chatsky, leaving boat for ball.[16]

14

But look at how the crowd is clearing,
How whispers speed around the hall . . .
The hostess sees a lady nearing,
In tow a weighty general.
She is unhurried, not loquacious,
Not cold, standoffish, not ungracious,
She does not stare with insolence,
And to success makes no pretence;
Reveals no petty affectation
Or imitative artifice,
She shows a quiet, simple grace,
And seems a faithful illustration
Of *comme il faut* (a phrase which I,
Shishkov[17] forgive, can't Russify).

15

The ladies gathered closer to her;
Old women smiled as she passed by,
The gentlemen were bowing lower,
Endeavouring to catch her eye.
In front of her, the girls stopped chasing
Across the room, while gravely raising
Shoulders and nose above them all,
The general impressed the hall.
None could have said she was a beauty,
Nevertheless, from head to foot,
None could have found in her what would,
In fashionable London city,
In that high autocratic court,
Be known as *vulgar* (I can not . . .

16

I'm very fond of this expression,
But own, I can't translate it yet,
It still feels like an innovation
And hardly suits our etiquette;
An epigram might serve it better . . .)
But let me turn now to our matter.
With carefree charm, our lady sat,
Engaged in amicable chat
With Nina Voronskoy, at table,
The Cleopatra of Neva,[18]
Who, though more beautiful by far,
With classic features, smooth like marble,
Could not eclipse her fellow guest,
For all the dazzle she possessed.

17

'Can it be possible?' thinks Eugene
'Can it be she? But no . . . and yet . . .
What! From the steppes, that outback region . . . ?'
He keeps his resolute lorgnette
Directed at her every minute
And dimly sees, reflected in it,
Looks he'd forgotten long ago.
'Excuse me, Prince, but do you know
That lady in the crimson beret
Talking with Spain's ambassador?'[19]
The Prince looks at Onegin: 'Ah!
You've been away a long time – very,
Wait, I'll present you, when they end.'
'But who is she?' 'My wife, dear friend.'

18

'You're married.' 'Oh, you did not know then?'
'How long?' 'About two years.' 'To whom?'
'To Larina.' 'Tatiana!' 'Oh then,
She knows you.' 'I live near her home.'
'In that case, come,' the Prince says, taking
His relative and friend, Onegin,
To meet his wife. The Princess looks
At him . . . and whatsoever shakes
Her soul, whatever her impression
Of him or the astonishment
She feels or the bewilderment,
Nothing betrays her self-possession.
Her tone remains as it had been,
Her bow is equally serene.

19

Not only did she not take flight now,
Or suddenly turn crimson, white . . .
She never even moved an eyebrow,
Nor pursed her lips a bit too tight.
Although Onegin looked most closely,
He found no trace in her that loosely
Recalled the girl that he had met.
He wanted to address her . . . yet
He could not . . . She then spoke, inquiring
How long had he been here, and whence,
And was it from their parts perchance;
Then to her husband turned, retiring.
With weary look she glided hence . . .
Eugene remained there, motionless.

20

Could it be she, the same Tatiana,
The very maiden he once met
In that remote and distant corner
And preached to in a tête-à-tête
With loftiness and exhortation,
When we embarked on our narration,
Was hers the letter he'd preserved,
In which her heart spoke, unreserved,
Out in the open, undeflected,
That little girl . . . a dream, maybe?
That little girl . . . the one whom he
Had, in her humble lot, neglected,
Could it be she who, now so bold,
Had, heedless, left him in the cold?

21

He leaves the packed hall hurriedly
And pensively he drives back home,
His tardy sleep is worried by
A dream, now sad, now full of charm,
He wakes; an invitation's brought;
His presence by Prince N is sought
At a soirée. 'My God, to her!
I will, I will, without demur!
He scrawls a courteous 'Yes, I'll be there.'
What's happening? In what strange dream
Is he now? What, deep down in him,
Has stirred his sluggish soul to fever?
Pique? Vanity? Or, once again,
Could it be love, that youthful pain?

22

The passing hours Onegin's counting,
For day to end he cannot wait.
But ten strikes,[20] he's already mounting
His carriage, soon he's at the gate.
He enters in a nervous manner,
There, on her own, he finds Tatiana,
Some minutes they together sit.
Once more Onegin cannot fit
A word in place. Embarrassed, sullen,
He scarcely can reply to her.
But all the time his mind's a-whirr.
A fixed idea he keeps on mulling.
And fixedly he looks, while she
Sits calmly and at liberty.

23

Her husband enters, interrupting
This most unpleasant tête-à-tête,
And joins Onegin in recapturing
Pranks, jokes enjoyed, when first they met.
They laugh together. Guests now enter
And with the large-grained salt of banter
The *grand monde*'s conversation sparks;
Around the hostess, light remarks
Are flashing without affectation.
While, interrupting them, good sense
Eschews banality, pretence,
Eternal truths, pontification,
And, in its free vivacity,
Shocks nobody's propriety.

24

Yet here was found the city's flower:
Nobles and fashion's exemplars,
Faces one meets with every hour,
And fools – a necessary class;
Here were, in mobcaps and in roses,
Elderly dames who looked ferocious;
Here there were several spinsters, who
Would never think to smile at you;
Here an ambassador was speaking
About some government affair;
Here was, with scented, greying hair,
An old man in the old way joking:
With first-rate wit and subtle play,
That seem somewhat absurd today.

25

Here was, to epigrams addicted,
An irritable gentleman,
Cross with the tea – too sweet a liquid –
With trivial ladies, vulgar men,
The foggy novel being debated,
The badge of which two sisters prated,[21]
The lies the journals told, the war,[22]
The snow, and wife he found a bore[23]
. . . .
. . . .
. . . .
. . . .
. . . .
. . . .

26

Here was Prolasov[24] whose distinction
Lay in his soul's depravity,
In every album you can mention
He wore your pencils down, Saint-Priest;[25]
There at the door a ball dictator,
Fit for a fashion illustrator,
Pink as a Palm Week cherub,[26] shone,
Tight-buttoned, mute and still as stone;
A jackanapes, a bird of passage,
With neck-cloth overstarched,[27] produced
A smile among the guests, seduced
By his fastidious poise and carriage,
But silent glances in the end
Confirmed he was by all condemned.

27

Throughout the evening my Onegin
Thought only of Tatiana, not
The shy young girl that he'd forsaken,
Simple and poor, by love distraught,
But the princess, so very different,
Now the goddess, so very distant,
Ruling the opulent Neva.
O humans! You're so similar
To Eve, our ancestress: what's granted
Does not appeal to you at all,
You hear the serpent's endless call
To where a secret tree is planted;
Forbidden fruit provides more spice,
Without it there's no paradise.

28

How changed Tatiana is, adapting
So resolutely to her role,
With what alacrity accepting
The codes of rank that cramp the soul!
Who'd dare to seek the tender creature
In this majestic legislator
Of every salon, one whose heart
Had once by him been torn apart?
Time was, when virginally grieving
For Eugene in the dark of night,
While Morpheus[28] was still in flight,
She raised her tired eyes moonward, dreaming
Of how together they might wend
Their humble journey to the end.

29

Love is for every age auspicious,
But for the virginal and young
Its impulses are more propitious
Like vernal storms on meadows sprung:
They freshen in the rain of passion,
Ripening in their renovation –
And life, empowered, sends up shoots
Of richest blooms and sweetest fruits.
But at a late age, dry and fruitless,
The final stage to which we're led,
Sad is the trace of passions dead:
Thus storms in autumn, cold and ruthless,
Transform the field into a slough,
And strip the trees from root to bough.

30

There is no doubt, alas, that Eugene's
In love with Tanya like a child,
And every day and night imagines,
In throes of love, some fancy wild,
Not harking to his mind's stern censures,
Each day up to her porch he ventures,
Into her entrance hall of glass;
He shadows her in every place;
He's happy if upon her shoulders
He casts a fluffy boa, if he
Touches her hand hot-bloodedly
Or motley liveries, like soldiers,
He separates before her or
Her handkerchief picks from the floor.

31

She does not mark, she does not heed him,
Though he might struggle, short of death,
To visit her she grants him freedom,
Elsewhere she scarcely wastes her breath;
Sometimes she'll bow out of politeness,
Sometimes she simply takes no notice.
There is no coquetry in her –
It is not brooked in her milieu.
Onegin pales, can hardly function.
She does not care or does not see.
Onegin pines away, is he
Already suffering from consumption?
All send him to the doctors, they
Prescribe a spa without delay.

32

He stays: beforehand he'd been ready
To warn his forebears to expect
That soon he'd be among them, yet she
Cares not a bit (such is their sex).
But he is stubborn, won't surrender,
Still hopes and keeps to his agenda.
Far bolder than a healthy man,
Unwell, he writes with feeble hand
The Princess an impassioned letter,
Although (in this I share his views)
He saw in letters little use;
But with his heart held in a fetter,
A missive could not be deferred.
Here is his letter, word for word.

Onegin's Letter to Tatiana

I can predict: I shall offend
You[29] with my secret, sad confession,
And I foresee your proud expression
Of bitter scorn for what I send.
What do I want? To what end, after
I've opened up my soul to you?
What wicked merriment, what laughter
I'll give, perhaps, occasion to!
When first I met you, I detected
A tender spark, I was affected,
But to the challenge dared not rise,
I'd curbed myself of that sweet habit,
And I had no desire to forfeit
The hateful freedom I so prize.
Yet one more thing drove us asunder . . .
Lensky, a hapless victim, fell . . .
And then, from all a heart finds tender
I tore my own; an alien soul,
Without allegiances, I vanished,
Thinking that liberty and peace
Could take the place of happiness.
My God, how wrong, how I've been punished!

To see you as each minute flies,
To follow you in all directions,
To capture with enamoured eyes
Your smiling lips, your eyes' reflections,
To listen and to understand
With all my soul your perfect nature,
To melt in torments at your hand,
Grow pale and waste away – that's rapture!

And I'm deprived of that: for you
I drag myself at random, wander,
Each day is dear, each hour too:
Yet I in futile dullness squander

The days my fate has counted off.
And they are burdensome enough.
I know: my end may well be dawning,
But so as to prolong my stay,
I must be certain every morning
That I shall see you that same day . . .

I fear that my meek supplication
Will be by your relentless gaze
Seen as a shameful machination –
I hear your furious dispraise.
If you but knew the frightful torment
To languish after your beloved,
To burn – while reason every moment
Tells you to quell your raging blood,
To wish to hold your knees, and, pouring
My tears out at your feet, to press,
Entreat, confess, reproach, imploring
All, all I've wanted to express,
To do so, feigning reservation,
To arm each glance and every phrase,
To look at you with cheerful gaze
And hold a placid conversation . . .

But let that be: I'm in no state
To struggle further with my passion;
My life depends on your decision
And I surrender to my fate.

33

He gets no answer to this letter,
A second and a third he sends,
But neither one fares any better.
At a reception he attends,
He's hardly entered than towards him
Tatiana comes, and she ignores him,

Says nothing, does not see him there.
What frost surrounds her, how severe!
How, holding back her indignation,
Her stubborn lips remain in place!
Onegin peers with searching gaze:
Where, where's the pity, perturbation?
The tear stains, where? No trace, no trace,
Anger alone has marked this face . . .

34

And, possibly the apprehension
That *monde* or husband might suppose
Some waywardness, some casual penchant . . .
And everything Onegin knows . . .
No hope! He drives from the reception,
Cursing his crazy self-deception;
Though part of it, he did not rue
Bidding the *monde* again adieu;
The silence of his study brought him
Remembrance of another time,
When in the loud *monde*'s pantomime,
Khandra had cruelly chased and caught him,
And seized him by the collar, then
Enclosed him in his gloomy den.

35

He read again, but all at random:
Manzoni, Gibbon[30] and Rousseau,
Madame de Staël, Chamfort[31] in tandem,
Bichat and Herder and Tissot.[32]
He read the sceptic Bayle,[33] who led him
To Fontenelle,[34] and when he'd read him,
He tried some authors of our own
Without rejecting anyone –

The almanachs, reviews that ever
Are drumming sermons into us,
And treating me with animus,[35]
But where, time was, I might discover
Such madrigals to me back then:
E sempre bene,[36] gentlemen!

36

But even while his eyes were reading,
His thoughts were far away, as old
Desires, dreams, sorrows kept invading
And crowding deep inside his soul.
Between the lines before him, printed,
His inward eye saw others hinted.
On these he concentrated most,
In their decipherment engrossed.
These were the secret legends, fictions
The heart's dark story had collected,
The dreams with all else unconnected,
The threats, the rumours, the predictions,
Or else some lengthy, crazy tale
Or letters from a fledgling girl.

37

And by degrees his thought and feeling
By lethargy are overcome,
Meanwhile, imagination's dealing
Its motley faro cards to him.
He sees on melted snow, recumbent,
As if asleep at some encampment,
A youth on his nocturnal bed
And hears a voice: 'Well then, he's dead!'

He sees past enemies forgotten,
Base cowards and calumniators,
A swarm of youthful, female traitors,
A group of former friends turned rotten,
And then a country house – where she
Sits at the window . . . constantly.

38

Such musings soon became a habit
And nearly drove him off his head
Or, failing this, made him a poet –
That would have been a boon, indeed!
Truly: by means of magnetism[37]
He almost grasped the mechanism
Of Russian poetry of the time –
This muddled neophyte of mine.
He looked a poet to the letter:
Ensconced before a blazing hearth,
He sat alone as flames would dart,
Hummed *Idol Mio, Benedetta,*[38]
And dropped into the fire, unseen,
A slipper or a magazine.

39

Winter, as warming air blew through it,
Was over now; the days rushed by;
And he did not become a poet,
Nor turn insane, nor did he die.
Enlivened by the spring's returning,
He leaves upon one cloudless morning
The shuttered rooms, where he had spent
The winter like a marmot pent.

From fireplace and the double windows,
By sleigh, past the Neva he flies.
Upon blue blocks of hewn-out ice[39]
The sun disports; in dirty cinders
The furrowed snow melts on the street:
Where, then, upon it with such speed

40

Is he proceeding? Oh, already
You've guessed, you're right: my unreformed
Eccentric's rushing to his lady,
To his Tatiana, unforewarned.
He walks in like a corpse, nobody
Is there to greet him in the lobby.
In the reception room there's not
A soul. A door he opens . . . what
Confronts him then, what makes him shudder?
Before him the Princess alone
Sits pale and unadorned, forlorn,
Immersed in what looks like a letter,
A flood of tears she softly sheds
With cheek on hand . . . Ah, what regrets,

41

What silent sufferings were reflected
In this quick moment of distress!
Who is it could not have detected
Poor Tanya in the new princess!
Eugene, the moment that he saw her,
Fell maddened with remorse before her.
She gave a start, said not a word
And looked at Eugene unperturbed

Without surprise or wrath . . . His fading
Appearance, his extinguished look,
Imploring aspect, mute rebuke
She takes in all. The simple maiden
Returns again now, reappears
With dreams and heart of former years.

42

She lets Onegin go on kneeling
And, looking at him fixedly,
Does not withdraw her hand unfeeling
That he is kissing avidly . . .
What is she dreaming of at present?
A long time passes by, quiescent,
At last she softly speaks again:
'Enough, get up. I must explain
Myself to you. I wonder whether,
Onegin, you recall, do you,
The garden and the avenue,
The hour when fate brought us together
And how you lectured me, so meek.
Today it is my turn to speak.

43

'I was much younger at that meeting
And better looking, to my mind,
I loved you then, was that upsetting?
And in your heart, what did I find?
What was your answer? Only sternness.
You'd never, would you, take in earnest
A little maiden's modest love.
My blood runs cold now – God above! –

The very moment I remember
Your chilling glance, that sermon . . . I'm
Not blaming you: at that dark time
You showed at least a noble temper
And you were right regarding me,
I thank you for your honesty . . .

44

'Admit that in our backwoods haven,
From empty rumour far away,
I was not to your liking . . . Say, then,
Why you're pursuing me today.
Why have you marked me for attention?
Might it not be because convention
Includes me in the social round,
Because I'm wealthy and renowned,
Because my husband's wounds in battle
Have gained him royal favour, fame?
Might it not be because my shame
Would feed the flames of tittle-tattle
And win you, in society,
Seductive notoriety?

45

'I weep . . . if you recall your Tanya,
There's one thing you should hear from me:
Your sharp reproach, unfriendly manner,
Your cold, unsparing homily,
All this, with which you made me cower,
I'd have preferred, had I the power,
To this offensive passion, to
The letters, tears I've had from you.

You showed my childish dreams compassion,
And you at least respected me
And my young age. But now, I see
You at my feet in coward fashion?
How with the heart and mind you have
Can you be paltry feeling's slave?

46

'This pomp, Onegin, these excesses,
The trumpery of hateful days,
My high society successes,
My fashionable house, soirées,
What do they mean? Oh, I'd surrender
At once this masquerade, this splendour,
With all its glitter, noise and smoke
For one wild garden and a book,
For our poor home, to me the dearest,
For all those places I recall,
Where I beheld you first of all,
And for the humble churchyard near us,
Where now a cross and branches shade
The grave where my poor nurse is laid . . .

47

'And yet that time was so auspicious
And happiness so near . . . But no,
My fate is settled. Injudicious
I may have been, but it is so.
With tears my mother begged, entreated
And I, poor Tanya, listless, ceded,
All lots were equal anyhow . . .
I married. Pray you, leave me now.

Your heart is honest and I prize it:
And there resides in it true pride
With candid honour, side by side.
I love you (why should I disguise it?),
But I am someone else's wife,
To him I shall be true for life.'

48

She goes. He stands in desolation
As if by thunder struck. In what
A sudden tempest of sensation
His heart's ungovernably caught!
But then a clink of spurs resounded,
Tatiana's husband he encountered.
And, reader, now, in this mischance,
In this unhappy circumstance,
We'll leave my hero to his meeting
For long ... forever ... in his track
We've roamed around the world and back.
On land again, let's send our greeting
To each and all. So, now, hurrah!
It's high time (you'll agree), by far.

49

Whatever, reader, your opinion,
A friend or foe, I wish to part
With you today like a companion.
Farewell. Whatever you may chart
Among these careless lines, reflections –
Whether tumultuous recollections
Or light relief from labour's yoke,
The lively image, witty joke

Or the mistakes I've made in grammar –
God grant you find here just a grain
To warm the heart, to entertain,
To feed a dream, and cause a clamour
With journals and their clientele,
Upon which, let us part, farewell!

50

Goodbye, strange comrade, now forever,
And you, my true ideal – now gone,
Goodbye, my lively, long endeavour,
Though slender work. With you I've known
The things that every poet covets:
Oblivion, when the tempest buffets,
Sweet talk of friends. So many days
Have passed since in a dreamy haze
I first saw young Tatiana near me,
With her, Onegin – and when I
Looked through the magic crystal's eye,
I could not yet distinguish clearly
The distant reach of the domain
That my free novel would attain.

51

But of those friends who, meeting, listened
To those first strophes that I wrote . . .
Some are no more now, some are distant,
As Sadi[40] once said in a note.
They've missed the fully fledged Onegin,
And she, from whom the model's taken
For dear Tatiana, she is gone . . .
Oh, much by fate has been undone!

Blest who betimes has left life's revel,
Whose wine-filled glass he has not drained,
Who does not read right to the end
Life's still, as yet, unfinished novel,
But lets it go, as I do my
Onegin, and bid him goodbye.

FRAGMENTS OF
ONEGIN'S JOURNEY[1]

FOREWORD

The omitted stanzas gave rise to frequent reproofs and gibes (no doubt most just and witty). The author candidly confesses that he deleted from his novel an entire chapter describing Onegin's journey through Russia. It was incumbent on him to indicate this omitted chapter by means of dots or a numeral; but in order to avoid confusion he decided it would be better to mark the last chapter as number eight instead of nine, and to sacrifice one of its closing stanzas:

> It's time: for peace the pen is asking;
> Nine cantos done, and ninth the wave
> That lifts my boat and sets it basking
> Upon the joyous seashore, safe –
> Praise be to you, O nine Camenae,[2] etc.

P. A. Katenin (whom a fine poetic talent does not prevent from being also a subtle critic) remarked to us that this deletion, while perhaps advantageous for the reader, spoils the plan of the entire work, since, as a result, the transition from Tatiana the provincial miss to Tatiana the grande dame becomes too unexpected and unexplained – an observation revealing the experienced artist. The author himself felt the justice of this, but decided to leave out the chapter for reasons important to him and not to the public. Some fragments have been published; we give them here with several adjoining stanzas.

E. Onegin leaves Moscow for Nizhny Novgorod:

1

... In front of him,
Makaryev,[3] kicking up a shindy,
Seethes with its rich emporium:
Pearls by the Indian imported,
Wines by the European watered,
The breeder from the steppe-land speeds
To sell his herd of cast-off steeds;
The gamester wagers all his cash on
His card decks and obliging dice,
The squire brings daughters ripe in size,
His daughters come with last year's fashion,
Each bustles, lies enough for two –
A trading spirit rules right through.

2

Ennui!

Onegin travels to Astrakhan, and thence to the Caucasus.

3

He sees the wayward Terek,[4] scoring
Its banks in their abrupt descent,
In front of him an eagle soaring,
A standing deer with antlers bent;
A camel lies in rocky shadows.
And a Circassian's steed through meadows
Races; the sheep of Kalmuks graze
Round nomad tents; Onegin's gaze

Takes in the far Caucasian masses.
The way is opened: war defied
The country's natural divide,
The perils of its mountain passes;
Where the Kura, Aragva[5] whirled,
There were the Russian tents unfurled.[6]

4

Now, watchman of the desolation,
Beshtu,[7] hemmed in by hills, is seen,
Sharp-peaked, at its eternal station,
And there Mashuk, now turning green,
Pours healing streams from its recesses;
Around its magic brooklets presses
A pallid swarm of invalids,
The victims, some of martial deeds,
Others of piles or Aphrodite;
These sufferers hope to reinforce
Life's thread at this prodigious source:
Coquettes – to drown the notoriety
Of wicked years, and ancient men –
To bring back briefly youth again.

5

Immersed in bitter meditation,
Amidst this melancholy crew,
Onegin looks with lamentation
Upon the waters' steamy flow,
And thinks, with sadness overclouded:
Why has no bullet in me landed?
Why is it I'm not old, infirm,
Like him, poor taxman at his term?

Why is it I'm not paralytic
Like him, the clerk of Tula town?
Why don't I in my shoulder bone
Feel just the slightest bit rheumatic?
I'm young, o Lord, there's life in me:
What's there to come? Ennui, ennui!

    Onegin then visits Tauris:

6

You, land of the imagination:
Saw Pylades, Orestes[8] strive,
And Mithridates[9] take his life;
There Mickiewicz sang his passion[10]
And midst the coastal cliffs afar
Recalled his Lithuania.

7

How beautiful, when day is dawning,
To see you, shores of Tauris, when
My ship reflects the star of morning –
Thus first you came into my ken;
In bridal brilliance apparent,
The sky behind you, blue, transparent,
The masses of your mountains shone,
Villages, trees and valleys spun
A pattern spreading out before me.
And there, among the Tatar dens . . .
What ardour roused my sleeping sense!
What magic longing caught me, bore me
What yearning pressed my flaming heart![11]
But with the past, Muse, let me part.

8

Whatever feelings then lay hidden
Within me – now they are no more:
They went or changed, no longer bidden . . .
Peace unto you, alarms of yore!
It seemed it was the wild I needed,
The pearl-edged waves that flowed, receded,
The noise of sea, the rocks' cascade,
And my ideal of proud, young maid,
And nameless torment, tribulation . . .
Now other days, now other dreams,
My springtime's fancies, high-flown themes
You've quietened down, with resignation,
And into my poetic glass
Much water have I mixed, alas.

9

I need another kind of image:
A sandy, sloping eminence,
Two rowans and a little cottage,
A wicket gate, a broken fence,
The sky when greyish clouds are passing,
The straw before the thresh-barn massing,
A pond beneath dense willow trees
And ducklings doing as they please;
I'm fond now of the balalaika
And, at the tavern's door, the pack
Of drunkards stamping the trepak.[12]
Now my ideal's a housewife – like her,
It's peace alone that I desire,
'And cabbage soup, while I'm the squire.'[13]

10

When recently in rainy weather
I dropped into the cattle yard . . .
But fie on such prosaic blather,
The motley dross of Flemish art!
Was such my habit in my heyday?
O fountain at Bakhchisaray,[14] say!
Were such the thoughts your endless sound
Communicated to my mind,
When, watching you in silent wonder,
Zarema first appeared to me
Midst empty halls of luxury? . . .
Three years since then, and who should wander
Along my tracks, if not Eugene,
Recalling me, though long unseen.

11

I lived in dust-submerged Odessa . . .
There for a long time skies are clear,
Abundant trade that knows no leisure
Readies its sails for every sphere;
By Europe all things are invaded,
The South shines out in variegated
And lively multiformity.
The tongue of golden Italy
Resounds along the merry pavement,
Where our imperious Slav walks cheek-
By-jowl with Frenchman, Spaniard, Greek,
Armenian, ponderous Moldavian
And son of Egypt, Morali,[15]
Corsair, retired now from the sea.

12

Our friend Tumansky[16] has depicted
Odessa in resounding rhyme,
But partiality restricted
His observations at the time.
Arriving in the town, our poet,
Armed with lorgnette, set off to know it,
Alone, above the sea – and then,
Employing an enchanting pen,
Extolled the gardens of Odessa.
All that is well and good, except
That round about is naked steppe;
In some few spots a recent measure
Has forced young boughs on sultry days
To mitigate the solar rays.

13

But where now is my rambling story?
Inside Odessa's dust bowl, I
Might well have said its 'dirty quarry',
And that would not have been a lie.
For five, six weeks a year Odessa,
At Zeus's tempest-bringing pleasure,
Is flooded, blocked, its conduits burst,
Into the thickest mud immersed,
With houses sinking two feet under;
Only pedestrians on stilts
Dare breach the cumulative silts;
The coaches and the people flounder,
And oxen, horns inclined, replace
The horses with their feeble pace.

14

But hammers are already cracking
The stones, and soon the sunken town
Will have acquired a novel backing
As if with armour plated down.
However, in this moist Odessa
There's something missing to refresh her;
Why, water! What would you have thought?
Some reconstruction must be wrought . . .[17]
But really, this is no great sorrow,
Particularly, you'll agree,
When wine's imported duty-free.
There's Southern sun and sea tomorrow . . .
Where better, friends, to spend your time
Or find a more propitious clime?

15

Time was, no sooner had day risen,
Marked by the naval cannonry,
Than, running down with expedition,
I'd leave the steep shore for the sea.
Then, by the briny breakers freshened,
Smoking a pipe near incandescent,
Like Muslims in their paradise,
Coffee with Eastern grounds I'd prize,
And leave then for a stroll. Already,
The generous casino[18] hums;
Cups clash; the sleepy marker comes
On to the balcony, unsteady,
With broom in hand, while at the hall
Two merchants, meeting, make their call.

16

Look now – the square has put on motley.
All is alive: the people there,
On business or without, run hotly,
But most of them with some affair.
The merchant, child of cautious daring,
Tells from the ensigns how he's faring,
Whether he's favoured by the skies
With sails that he can recognize.
What novel wares from sundry nations
Have entered into quarantine?
Where are the promised casks of wine?
What news of plague and conflagrations?
Of famine or another war,
Or something new, but similar?

17

But we, young fellows, blithely standing
Alongside anxious merchants, had
Eyes only for the vessel landing,
That brought us oysters from Tsargrad.
Has it arrived? What joy, what pleasure!
Youth, avaricious beyond measure,
Flies off to swallow from the shell
The cloistered molluscs, live and well,
Besprinkling them with lemon lightly.
Noise, arguments – light wine is brought
Straight from the cellars to our board,
Where good Oton[19] serves us politely.
The hours fly by, while the account
Reaches unseen a grim amount.

18

But evening's blue already thickens,
The opera now calls to us,
Rossini, Europe's darling, beckons –
Th' intoxicating *Orpheus*.
To criticism inattentive,
Selfsame as ever, new, inventive,
He pours out tunes that effervesce,
Cascade and flow and incandesce,
They burn like youthful lovers' kisses
In flames of love, in luxury,
Or like the spurt and golden spray
Of an Aí when out it fizzes . . .
But, gentlemen, who can define
Do-re-mi-sol in terms of wine?

19

But are these all its delectations?
What of the quizzical lorgnette?
What of the backstage assignations?
The prima donna, the ballet?
The box where, in her beauty shining,
A trader's youthful wife,[20] reclining,
Disdainful and in languid pose,
Whom pressing throngs of slaves enclose?
She hears, hears not the cavatina,
Nor the entreaties or the jests,
Halfway with flattery expressed . . .
While just behind her in a corner
Her husband dozes, shouts 'encore',
Yawns – and begins again to snore.

20

At last there thunders the finale;
The noisy audience greets the night;
The square to which the people rally
Is lit by stars and lantern light.
Ausonia's[21] sons are gently singing
A playful tune that goes on ringing
Inside their heads and will not leave,
While we roar out the recitative.
But it is late. Odessa's sleeping;
The night is warm and mute and still.
The moon has risen, and a veil,
Diaphanously light, is draping
The sky. All's silent; save the roar
Of Black Sea waves upon the shore . . .

21

And so I lived then in Odessa . . .

CHAPTER X[1]

1

A ruler, timorous and wily,
A balding fop, of toil a foe,
Minion of Fame by chance entirely,
Reigned over us those years ago.[2]

....

2

We knew him not at all so regal,
When cooks, who were not ours, were sent
To pluck our double-headed eagle,
Where Bonaparte had pitched his tent.[3]

....

3

The storm of 1812 descended –
Who was our rock here, who our rod?
Was it the rage the people vented?
Winter, Barcláy[4] or Russia's God?

....

4

But God did help – murmurs abated,
And, shortly, by the force of things,
In Paris we had congregated
And Russia's Tsar was king of kings.[5]

....

5

And as he fattened,[6] life grew heavier,
O you, our stupid Russian folk,
Say, why for God's sake did you ever

....

6

Maybe, O shibboleth of the nation,
I'll dedicate an ode to you,
It seems, though, in anticipation
A high-born rhymester's done it, too.[7]

....

To Albion the seas are granted[8]

....

7

Maybe the fraud,[9] his rents forgetting,
Will move into a monastery,
Maybe Tsar Nicholas, regretting,
Will set Siberia's captives free[10]

....

Maybe they will repair the highways

....

8

This man of fate, through wars progressing,
Before whom Europe's kings would fawn,
This horseman, crowned with papal blessing,
Gone like a shadow of the dawn,
....
Exhausted on the rack of leisure[11]

9

The Pyrenees shook with foreboding,
Naples' volcano was astir,
The one-armed prince was up and nodding
From Kishinev to the Morea.
....
L's dagger . . . B's shadow[12]

10

I'll curb all comers with my people. –
Our Tsar said in the congress hall,
....
And does not give a damn about you,
You're Alexander's menial.[13]

11

Toy regiment of Peter-Titan,
A guard of old mustachios,
Whose fake protection of a tyrant
Betrayed him to his deadly foes.[14]

12

Russia again returned to quietness,
Still more the Tsar went revelling,
But sparks of quite another brightness,
Perhaps a long time smouldering,[15]
....

13

Foregathering at private meetings,
Over a Russian vodka, wine,
They would, reciprocating greetings,[16]
....

14

Grandiloquent and trenchant pleaders,
This group of friends would congregate
At either turbulent Nikita's
Or cautious Ilya's to debate.[17]
....

15

Mars, Bacchus, Venus were his pleasures:
Here Lunin with audacity
Put forward his decisive measures,[18]
And muttered in a reverie.
Noëls were brought and read by Pushkin,[19]
While melancholical Yakushkin,[20]
Had silently, it seemed, laid bare
A dagger meant to slay the Tsar.

With only Russia in his vision,
Pursuing his ideal, the lame
Turgenev[21] hearkened to their aim
And, hating slavery's oppression,
Predicted that this noble folk
Would free the peasants from their yoke.

16[22]

All this on the Neva, iced over;
But where much sooner shines the spring
On Kamenka[23] in shady cover
And on the hilltops of Tul'chin,[24]
Where Wittgenstein's detachments quartered,
On plains by the Dnieper watered
And on the steppeland of the Bug,
These things took on a different look.
There Pestel[25] . . . for the tyrants,
And a cool-headed general[26]
Gathered supporters to his call,
And Muryavyov,[27] to him inclining,
Hastened with strength and boldness to
See the uprising carried through.

17

At first, these plots, initiated
'Twixt a Lafitte and a Cliquot[28]
Were in a friendly tone debated
And the rebellious science was slow
To kindle a defiant passion,
All this was mere ennui and fashion,
The idleness of youthful minds,
Games that a grown-up scamp designs,

It seemed . . .
But gradually . . .
From cell to cell . . .
And soon . . . by a secret network
Russia . . .
Our Tsar was dozing . . .

Notes

Pushkin added a series of notes to his edition of *Eugene Onegin*. I have referred to several of these in the Notes below, but have not translated them as a whole because they include long quotations, often from secondary poets, which themselves would require further annotation, and would, I think, interest only a tiny minority of readers.

I am indebted to the commentaries on *Onegin* by Vladimir Nabokov, Yuri Lotman and N. L. Brodsky.

1. 'Steeped in vanity, he had even more the kind of pride that will accept good and bad actions with the same indifference – the result of a feeling of superiority, perhaps imaginary. (From a private letter.)' There is no known source for this quotation.

DEDICATION

1. Addressed to P. A. Pletnyov (1792–1865), man of letters and minor poet, in later years academician and rector of St Petersburg University. He met Pushkin in 1817 and remained one of his closest friends. From 1825 he was his principal publisher and, after the poet's death, his first biographer.

CHAPTER I

1. *And it hurries . . . Prince Vyazemsky*: The epigraph is from 'The First Snow' (1819), a poem by Pushkin's close friend Prince Pyotr Vyazemsky (1792–1878), mentioned several times in *Onegin* and appearing in person in Chapter VIII. The 'it' is 'youthful ardour', compared to the intoxication of a sleigh ride.
2. *Zeus*: Supreme god of the ancient Greek pantheon.

3. *Ruslan and Lyudmila*: (1820) A mock-epic and Pushkin's first major work. Pushkin signals his return to a light-hearted manner after a series of impassioned Romantic poems.

4. *But now the North's unsafe for me*: Pushkin's note 1 to the chapter reads: 'Written in Bessarabia', his initial place of exile.

5. *Madame ... passed on her trust*: Refugees from revolutionary France were employed as tutors by aristocratic families.

6. *the Summer Park*: The Summer Gardens, a fashionable park in St Petersburg.

7. *Juvenal*: (*c.* 42–*c.* 125 AD), Roman satirical poet, popular with the Decembrists (see Introduction) for his denunciations of despotism and depravity.

8. *the Aeneid*: Epic poem by Roman poet Virgil (70–19 BC).

9. *Homer*: Ancient Greek poet, somewhere between the twelfth and seventh centuries BC, supposed author of the *Iliad* and the *Odyssey*.

10. *Theocritus*: Ancient Greek poet of idylls, third century BC. Russian pre-Romantics, seeking a national alternative to Russian rococo, drew on Homer and Theocritus. Decembrist economists, on the other hand, dismissed the entire classical poetic tradition as of no practical use.

11. *Adam Smith*: Scottish economist (1723–90) who influenced the Decembrists.

12. *in the land ... The simple product*: A principal tenet of physiocrat economic theory, originating in eighteenth-century France, according to which national wealth was based on the '*produit net*' of agriculture.

13. *Ovid*: Roman poet (43 BC–16 AD), author of *Metamorphoses* and *The Art of Love*, with whom Pushkin felt a kinship during his exile. Ovid died in exile on the Black Sea.

14. *[9]*: The omitted stanzas are of three kinds: those written and dropped; those which Pushkin intended to write but never got round to; and fictitious ones in the ironic manner of Sterne, Byron and Hoffmann. Together they constitute an invisible subtext.

15. *Faublas*: A sixteen-year-old seducer of young wives in a picaresque novel by Louvet de Couvrai (1760–97). But none of the husbands in the novel can be described as 'cunning'.

16. *bolivar*: A silk hat with a wide, upturned brim, named after Simón Bolivar (1783–1830), the Latin American liberator and idol of European liberals in the 1820s and of Latin American revolutionaries today.

17. *Bréguet*: A repeater watch, invented by Parisian watchmaker

Abraham Louis Bréguet (1747–1823). A spring mechanism allowed the watch, while shut, to strike the hour or minute. A real dandy would not have carried one.

18. *'Away, away'*: The postilion's cry to pedestrians.

19. *Talon's*: A restaurant on the Nevsky Prospekt owned by a Frenchman until 1825.

20. *Kaverin*: Pyotr Kaverin (1794–1855), hussar and duellist, school friend and companion of Pushkin during his early Petersburg years, student at Göttingen (1810–11) and Decembrist.

21. *comet wine*: Champagne of vintage comet year 1811.

22. *bloody roast beef*: Fashionable in the early decades of the nineteenth century.

23. *Strasbourg pie, that keeps forever*: Made from goose liver and imported in tins, therefore 'kept forever'. Tinned food was invented during the Napoleonic wars.

24. *ananas*: Pineapple, an expensive taste throughout the nineteenth century.

25. *Limburg's cheese's living mass*: Sharp, strong, soft and runny Belgian cheese, hence perhaps the epithet 'living' or, alternatively, because of the 'living dust' of microbes that covered it.

26. *liberty's admirers*: The Russian has: 'Where everyone, breathing liberty', a Gallicism from *'respirer l'air de la liberté'*. At the Decembrist rising, the poet Ryleyev remarked: 'We are breathing freedom.'

27. *Cleopatra, Phaedra ... Moëna*: It is unclear what work Cleopatra figured in. Phaedra: heroine of an opera adapted from Racine's eponymous tragedy. Moëna: heroine of Ozerov's tragedy *Fingal*.

28. *Fonvizin*: Denis Fonvizin (1745–92), author of *The Minor*, a satirical play about cruelty, smugness and ignorance.

29. *Knyazhnin*: Yakov Knyazhnin (1742–91), imitator of French tragedies and comedies.

30. *Ozerov*: Vladislav Ozerov (1769–1816), author of five tragedies in the French style, including *Fingal* (note 27 above), considered 'very mediocre' by Pushkin, who put his success down to the acting of Yekaterina Semyonova, whom he regarded highly.

31. *Katenin*: Pavel Katenin (1792–1853), playwright, critic and Decembrist, translated Corneille's *Le Cid*, firing Decembrist ideals. See Chapter I, stanza 18.

32. *Shakhovskoy*: Prince Alexander Shakhovskoy (1777–1846), theatre director and author of comedies satirizing contemporary writers.

33. *Didelot*: Charles Louis Didelot (1767–1837), well-known ballet master in St Petersburg.

34. *Terpsichore*: Ancient Greek goddess of dance.

35. *Istomina*: Avdotya Istomina (1799–1848), prima ballerina of Petersburg ballet with whom Pushkin was smitten, pupil of Didelot.

36. *Aeolus*: Ancient Greek god of wind.

37. *even Didelot's boring stuff*: Pushkin in his note 5 comments: 'A feature of chilled feeling, worthy of Childe-Harold. Didelot's ballets are filled with a liveliness of imagination and unusual charm. One of our romantic writers found in them far more poetry than in the whole of French literature.' This 'romantic writer' was Pushkin himself.

38. *Tsargrad*: Old Russian name for Constantinople.

39. *Perfumes*: A fashionable novelty at the beginning of the nineteenth century.

40. *Rousseau*: Jean-Jacques Rousseau (1712–78), French writer and philosopher. In his note 6 Pushkin quotes at length from the description in Rousseau's *Confessions* of Grimm's toiletry.

41. *Grimm*: Melchior Grimm (1723–1807), French encyclopedist of German extraction.

42. *Chaadaev*: Pyotr Chaadaev (1794–1856), dandy and libertarian thinker, later a mystic, influenced the young Pushkin, famous for his later *Philosophical Letters*, contrasting Russian history unfavourably with the West, with which Pushkin disagreed. The journal carrying the first *Letter* was suppressed, Chaadaev being declared insane and placed under house arrest.

43. *pantalons, frac and gilet*: These were relatively new items of clothing at the beginning of the nineteenth century as yet without Russian names.

44. *Chevalier Gardes*: A privileged regiment of heavy cavalry created under Paul I to counterbalance the already existing Horse Guards regiment. Chevaliers Gardes were distinguished by their tall height and embroidered uniforms. However, in a manuscript note Pushkin mentions that in fact they wore court dress and shoes, but he included the spurs to give the picture a poetic touch.

45. *Diana*: Virgin goddess of the moon in ancient Rome.

46. *Flora*: Ancient Roman goddess of spring and flowers.

47. *Elvina*: Conventional name in erotic poetry of the time.

48. *Armida*: Chief heroine of the epic poem *La Gerusalemme liberata* (*Liberated Jerusalem*, 1580) by Torquato Tasso (1544–95), here meaning an enchantress.

49. *Okhta*: An outlying region of St Petersburg, populated by Finns supplying the capital's dairy needs. The 'Okhta girl' is a milkmaid.

50. *vasisdas*: A window-pane. 'Vasisdas' has been taken to be a corruption either of *fortochka*, a ventilation-pane used in Russian windows, or of the French word *vasistas* (a small spy-window), which in turn is a corruption of the German *was ist das?* Pushkin keeps the more German spelling no doubt because the baker is German.

51. *khandra*: Russian for 'chondria', as in 'hypochrondia'.

52. *Childe Harold*: The disillusioned and languid hero of Byron's first great narrative poem, *Childe Harold's Pilgrimage* (1813), which brought him fame.

53. *boston*: A member of the whist family. Russian boston differs only slightly from ordinary boston.

54. *bon ton*: The Russian has 'higher tone', meaning well-bred conversation and manners. A near English equivalent would be 'good form'.

55. *Say and Bentham*: Jean-Baptiste Say (1767–1832), French publicist and economist, follower of Ricardo and Adam Smith, author of *Traité d'économie politique* (*A Treatise on Political Economy*, 1803). Jeremy Bentham (1748–1832), liberal English publicist and jurist.

56. *Capricious ladies ... spleen*: In note 7 Pushkin remarks: 'The whole of this ironic strophe is nothing other than a subtle form of praise for our fair compatriots. So Boileau, in the guise of reproach, praises Louis XIV. Our ladies combine enlightenment with amiability, and strict purity of morals with that Eastern charm that so captivated Mme de Staël (see *Dix ans d'exil*).' Posthumously published in 1818, the latter work describes de Staël's visit to Russia in 1812.

57. *How often ... bright*: Pushkin's note 8 refers the reader to Nikolai Gnedich's (1784–1833) idyllic poem 'The Fishermen' (1822) for its 'charming description' of the Petersburg night, from which he quotes at length.

58. *the Poet*: An ironic reference, underlined by the capital 'P' and the archaic Russian spelling, to Mikhail Muravyov (1757–1807), an insignificant poet and founder of Russian Sentimentalism. In his note 9, Pushkin quotes the lines of Muravyov's poem 'To the Goddess of the Neva', from which he lifts the phrase 'leaning on the granite'.

59. *Millionaya*: A street in Petersburg, alluding to Katenin's habit of

returning from the theatre at this hour to his regimental barracks on Millionaya Street.

60. *Brenta*: River with Venice at its delta.

61. *Albion's proud poetry*: Byron's poetry.

62. *Petrarch*: Francesco Petrarca (1304–74), Italian poet.

63. *Above the sea, forever roaming*: Pushkin's note 10 has: 'Written in Odessa.' It was from here that Pushkin sought to escape from Russia.

64. *my Africa*: In his note 11 Pushkin refers the reader to the first edition of the chapter, where he provides an extended footnote on his African forebears.

65. *Salgir*: A river in the Crimea. The captive maids are the harem girls of Pushkin's narrative poem *The Fountain at Bakhchisaray* (1824). The 'maid of the mountain' is the Circassian heroine of his poem *The Captive of the Caucasus* (1822). In Chapter VIII of *Onegin* he reviews his literary heroines up to the point where they transmogrify into Tatiana.

CHAPTER II

1. *Endowed with Göttingenian soul*: Göttingen university, where Lensky studied, was one of the most liberal universities, not just in Germany, but in Europe as a whole. Situated on Hanoverian territory, it was subject to English law. The future Decembrists Pyotr Kaverin (see Chapter I, stanza 16, and note 20) and N. I. Turgenev (see Chapter X, stanza 15, and note 21) studied there.

2. *Kant*: Immanuel Kant (1724–1804), German philosopher, author of three Critiques – of *Pure Reason, Practical Reason* and *Judgement*. His emphasis on imagination and genius in the third Critique influenced the Romantic movement in Germany and beyond.

3. *vessel*: The Church Slavonic use of this term, which adds to the heightened language of this stanza, can mean 'weapon', which is what is meant here.

4. *Schiller, Goethe*: Friedrich Schiller (1759–1805), German poet, philosopher, historian and dramatist. His early plays *Die Räuber* (*The Robbers*, 1781) and *Kabale und Liebe* (*Intrigue and Love*, 1784) and his idealist poetry fired the Romantics throughout Europe. He later joined Goethe in Weimar to promote a classical aesthetic. Johann Wolfgang von Goethe (1749–1832), German poet, dramatist, novelist and scientist. His masterpiece *Faust* and his novel *Wilhelm Meisters Lehrjahre* (*Wilhelm Meister's*

Apprenticeship, 1795–6) strongly influenced the Romantics in Germany, although he came to see himself (with Schiller) as a defender of classical values. Pushkin's knowledge of German literature was largely drawn from Mme de Staël's *De l'Allemagne* (*On Germany*, 1813), which put a Romantic gloss on Kant, Schiller and Goethe. His ability to read German was very limited.

5. *Richardson*: Samuel Richardson (1689–1761), English novelist, author of *Pamela or Virtue Rewarded* (1740), *Clarissa Harlowe* (1748) and *Sir Charles Grandison* (1754).

6. *A Lovelace for a Grandison*: Respectively villain of *Clarissa Harlowe* and hero of *Sir Charles Grandison* (see note 5 above).

7. *She shaved the conscripts' foreheads*: Shaving foreheads was the way of marking out recruits for the army, thereby getting rid of unwanted serfs, who were torn away from their families and often had to serve for life.

8. *shed tears . . . buttercups*: A way of atoning for sins: the number of teardrops represents the number of sins.

9. *kvas*: Russian national soft drink (sometimes mildly fermented), usually made of leavened rye, dough or rye bread with malt. In other varieties honey or fruit is used.

10. *a second crown*: The first crown is the wedding crown.

11. *barin*: Squire or landowner.

12. *penates*: (Latin) guardian deities of the household.

13. *Ochakov medal*: Ochakov, on the Black Sea, was seized from the Turks in 1788 by Suvorov, under whom Larin served. The commemorative medal was given to all officers taking part in the campaign. Brigadier (a general's rank) Larin might have expected the more illustrious 'order'. Pushkin might have wanted thereby to keep Larin ordinary.

14. *Lethe*: River of fortgetfulness in Greek mythology.

15. *Aonia's maids*: The Muses in Greek mythology. Aeonia was a region of ancient Boeotia, containing the mountains of Helicon and Cithaeron, sacred to the Muses.

16. *will pat the old man's laurel crown*: Alongside the ignoramus, Pushkin addresses his future devotee. In the 'old man' Pushkin optimistically envisages his own future. A Latin teacher at Pushkin's *lycée*, when introducing a classical text, would always remark: 'Let's pat the old man on the head.'

CHAPTER III

1. *Elle était fille* . . . *Malfilâtre*: 'She was a girl, she was in love.' A line from *Narcisse, ou l'île de Venus* (*Narcissus, or the Island of Venus*, 1768), a posthumous poem in four cantos by the second-rate French poet Jacques Charles Louis Clinchamp de Malfilâtre (1733–67), probably taken by Pushkin from Laharpe's anthology of ancient and modern literature used at Pushkin's *lycée*.

2. *Jam in small dishes*: Home-made preserves – cherry, raspberry, strawberry, gooseberry, red and blackcurrant – were presented to guests in small glass dishes on a tray. In a variant Pushkin has 'with but one spoon for all'. The guests would transfer their helpings (by means of that spoon) on to their respective saucers and then would eat the jam with their teaspoons or mix it with their tea.

3. *board*: Pushkin omitted the rest of the stanza in the final version, though it exists in his fair copy.

4. *Svetlana*: Heroine of Vasily Zhukovsky's ballad of the same name (1812). Zhukovsky (1783–1852) was Russia's outstanding Romantic poet, a friend and protector of Pushkin and a mentor of Nicholas I's son and heir. *Svetlana* was a free adaptation of Gottfried August Bürger's (1747–94) ballad *Lenore* (1773).

5. *The lover of Julie Wolmar*: St Preux, hero of Rousseau's *Julie, ou la Nouvelle Héloïse* (*Julie, or the New Héloïse*, 1761). Julie and St Preux are lovers, but only until she marries and assumes her husband's name, Wolmar.

6. *Malek Adhel*: Hero of *Mathilde, ou Mémoires tirés de l'histoire des croisades* (*Mathilde or the Crusades*, 1805), a novel by Sophie Cottin (1774–1807), described by Pushkin in his note as 'mediocre'. Malek Adel is a Muslim general at the time of the Third Crusade who falls in love with Princesse Mathilde, sister of Richard Lionheart.

7. *de Linar*: 'Hero of baroness Krüdener's delightful tale,' notes Pushkin. The tale in question is *Valérie, ou Lettres de Gustave de Linar à Ernest de G.* (*Valérie, or Letters from Gustave de Linar to Ernest de G.*, 1803). Mme von Krüdener (1764–1824) was a German novelist and mystic who wrote in French. De Linar, a dark-haired and violent young Swede, is the unrequited lover of Countess Valérie (probably from Livonia), who, like Julie in *La Nouvelle Héloïse* (see note 5 above), remains faithful to her older husband. She marries at fourteen and meets de Linar at sixteen.

8. *Werther*: Hero of Goethe's *Die Leiden des jungen Werthers* (*The Sorrows of Young Werther*, 1774). Werther commits suicide after failing to win the love of Lotte, who is married to his friend.

9. *Grandison*: Hero of Richardson's *Sir Charles Grandison* (1754).

10. *Delphine*: Eponymous heroine of Mme de Staël's novel *Delphine* (1802). It has been suggested, but not accepted, that the Delphine mentioned by Pushkin belongs to a story by Marmontel, *L'Ecole de l'amitié* (*School of Friendship*, 1792), translated in 1822 by Nikolai Karamzin (1766–1826), an important predecessor of Pushkin. In Mme. de Staël's novel Delphine is a widow of twenty-one whose admirer she gives up out of consideration for his wife.

11. *Clarissa*: Heroine of Richardson's *Clarissa Harlowe* (1748).

12. *The British Muse's tales*: Romanticism was in Russia largely taken to be an English trend in European literature.

13. *the pensive vampire*: Pushkin comments in his note: 'A tale wrongly attributed to Lord Byron.' During a stay in Switzerland in 1816 Byron, Shelley, Mary Shelley and Byron's physician Polidori competed in writing horror stories of which the most successful and famous was Mary Shelley's *Frankenstein*. Byron composed a fragment, *The Vampyre*, which Polidori later turned into a novel (1819).

14. *Melmoth*: Pushkin's note: 'Melmoth, Maturin's work of genius.' Charles Robert Maturin (1782–1824), an Irish clergyman, wrote *Melmoth the Wanderer* (1820), a long Satanic horror tale.

15. *The Wandering Jew*: The legend of the Wandering Jew was common at the time. Pushkin's sources are probably Mathew Lewis's (1775–1818) *The Monk* (1796) and Jan Potocki's (1761–1815) enormous novel *The Manuscript Found in Saragossa*, published between 1803 and 1814.

16. *the Corsair*: Hero of Byron's poem of the same name.

17. *Sbogar*: Hero of Charles Nodier's (1780–1844) *Jean Sbogar* (1818). Sbogar is the Dalmatian chief of a robber band who redistribute wealth in favour of the 'common good'.

18. *Coquettes . . . more assuredly*: An imitation of the French poet Evariste de Parny's 'La Main' ('The Hand'). Parny (1753–1814) was renowned for his elegant love poetry. See lines 13–14 of stanza 29.

19. *The Well-Meaner*: Pushkin's note reads: 'A journal edited by the late A. Izmailov in a rather slipshod way.' Pushkin and his friends treated the journal as a joke and privately read line 4 as 'With a phallus in their hand'.

20. *seminarist ... in yellow shawl*: In this case a seminarist is a learned woman.

21. *Bogdanovich*: Ippolit Fedorovich Bogdanovich (1743–1803), poet, author of *Dushen'ka* (1783–9), based on the story of Cupid and Psyche; regarded as the founder of 'light poetry' and valued by Pushkin for opening up poetry to popular speech. His influence on Pushkin is felt in *Ruslan and Lyudmila* (1820).

22. *tender Parny's*: Evariste Désiré Desforges, Chevalier de Parny (1753–1814) French poet. He used the word *tendre* profusely in his elegies.

23. *Bard of The Feasts*: Yevgeny Abramovich Baratynsky (1800–1844), an outstanding poet of Pushkin's period. *The Feasts* was written in Finland in 1820, where he was serving as a private in the army, having been expelled from military school for theft. It evokes the ebullient days spent in St Petersburg in 1819, when he got to know Pushkin. But he was more famed as an elegiac poet.

24. *Der Freischütz*: Opera by Carl Maria von Weber (1786–1826), a popular import when Pushkin was writing his third chapter.

25. *The rosy seal*: A round piece of sticky paper used to seal envelopes.

26. *Song of the Girls*: Invented by Pushkin, but adapted from folk songs he heard on his family estate at Mikhailovskoye. This is a wedding song where the bridegroom is symbolized by cherries and the bride by berries. It has the double effect of keeping the girls from eating the fruit and adding to Tatiana's situation.

CHAPTER IV

1. *La morale ... Necker*: 'Morality is in the nature of things.' Jacques Necker (1732–1804) was a politician and financier, minister in Louis XVI's government at the beginning of the French Revolution and father of Mme de Staël, who quotes Pushkin's epigraph in her *Considérations sur les Principaux Evénements de la Révolution Française* (*Considerations on the Principal Events of the French Revolution*, 1818).

2. *Chateaubriand*: François-René de Chateaubriand (1768–1848), French Romantic writer and politician, author of the novel *René* (1802).

3. *Qu'écrirez-vous ... Annette*: 'What will you write on these tablets?' ... 'Ever yours, Annette.'

4. *Tolstoy*: Count Fyodor Petrovich Tolstoy (1783–1875), artist.

5. *a madrigal*: In this context is a complimentary poem written for society albums.

6. *And, river-like . . . verities*: A rare example of a two-rhyme octet resembling the Italian sonnet, which I render imperfectly – ababaabb. A similar, but less exact version is to be found in Chapter V, stanza 10.

7. *Yazykov*: Nikolay Mikhailovich Yazykov (1803–47), Romantic poet.

8. *an awesome critic*: The critic is Wilhelm Küchelbecker (1797–1846), who in an essay of 1824 denounced the elegy and praised the ode.

9. *The Other Version*: The reference is to *Chuzhoy tolk* (1795), a satirical verse narrative by Ivan Dmitriyev (1760–1837). The title may be translated as 'The Other Opinion' or 'The Opinion of Others'. The poem ridicules the overblown style of the ode, attributing mercenary aims to its authors. The satirist and the lyric poet are characters in the poem.

10. *36*: Stanza 36 was published only in the separate edition of Chapters IV and V.

11. *Gulnare*: Byron. Gulnare is the heroine of *The Corsair*.

12. *Then drank . . . dressed*: Omitted in the final text. After 'And dressed' there follows in Pushkin's fair copy: 'but you'd not care to don/ The article that he put on'.

13. (*You've guessed . . . 'petals'*: Pushkin parodies a hackneyed rhyme which he himself used elsewhere: morozy/rozy, frosts/ roses. The suggestion is perhaps reddening of the cheeks in the cold. The rhyme is irreproducible. Having used settles/petals before, in Chapter 1, stanza 16, I decided to use it again here, hoping that the reader might remember it. In neither case is it a hackneyed rhyme, but in both cases the context is frost. Compare a similar rhyme in Chapter IV, stanza 44, where Pushkin rhymes 'sladost' with 'mladost', sweetness/youth: 'Dreams, dreams! Where is your sweetness?/Where is its stock rhyme, youth?' which I have translated, this time more successfully, I think, as: 'Where are my dreams, the dreams I cherished?/What rhyme now follows, if not 'perished' since 'cherished' and 'perished' have a more hackneyed ring in English. I have used the same rhyme in Chapter VII, stanza 28. What Pushkin is getting at in both cases is the paucity of rhymes in the Russian poetry of his time.

14. *Pradt and Scott*: Dominique de Pradt (1759–1837), French political writer and priest to Napoleon; later a liberal under the Restoration. Sir Walter Scott (1771–1832), Scottish poet and

father of the historical novel, who influenced Pushkin in the writing of his own historical novel *The Captain's Daughter* (1836). Pushkin read Scott in French translations.

15. *Aï*: Aï or Ay is the name of a town in the Marne Department of Northern France, where this champagne originates.

16. *'Between the wolf and dog'*: A translation of *entre chien et loup*, meaning dusk or the time of day when it is too dark for a shepherd to distinguish his dog from a wolf.

17. *Lafontaine*: Not the fabulist Jean de Lafontaine, but August Lafontaine (1759–1831), a mediocre German writer, 'author of numerous family novels' (Pushkin's note), popular in Russia at the end of the eighteenth century.

CHAPTER V

1. *Never know . . . Zhukovsky*: Epigraph from concluding lines of Zhukovsky's ballad *Svetlana* (1812), which was considered a model of Romantic poetry based on folklore. Svetlana shadows Tatiana in this chapter.

2. *kibitka*: A hooded carriage.

3. *One poet*: In a note Pushkin refers to Vyazemsky and his poem 'The First Snow' (1819). The epigraph from Chapter I is likewise taken from Vyazemsky's poem.

4. *Finnish Maid*: A reference to a fragment of Baratynsky's poem *Eda* (1825).

5. *With curious gaze . . . tomcat chants*: Dish-divining took place at Yuletide and Twelfth Night. Divining times were divided between 'holy evenings' (25–31 December) and 'fearful evenings' (1–6 January). Tatiana chose the second period. Girls and women dropped rings into a dish containing water that was then covered with a cloth. As each is removed, a song is sung. The one sung for Tatiana predicts unhappiness and death. Tomcat songs foretell marriage, as Pushkin remarks in a note. In these the tomcat invites the she-cat to join him on his comfortable stove.

6. *training a mirror on the moon*: Another method of divination whereby a future husband was supposed to appear in the mirror's reflection.

7. *Agafon*: In this context a comical peasant's name, derived from the Greek Agathon. As Pushkin points out in his note 13 to Chapter II, concerning his choice of Tatiana's name, 'sweet-sounding' Greek names are only used by the common people.

Asking the name of the first pedestrian Tatiana comes across is another ritual for discovering the name of her future intended.

8. *fear assailed Tatiana . . . Felt fear as well*: In her dream Svetlana, heroine of Zhukovsky's ballad (see above), conjures up her lover only to be carried off by him to his grave. This reference presages Tatiana's nightmare.

9. *We won't tell fortunes all night through*: See Chapter IV, note 6 on the two-rhyme octet in Italian sonnets.

10. *Her silken girdle she unknotted*: Unknotting her girdle is a magical act like taking off a crucifix. It is an invitation to the secret world of superstition. Russians would often wear a belt in the bathhouse to ward off evil spirits.

11. *Lel*: Artificial god of love derived by eighteenth-century writers from chants and cries associated with wedding ceremonies (*lyuli*, *lel'*, *lelyo*).

12. *Ladies' Fashion*: The full title is *Journal of Ladies' Fashions* and refers to the French publication *Journal des dames et des modes* (1797–1838), which set the fashions throughout Europe. Tatiana, as Pushkin points out in Chapter III, stanza 26, line 6, did not read Russian journals, nor did a specific women's fashion journal exist in Russia.

13. *Martin Zadek*: A fictitious person probably invented in Switzerland in the eighteenth century. His book of prophecies and divinations, the impressive title of which is too long to reproduce here, was translated from German into Russian and published in three separate editions (1814, 1821, 1827).

14. *Malvina*: A novel by Mme Cottin (1773–1807).

15. *Petriads*: Pushkin gives this ironic, high-sounding name to the various mediocre poems on Peter the Great current at the time.

16. *Marmontel*: Jean-François Marmontel (1723–99), French author; volume 3 of his complete works, all of which Pushkin possessed, contained his *Contes moraux* (*Moral Tales*).

17. *her crimson hands extending*: Pushkin comments in his note 34: 'A parody of well-known lines by Lomonosov: Dawn with crimson hand/From morning's tranquil waters'. These are the opening lines of a Lomonosov ode celebrating Empress Elizabeth's ascent to the throne. Pushkin's parody recalls the discussion of the ode in Chapter IV, stanza 33. Lomonosov's 'crimson hand' derives from Homer's 'rosy-fingered dawn'. M. V. Lomonosov (1711–65) was a scientist, poet, creator of the modern literary language and founder of Moscow University.

18. *britska*: A light carriage.

19. *Pustyakov*: Most of the names in this stanza are farcical, largely
      deriving from the comedies of Fonvizin (see note 28 to Chapter I).
      Pustyakov means Trifle, Gvozdin Basher, Skotinin Brute, Petush-
      kov Rooster or Cockahoop. Buyanov (Rowdy) is the hero of a
      skittish poem *The Dangerous Neighbour* by Pushkin's uncle
      Vasily Pushkin (1770–1830). This allows his nephew to intro-
      duce Buyanov here as his cousin.

20. *Kharlikov*: Another comic name meaning 'Throttle'.

21. *Réveillez-vous, belle endormie*: 'Awake, sleeping beauty.'

22. *pie*: The pie or pirog was either a meat or cabbage pie and
      traditional for a nameday feast.

23. *blanc-manger*: Nabokov writes in his Commentary: 'blanc-
      manger (pronounced as in French): This almond-milk jelly (an
      old French and English sweet, not to be confused with our
      modern 'blancmange') might be artificially coloured. Its presence
      (as well as the presence of Russian champagne) at Dame Larin's
      festive table stressed both the old-world style of her household
      and a comparative meagreness of means.

24. *Tsimlyansky*: A sparkling wine from Tsimlyanskaya Stanitsa, a
      Cossack settlement on the Don.

25. *Zizi*: Zizi or Yevpraksia Vulf (1809–83) was the youngest daugh-
      ter of the large Osipov family headed by Praskovia Osipov,
      widow of Nikolay Vulf and Ivan Osipov. The Osipovs were
      Pushkin's nearest neightbours during his exile at Mikhailovskoye
      (1824–6). He courted fifteen-year-old Zizi and several other mem-
      bers of the clan. Later, in 1829, the two briefly became lovers.

26. *omber*: A card game of Spanish origin, popular in Europe in the
      seventeenth and eighteenth centuries.

27. *Albani*: Francesco Albani (1578–1660), Italian painter popular
      in the eighteenth century.

28. *'I'll go no more a-roving*: I have allowed myself a quote from
      Byron (1788–1824), since he is omnipresent in the text, from his
      poem 'So, we'll go no more a-roving'.

CHAPTER VI

1. *La, sotto ... non dole*: 'There, where the days are cloudy and
      short, A race is born for whom death is not painful.' A quotation
      from Petrarch's *In vita di Laura*, Canzone XXVIII, which misses
      out the middle line: 'Nemica naturalmente di pace' ('By nature
      the enemy of peace'). The omission allows the quotation to refer
      more easily to Pushkin's own generation.

2.   *To die from him will be delightful*: Love for a villain was a common theme in contemporary Romantic literature and folk-lore (cf. Maturin's *Melmoth the Wanderer*).

3.   *Hetman*: Headman or captain, from the Polish *hetman*.

4.   *He's even honest ... every stage*: Quotations from Voltaire (1694–1778): 'et même devint honnête homme' (*Candide*, 1759); '. . . combien le siècle se perfectionne' (opening of Canto 4 of *La Guerre Civile de Genève* ((*Civil War in Geneva*)) 1768).

5.   *Regulus*: Roman general Marcus Atilius Regulus (d. *c*.250 BC), captured by the Carthaginians and sent to Rome with harsh terms of peace. Once there, he advised the Senate to continue the war and returned to Carthage, as he had promised, to face execution.

6.   *chez Véry*: Pushkin's note 37: A Parisian restaurateur.

7.   *Sed alia tempora*: Latin: 'But times are different.'

8.   *Where bird cherry, acacia climb*: Nabokov, with customary botanical expertise, translates 'bird cherry' as 'racemosa' and 'acacia' as 'pea tree'. He finds 'racemosa' more exact than 'bird cherry' and points out that the 'acacia' of northern Russia (where the story takes place) is imported from Asia, has yellow flowers and is therefore not a true acacia, but a 'pea tree'. (The more familiar acacia of southern Russia has a white blossom.) Nabokov refers to the 'yellow' epithet in the following couplet by Konstantin Batyushkov (1787–1855), which Pushkin is parodying:

> In the shade of milky racemosas
> And golden-glistening pea trees
> (Nabokov's translation)

He may be right, but I have preferred the more recognizable 'bird cherries' and 'acacias'. Batyushkov (1787–1855) was one of Pushkin's predecessors from whom he learned standards of harmony and precision (see Introduction, p. xii).

9.   *planting cabbages, like Horace*: 'Planting cabbages' is taken from the French *planter des (ses) choux*, meaning 'to cultivate a rural life', which Horace lauded on his withdrawal from Rome to a country estate given to him by Gaius Cilnius Maecenas, adviser to the emperor Augustus.

10. *cartel*: A written challenge which the duellist's second delivers to the former's opponent. Lensky's second is Zaretsky.

11. *And there it is – public opinion*: Pushkin's note 38: 'A verse of

Griboyedov's.' The verse comes from the comedy *Woe from Wit* (finished, but not published, in 1824) by Alexander Griboyedov (1795–1829) in which the hero, Chatsky, is hounded by the rumour that he is mad. Only fragments of the play were published during the author's lifetime. The whole play, still with cuts, appeared posthumously in 1833. Pushkin knew it from manuscripts which were widely circulated. The fact that Pushkin has not italicized the quotation means that he has assimilated it to his own viewpoint rather than treating it as a comment from outside.

12. *A temple or a thigh to claim*: The duellist would aim at his opponent's leg if he wished to satisfy his honour with a simple wound. He would aim at his head if he wished to kill him.

13. *[15, 16]*: The omitted stanzas, 15 and 16, deal with the theme of jealousy.

14. *Delvig*: Baron Anton Delvig (1798–1831), a minor poet, one of Pushkin's closest friends and a classmate at the *lycée*.

15. *his verse . . . ready for your gaze*: Every phrase of Lensky's poem is a stereotype of contemporary elegiac poetry, including Pushkin's own early verse, and translations from French and German poetry. Nevertheless, as elsewhere in the novel, parody blends with genuine feeling. The 'arrow' in line 9 is not a poetic synonym for 'bullet', but a conventional literary euphemism for death.

16. *Romantic*: By 'Romantic' Pushkin meant something more full-blooded and realistic, as he explains in his preface to his historical drama *Boris Godunov*. 'Obscurely' and 'limply' are terms used by Pushkin's friend the poet Wilhelm Kükhelbeker (1797–1846) in his attack on elegiac poetry.

17. *Lepage's fatal tubes*: Jean Lepage (1779–1822) was a Parisian gunsmith.

18. *The pistols . . . to the place*: A Lepage pistol had six edges on the outside of the barrel; the inside was smooth. Powder was poured into the barrel through the opening and secured with a wad. The bullets were inserted with the help of a mallet and ramrod. The flint, which was held in place by a special screw, was raised and tiny grains of powder were poured on to the pan, a steel shelf near an opening in the breech. The powder would burst into flame when struck and ignite the powder charge inside the barrel, causing the bullet to be fired. One of the seconds would load the pistols, while the other observed him.

19. *To call his people*: Presumably inaccuracy on the part of Pushkin, since Onegin has brought no men with him, only Guillot.

20. *[38]*: This omitted stanza reinforces the previous one by suggesting that Lensky might have become a Kutuzov (the Russian general who defeated Napoleon), a Nelson, a Napoleon in exile or a Ryleyev (Pushkin's Decembrist friend) executed by Nicholas I on the gallows.

21. *But, reader ... monument is laid*: This stanza is written in a traditional elegiac mode. Lensky is buried here because, as a duellist, his grave is not allowed in consecrated ground.

22. *And wonders: 'How did Olga suffer?'*: It is Pushkin who is doing the wondering, since the townswoman has no idea who Olga, Tatiana and Onegin are.

23. *cherished ... perished*: Pushkin's stock rhyme here is in Russian 'sladost'/'mladost', 'sweetness'/'youth' (he employs an archaic word for 'youth'). I have substituted 'cherish'/'perish' because these are hackneyed Romantic terms in English and are often used by Pushkin.

24. *my thirtieth year*: Pushkin was twenty-eight when he wrote this stanza.

25. *In that intoxicating ... together now*: Pushkin points out in his note 40 that in the first edition of the novel the last two lines of stanza 46 were different and linked with another stanza, 47, all of which he quotes. This version reinforces the anger and satire of the previous stanza:

Stanza 46, lines 13–14:

Midst swaggerers bereft of soul,
Midst fools who shine in every role,

Stanza 47

Midst children, crafty and faint-hearted,
Spoiled and alive to every ruse,
Ludicrous villains, dull, outsmarted
And judges, captious and obtuse,
Midst the coquettes, devout and fervent,
Midst those who play the part of servant,
Midst modish scenes that daily hail
Polite, affectionate betrayal;
Midst the forbidding dispensations
Of cruel-hearted vanity,
Midst the banal inanity

> Of schemes, of thoughts and conversations,
> In that intoxicating slough,
> Where, friends, we bathe together now.

The last two lines are the same as the final couplet of the present stanza 46.

CHAPTER VII

1. *Dmitriyev ... Baratynsky ... Griboyedov*: The first epigraph is from Ivan Dmitriev's (1760–1837) poem *The Liberation of Moscow* (1795), the second from Baratynsky's *The Feasts*, the third from Griboyedov's *Woe from Wit*. Dmitriev's poem is an official ode. Baratynsky's gives an ironic representation of private mores. Griboyedov's play, banned by the censor, is a biting satire on Moscow social life. Together they symbolize three contradictory aspects of contemporary Moscow.

2. *Lyovshin*: Vasily Lyovshin (1746–1826), a Tula landowner and prolific author of a vast range of subjects. Known in the 1820s for his books *Flower Gardens and Vegetable Gardens* and *A Manual of Agriculture* (1802–4). The school's 'fledglings' are gentry and country landowners.

3. *Priam*: Last king of Troy, a venerable and kind ruler.

4. *'tomfoolery'*: A simple card game, played today in Russia mainly by children.

5. *a cast-iron statuette ... hat*: Certain to be Napoleon in classic pose.

6. *Juan and the Giaour*: Poems by Byron.

7. *three novels of the hour*: In a draft Pushkin refers to 'Melmoth, René, Constant's Adolphe' as three novels which Onegin always took with him.

8. *Circe*: Sorceress in Homer's *Odyssey* who turns men into swine. Here the meaning is 'coquette'.

9. *philosophic measurement*: The Russian has 'philosophic tables', which is perhaps an ironic reference to Charles Dupin's 'statistical tables' showing the economic growth of European states including Russia in his book *Forces productives et commerciales de la France* (Paris, 1827), which was popular in Russia.

10. *automedons*: Ironic reference to Achilles' charioteer in the *Iliad*.

11. *Petrovsky Castle*: Built in 1776, then rebuilt in 1840, the castle was roughly two miles from Moscow. Napoleon stopped here

on his way to Moscow from St Petersburg. When the fire broke
out in Moscow, he took up residence in the castle. The Larins
followed the same route in their journey to Moscow, passing
Petrovsky Castle on their left.

12. *turnpike pillars*: The turnpike pillars belonged to a triumphal
arch, celebrating victory over Napoleon, which was still un-
finished when the Larins entered Moscow.

13. *street lamps*: The streets were illumined by oil-lit lamps attached
to striped pillars. These were lit at dusk and extinguished in the
morning by a special staff. They gave out a dullish light.

14. *Bokharans*: Originating in Bokhara, Central Asia, they sold
Eastern goods in Russia. Their shawls were very popular among
Russian women in the 1820s.

15. *Cossack messengers*: Cossacks were employed to take errands
by horse.

16. *gates where lions curl*: Heraldic animals made of iron or alabaster
and painted green with no connection to the sculpted lion, nor
any necessary resemblance to a real one.

17. *Crosses where flocks of jackdaws swirl*: According to the censor,
the Metropolitan of Moscow took offence at Pushkin's reference.
The censor replied that, as far as he knew, jackdaws did indeed
alight on church crosses, but that this was a matter for the Chief
of Police, who allowed this to happen. The complaint went to
the Tsar's minister, Count Benkendorf, who politely advised the
Metropolitan not to meddle in trivialities beneath his dignity.

18. *39, 40*: There is no stanza missing here. Pushkin is probably
trying to convey a sense of passing time.

19. *St Khariton*: A Muscovite identified his address by its proximity
to this or that church. The saint in question was a martyr in the
Orient, under Diocletian, in about AD 303. Pushkin had spent
several years in this residential quarter as a child. The parish was
in east Moscow, which explains why the Larins, who entered
Moscow by the western gate, had to traverse the entire city.

20. *grey-haired Kalmyk*: The Kalmyks were originally a Mongolian
people who moved westwards in the seventeenth century and
were absorbed into the province of Astrakhan in south-west
Russia in the eighteenth century, later to become a republic
under the Soviets. It was an aristocratic fashion in the eighteenth
century to keep a Kalmyk boy in the household, a practice that
had fallen into disuse when the Larins arrived, so that the original
boy is here an old man. Only a few very rich houses employed a
special doorman; in most cases one of the household staff would

take over this function like the Kalmyk here, who is still engaged in a household task as he does so.

21. *Pachette*: A Frenchified (and comic) version of the purely Russian *Pasha*.

22. *St Simeon's*: St Simeon's was in the same parish as St Khariton. St Simeon Stylites the Elder (390?–459) was a Syrian hermit who spent thirty-seven years on a pillar.

23. *And since I pulled you by the ears*: A slightly altered quotation from Griboyedov's *Woe from Wit*, a recurrent source for this chapter, starting with the epigraph.

24. *Lyubov Petrovna, Ivan Petrovich . . . Semyon Petrovich*: These three are siblings.

25. *Monsieur Finemouche*: Probably a French tutor.

26. *Pomeranian dog*: The custom of keeping house dogs went back to the second half of the eighteenth century.

27. *clubber*: The reference is to the prestigious English club, a private establishment founded in 1770, famed for its good food and gambling.

28. *graces of young Moscow*: An ironic reference to three maids of honour, known in Moscow as the 'three graces'.

29. *The 'archive boys'*: A designation coined by Pushkin's friend S. Sobolevsky for a circle of writers inspired by the German philosopher Friedrich Wilhelm Joseph von Schelling (1775–1854) known as the *lyubomudry* ('lovers of wisdom' – a Russified version of 'philosophy' or 'philosopher'). The majority of them served in the archive of the Ministry of Foreign Affairs. Despite the satire here, Pushkin was by no means hostile to the group, who included the outstanding men of letters Prince Vladimir Odoyevsky, Stefan Shevyryov and Dmitri Venevitinov.

30. *Vyazemsky*: Pushkin has already referred twice to his friend Vyazemsky – in the epigraph to Chapter I and in lines 6–7 of Chapter III. Here he makes him a member of the cast just as he had done with his friend Kaverin in Chapter I, stanza 16. But, apart from the joke, Vyazemsky appears here as the only surviving figure of any substance in the 'desert' of Russian social life after the collapse of the Decembrist revolt.

31. *an old man*: Vyazemsky suggested that this is the poet Ivan Dmitriyev (see epigraph).

32. *Melpomene*: The Greek Muse of tragedy. Pushkin took a negative view of Russian tragedy at the time, arguing for a Shakespearean theatre in place of bad imitations of Racine.

33. *Thalia*: The Greek Muse of comedy. Given the banning of

Griboyedov's *Woe from Wit* and the general stagnation of comic drama in the mid-1820s, Pushkin took a sceptical view of Russian comedy, too.

34. *the Assembly*: The Russian Assembly of Nobility, founded in 1783.

CHAPTER VIII

1. *Fare thee well . . . well*: The opening of Byron's poem 'Fare Thee Well' from the cycle *Poems of Separation*, 1816.

2. *The lycée* Established by Alexander I in 1810 in the grounds of the Summer Palace outside St Petersburg to educate young gentlemen destined for a professional career. Pushkin boarded there from 1811 to 1817, regarding the school as his real home, and celebrated the date of its opening, 19 October 1811, with anniversary poems from 1817 until the year of his death. The model of the *lycée* was taken from France.

3. *Apuleius*: Lucius Apuleius, Roman author (*c.* AD 125–180), whose fantastic and erotic tale *The Golden Ass* was popular in the eighteenth century in Russia. Pushkin read it in French.

4. *Cicero*: Marcus Tullius Cicero (106–43 BC), renowned Roman writer, politician and thinker.

5. *Derzhavin*: Gavrila Derzhavin (1743–1816), Russia's first out-standing poet. As a schoolboy, Pushkin enthralled the ancient man with his recitation of his poem 'Recollections at Tsarskoe Selo' at a public examination at the *lycée* in 1815.

6. *joined the dust*: Pushkin excluded the remaining ten lines of this stanza together with several others that were to follow stanza 1. They offered a more extended and detailed poetic autobiography.

7. *The noise and feasts . . . excursions*: This probably refers to the Green Lamp, a libertarian organization of young noblemen that Pushkin joined after leaving the *lycée* and that, already conspiratorial, foreshadowed the Decembrist movement.

8. *But I seceded . . . fled afar*: Pushkin refers here to his exile through the prism of his Romantic narrative poems, *Prisoner of the Caucasus* (1820–21) and *The Gipsies* (1824), where the hero voluntarily flees from civilization.

9. *Leonora*: Heroine of the much-translated *Lenore* by Bürger.

10. *Tauris*: The Crimea, where Pushkin spent three weeks during his first year of exile.

11. *The Nereids*: In Greek mythology, sea nymphs, the fifty daughters of Nereus and Doris.

12. *Moldavia*: Part of the province of Bessarabia, where Pushkin was exiled 1820–24. *The Gipsies* (1824), written later in Odessa and Mikhailovskoye, his family estate, drew its material from the environs of Kishinev, capital of Bessarabia.

13. *Then suddenly . . . French book*: This refers to the third stage of Pushkin's exile at his family estate at Mikhailovskoye, when the Muse is transformed into Tatiana.

14. *A Harold, Quaker, Pharisee*: 'Harold: i.e. Byron's Childe Harold. Quaker: a member of the religious society of friends, founded by George Fox in 1648–50, adopting peaceful principles and plain living. Pharisee: originally a member of an ancient Jewish sect distinguished by its strict obsevance of tradition and written law; latterly, a self-righteous person or hypocrite.

15. *Demon*: A reference to Pushkin's poem 'The Demon' (1824).

16. *leaving boat for ball*: An allusion to Griboyedov's *Woe from Wit*, referring to the hero Chatsky's return to Moscow in 1819 after three years abroad.

17. *Shishkov*: Admiral Alexander Shishkov (1754–1841), leader of the Archaist group of writers who contested the inclusion or adaptation of French vocabulary into Russian.

18. *The Cleopatra of Neva*: Probably Countess Yelena Zavadovsky, whose cold, queenly beauty was the talk of society.

19. *Spain's ambassador*: An anachronism. There was no Spanish ambassador in St Petersburg in 1824, when Chapter VIII takes place. A new ambassador appeared in 1825, when Russia resumed diplomatic relations with Spain, broken off during the Spanish revolution. This and similar anachronisms in the last two chapters suggest that Pushkin wanted to set a post-Decembrist background to his story.

20. *ten strikes*: Ten o'clock. Onegin visits at the earliest opportunity. Normally, guests would arrive at a soirée much later.

21. *The badge of which two sisters prated*: The badge is a court decoration inscribed with the royal monogram granted by the Tsar to women who became ladies-in-waiting to the Empress. In an unpublished version of this stanza the sisters are referred to as orphans. When their father, General Borozdin, died, leaving them penniless, the Tsar took them under his wing.

22. *the war*: The reference is presumably to the war with Poland of 1830, another anachronism.

23. *he found a bore*: Omitted lines: there are a number of variants behind stanzas 23–6 that either reinforce the civility surrounding Tatiana in stanza 23 or sharpen the satire of stanzas 24–6.

24. *Prolasov*: Prolasov or Prolazov is derived from 'prolaz' or 'pro-laza', meaning 'climber' or 'sycophant'. He is also a ridiculous figure in eighteenth-century Russian comedies and popular prints.

25. *Saint-Priest*: Count Emmanuil Saint-Priest (1806–28) was a hussar and fashionable cartoonist, son of a French émigré.

26. *Palm Week cherub*: Paper figures of cherubs (glued to gingerbread, etc.) sold at the annual fair during Palm Week, the week preceding Easter.

27. *A jackanapes ... overstarched*: The reference is possibly to Thomas Raikes, an Englishman who claims he met Pushkin in 1829. Beau Brummell had set the fashion for a lightly starched cravat in the first decade and a half of the century. Overstarching, which became the fashion in the late twenties, in France and Russia, was considered vulgar.

28. *Morpheus*: God of sleep.

29. *I shall offend you*: An echo of St Preux's letter to Julie (part 1, letter 2) in Rousseau's *La Nouvelle Héloïse*: 'Je sens d'avance le poids de votre indignation ...'

30. *Manzoni, Gibbon*: Alessandro Manzoni (1785–1873), Italian novelist, author of *I Promessi Sposi* (*The Betrothed*, 1825–7), which laid the basis for modern literary Italian. Edward Gibbon (1737–94), English historian. Onegin would have read his *Decline and Fall of the Roman Empire* (1776–88) in a French translation.

31. *Chamfort*: Sébastien Roch Nicolas Chamfort (1741–94), author of *Maximes et Pensées* (*Maxims and Thoughts*, 1803). Pushkin liked his aphorisms.

32. *Bichat and Herder and Tissot*: Marie Francois Xavier Bichat (1771–1802), French anatomist and physiologist. Johann Gottfried Herder (1744–1803), German philosopher and critic, notable collector of folk songs, and writer on history, literature and language. Simon André Tissot (1728–97), famous Swiss doctor, author of *De la santé des gens de lettres* (*On the Health of Men of Letters*, 1768).

33. *Bayle*: Pierre Bayle (1647–1706), French philosopher, author of famous *Dictionnaire historique et critique* (*Historical and Critical Dictionary*, 1697).

34. *Fontenelle*: Bernard le Bovier de Fontenelle (1657–1757), French sceptical philosopher, author of *Entretiens sur la pluralité des mondes* (*Conversations on the Plurality of Worlds*, 1686), the Russian translation of which was banned by the Church.

35. *The almanachs ... treating me with animus*: Almanachs, unlike journals or reviews, appeared irregularly and were more like anthologies. While he was writing Chapter VIII, Pushkin came under attack from the main literary journals, especially *The Northern Bee*, edited by the police spy Bulgarin.

36. *E sempre bene*: 'And excellently'.

37. *magnetism*: 'Magnetism' became a fashionable word at the time to designate immaterial influences.

38. *Idol Mio, Benedetta*: The barcarolle was popular in Russia at the time. Pushkin's neighbours at Trigorskoye enjoyed singing Kozlov's poem 'Venetian Night' to the tune of a gondolier's recitative ('Benedetta sia la madre' ('Blest be the mother')). 'Idol mio' is probably a duet by the Italian composer Vicenzo Gabusi: 'Se, o cara, sorridi' ('If you were to smile, my dear'), the refrain of which is: 'Idol mio, piú pace non ho' ('My idol, I have no peace any more').

39. *blue blocks of hewn-out ice*: In winter huge blocks of ice were cut from the Neva to be stored in refrigerators. During the March thaw sledges would transport them to buyers.

40. *Sadi*: Sadi or Saadi (b. between 1203 and 1210, d. 1292) was a Persian poet, born in Shiraz. Pushkin's quotation from Saadi gave cause to official suspicion that he was referring to the Decembrists.

FRAGMENTS OF ONEGIN'S JOURNEY

1. *Fragments of Onegin's Journey*: This was originally intended to be chapter VIII (with the preceding chapter in the present volume intended as chapter IX). It was published separately and includes stanzas written at various times. The description of Odessa was composed in 1825 while Pushkin was working on Chapter IV. The beginning of the published text was written in the autumn of 1829 and the final stanzas were completed on 18 December 1830, when Pushkin was staying at his Boldino estate. The Foreword first appeared in a separate 1832 edition of Chapter VIII. In the 1833 edition of the entire novel Pushkin included the Foreword and the Journey after his Notes. It is unclear whether a completed version of the Journey ever existed despite Pushkin's reference to it in the Foreword.

The route of the Journey is unclear. It is possible that Onegin spent some time abroad. He is away for some three and a half years. Since the surviving stanzas of the Journey represent him rushing from place to place, driven by ennui, it is unlikely that he spent all of that time in Russia. Moreover, his return to St Petersburg is compared with Chatsky's leap from 'boat to ball' in Chapter VIII, stanza 13, line 14.

Some of the stanzas were omitted with an eye to censorship, especially Onegin's visit to the notorious military settlements set up by Count Arakcheev (1769–1854), Alexander I's military adviser. These were harsh detention centres to which peasants were conscripted. Katenin (see below) wrote to Annenkov, Pushkin's first biographer, on 24 April 1853, that the poet had decided to sacrifice the entire chapter because of the violence of his comments. In his Foreword Pushkin is silent about his intentions and simply acknowledges Katenin's very different criticism of the omission there. Since Novgorod was one of the locations of these settlements, it has been suggested that Onegin's visit to them coincides with his stay in the town. In other words, the Fragments may have begun with such a visit. It is possible that Onegin also saw the settlements outside Odessa, the town that takes up most of the Journey. Pavel Ivanovich Pestel' (1793–1826), one of the leaders of the Decembrists in the South, wanted to foment a revolt in these camps (see Introduction, p. xxii).

2. *nine Camenae*: Roman water nymphs identified with the nine Greek Muses.

3. *Makaryev*: Annual fair originating outside the Makaryev monastery some sixty miles east of Nizhny and transferred into the town in 1817.

4. *Terek*: Caucasian river.

5. *Kura, Aragva*: Caucasian rivers. The Kura is the most important river in Transcaucasia.

6. *There were the Russian tents unfurled*: The Caucasus was first annexed by Peter the Great in 1722.

7. *Beshtu*: One of the five peaks of Besh Tau, a mountain, another one of which is Mashuk.

8. *Pylades, Orestes*: In Greek mythology, Orestes, accompanied by his friend Pylades, sails to Tauris to seek absolution from matricide. The rule of the small kingdom requires all strangers to be sacrificed to Diana, the local deity. Each of the two friends wants to die in the place of the other.

9. *Mithridates*: King of Pontus, who in 63 BC ordered a Gallic mercenary to kill him.

10. *Mickiewicz sang his passion*: Adam Bernard Mickiewicz (1798–1855), Polish poet, spent four and a half years in Russia, visiting

the Crimea in 1825 and composing the *Crimean Sonnets*. A friend of Pushkin until the Polish uprising of 1830, the suppression of which Pushkin enthusiastically supported.

11. *What yearning pressed my flaming heart*: Pushkin was in love with a daughter of the Raevsky family, with whom he was staying.

12. *trepak*: An energetic peasant dance.

13. '*And cabbage soup, while I'm the squire*': Quotation from the poet Antiokh Dimitrievich Kantemir's (1708–44) fifth satire, 'On Human Depravity in General', in literal translation: 'A pot of cabbage soup, but I'm the big one, master of the house.' A similar Russian proverb reads: 'My fare is plain, but I am my own master.'

14. *O fountain at Bakhchisaray*: Pushkin's narrative poem *The Fountain at Bakhchisaray*, composed in 1822 and published in 1824. Zarema is one of two female characters.

15. *Morali*: Born in Tunis, Morali (Ali) was a sea captain, suspected of piracy. He cut an extravagant figure in Odessa and was a close friend of Pushkin who referred to him as the Corsair (hero of Byron's eponymous poem).

16. *Tumansky*: Vasily Ivanovich Tumansky (1800–1860), a minor poet, worked with Pushkin as a clerk for Count Vorontsov, Pushkin's employer in Odessa.

17. *Why, water . . . must be wrought*: Water was transported to the town for about two miles uphill in small barrels. Later, aqueducts were used.

18. *casino*: Pushkin spells 'casino' in Western letters. It was called 'casino de commerce', where not only gambling, but all manner of financial transactions took place, and it doubled as a ballroom.

19. *Oton*: Russian version of Automne or Autonne, the name of a well-known French restaurateur in Odessa.

20. *A trader's youthful wife*: Probably Amalia Riznich, one of Pushkin's Odessa loves.

21. *Ausonia*: Italy.

CHAPTER X

1. *Chapter X*: Pushkin composed this politically explosive chapter in 1830, but burned most of it. Historical in character, it has nothing to do with the previous narrative, although there is evidence to suggest that Onegin might turn up, possibly as a Decembrist.

2. *A ruler ... those years ago*: Pushkin's attitude to Alexander I changed over the years as the latter became more reactionary. 'Those years ago' refers to the defeats of 1805–7, at Austerlitz and Eylau, when Alexander signed the humiliating Tilsit peace treaty with Napoleon.

3. *To pluck ... pitched his tent*: Alexander's authority was drastically undermined by these losses and the initial failures of the 1812 war, symbolized here by the 'plucking' of the Russian eagle. Napoleon's tent refers to the one he constructed on a raft in the middle of the Neman river where he conducted the negotiations of the Tilsit peace treaty. By appearing here several minutes before Alexander, Napoleon played the host, so humiliating the Tsar with his cheerful welcome.

4. *Barclay*: Prince Mikhail Bogdanovich Barclay-de-Tolly (1761–1818) commanded the Russian armies during the first part of the war, but his policy of retreat gave rise to accusations of treachery.

5. *king of kings*: A paraphrase of Agamemnon's title in the *Iliad*, often applied to Alexander I during the period 1813–15 by official publications. Another provenance is a song sung in the French opera in 1814.

6. *as he fattened*: The Russian says simply: 'And the fatter, the heavier', but it seems likely that the reference is to Alexander, whose personal 'fatness' after victory creates greater 'heaviness' for the Russian people.

7. *Maybe ... done it, too*: The Russian word for 'maybe' is the colloquial and popular *avos*, meaning 'on the off-chance'. The 'high-born rhymester' is Prince Dolgoruky (1764–1823), a satirical salon poet who addressed a poem to the word. Pushkin may have come across Byron's use of 'shibboleth' in *Don Juan*, XI, 12, 1–2: 'Juan, who did not understand a word / Of English, save their shibboleth, "God damn!"'

8. *To Albion the seas are granted*: Britain's defeat of the French (and Spanish) at Trafalgar in 1805 ensured its supremacy over the seas.

9. *the fraud*: The reference is either to Prince A. N. Golitsyn (1773–1844) or to M. L. Magnitsky (1778–1855). Golitsyn changed from an atheist in his early years to an adherent of 'official mysticism', founding the 'Biblical Society' and becoming Minister for National Education and Spiritual Affairs. Magnitsky was notorious for his monetary greed.

10. *Maybe Tsar Nicholas ... free*: In 1830 Pushkin continued to hope for Tsar Nicholas's mercy towards the exiled Decembrists. Here the tone is ironical.

11. *This man of fate ... rack of leisure*: The 'man of fate' is Napo-
     leon. The pope attended his coronation in Paris. 'Rack of leisure'
     refers to Napoleon's imprisonment on St Helena.
12. *The Pyrenees ... B's shadow*: The stanza refers to two revol-
     utions of 1820 that shook post-Napoleonic Europe and influ-
     enced Decembrism in Russia. The Spanish revolution was
     defeated in 1823 by the French, mandated by the Holy Alliance
     of France, Austria, Russia and Prussia. The Neapolitan was
     crushed by Austria in 1821, assisted by England and France.
     The 'one-armed prince' was general Alexander Konstantinovich
     Ipsilanti (1792–1828), a Greek serving in the Russian army, who
     lost his arm in the battle of Dresden. In 1821 he led an abortive
     rising of the Greeks in Turkish Moldavia. Pushkin knew Ipsilanti
     in Kishinev and supported his endeavours, but was later disillu-
     sioned with him. Pushkin uses the former name Morea for the
     Peloponnese. From Kishinev Ipsilanti directed a secret society
     known as the Hetairae, which had its headquarters in the Pelo-
     ponnese and fomented a rising there. 'L' refers probably to Louis
     Pierre Louvel (1783–1820), a saddler, who planned to kill all
     the Bourbons, assassinating 'B', duc de Berry, heir to the French
     throne in Paris, on 13 February 1820.
13. *Our Tsar said ... Alexander's menial*: Alexander attended four
     congresses aimed at crushing revolution in Europe: in Aachen
     (1818), Troppau (1820), Laibakh (1821) and Verona (1822). At
     Laibach the Neapolitan revolution was the main concern, while
     the Verona congress planned the intervention in Spain. 'Alex-
     ander's menial' is Count Arakcheev, the Tsar's most powerful
     adviser. See note 1 to 'Fragments of Onegin's Journey.
14. *Toy regiment ... deadly foes*: The stanza refers to the Semyon-
     ovsky regiment founded by Peter the Great (1672–1725),
     who modelled it on the half-boy, half-toy regiment that he
     created in his boyhood. The 'tyrant' was the mad Paul I (1754–
     1801, father of Alexander I and Nicholas I), slain by a gang of
     courtiers with the connivance of the Semyonovsky regiment, who
     were meant to be guarding him. The same regiment staged a
     rebellion in 1820, foreshadowing the Decembrist movement.
     Sergei Muravyov-Apostol (1796–1826) and Mikhail Bestuzhev-
     Riumin (1801–26), the hanged Decembrists leaders, had served
     in it.
15. *Russia again returned ... smouldering*: The Semyonovsky revolt
     was quelled, but the Decembrist movement had begun. Pushkin's
     image of the 'spark' responds to a line in a poem sent to him

from Siberia by the Decembrist Prince Alexander Odoevsky: 'From a spark a flame will burst'.

16. *Foregathering . . . reciprocating greetings*: The reference is to the conspiratorial 'Russian lunches' held by the Decembrist Ryleyev, who liked to stress his Russianness by serving only Russian food and drink.

17. *Nikita's . . . debate*: Nikita Mikhailovich Muravyev (1796–1843) was one of the most active members of the secret societies, formulating a plan for a constitution. He was sentenced to twenty years' hard labour. Pushkin knew him in the *lycée*. Ilya Andreyevich Dolgorukov (1798–1848) was a member of the Union of Welfare, one of the main Decembrist organizations. No action was taken against him as a result of the intervention of his commanding officer, Grand Duke Mikhail Pavlovich.

18. *Lunin . . . decisive measures*: Mikhail Sergeyevich Lunin (1787–1845), guards officer, reveller and member of all the Decembrist societies. His 'decisive measures' refer, it seems, to a plan for assassinating the Tsar put forward by him in 1816. Pushkin befriended him on leaving the *lycée*.

19. *Noëls were brought and read by Pushkin*: Pushkin was not present here, since he was not admitted to conspiratorial meetings. In any case, the occasion he refers to took place in Moscow in 1817. But he read his noëls at other gatherings. The noël is a French Christmas carol with a topical reference. Pushkin's noëls were political parodies of the form. Only one remains.

20. *Yakushkin*: Pushkin met Ivan Dmitrievich Yakushkin (1793–1857) in 1829 in St Petersburg and again in the South. One of the topics of the Moscow meetings in 1817 was Alexander's rumoured plan to move his residence to Warsaw and transfer part of Russia to Poland. It was this prospect that fired Yakushkin's impulse to assassinate him. Portraits of Yakushkin give an impression of dejection, apparently caused by unhappy love.

21. *the lame Turgenev*: Nikolai Ivanovich Turgenev (1789–1871), Decembrist. Pushkin saw the brothers Turgenev, Alexander and Nikolai, frequently in St Petersburg between 1817 and 1820, writing his famous ode 'Liberty' (1817) in their flat. Nikolai's influence can also be felt in the poem 'The Village' (1819), which deplores serfdom. The emancipation of the serfs motivated Nikolai's entire career. In 1824 he left for Western Europe, returning in 1856, when the Decembrists were amnestied. The limp in his left foot was the result of a childhood illness.

22. *16*: This stanza is defective. There is a gap of two syllables in the

middle of line 9, indicated by dots. Nor does the last word in line 9, 'tiranov' ('tyrants'), rhyme with the last word in line 12, 'sklonyaya' ('inclining'/'persuading') except on the second syllable ('a'/'ya'), although they fit metrically. My 'tyrants'/ 'inclining' misrhyme in a similar way. The stanza moves from the activities of the Northern Society of the Decembrists to those of the South.

23. *Kamenka*: An estate on the Dnieper, belonging to V. L. Davydov, where the Southern Decembrists met and Pushkin stayed during his exile in Kishinev.

24. *Tul'chin*: a small town in the Podolsk province housing the headquarters of the Second Army under the command of Count Wittgenstein (1768–1842) and the central group of the Southern Society.

25. *Pestel'*: Pushkin met Pestel' in Kishinev, remarking that he was one of the most original minds he knew.

26. *a cool-headed general*: Sergei Grigor'evich Volkonsky (1788–1865), a leader of the Southern Society, sentenced to twenty years' hard labour.

27. *Muryavyov*: To be distinguished from Nikita Muravyov in note 17 above. He is Sergei Ivanovich Muravyov-Apostol, mentioned in note 14.

28. *'Twixt a Lafitte and a Cliquot*: This means during either dinner or supper: the meal would begin with Lafitte, a dry wine, and end with champagne, Cliquot.